Tom Holt was bor⬛ ⬛⬛⬛⬛ ⬛⬛⬛⬛⬛⬛ much given to b⬛⬛⬛⬛ ⬛⬛⬛⬛⬛⬛ studied at Westminster School, Wadham College, Oxford and the College of Law. He produced his first book, *Poems by Tom Holt*, at the age of thirteen, and was immediately hailed as an infant prodigy, to his horror. At Oxford, Holt discovered bar billiards and at once changed from poetry to comic fiction, beginning with two sequels to E. F. Benson's *Lucia* series, and continuing with his own distinctive brands of comic fantasy in *Expecting Someone Taller*, *Who's Afraid of Beowulf?*, *Flying Dutch*, *Ye Gods!*, *Here Comes the Sun*, *Grailblazers* and *Faust Among Equals*. He has also written two historical novels set in the fifth century BC, the well-received *Goatsong* and *The Walled Orchard*, and has collaborated with Steve Nallon on *I, Margaret*, the (unauthorised) autobiography of Margaret Thatcher.

Somewhat thinner and more cheerful than in his youth, Tom Holt is now married, and lives in Somerset.

FLYING DUTCH
'Witty and eccentric . . . dazzling, neat, frivolous'
Time Out

YE GODS!
'Great fun'

City Limits

OVERTIME

TOM HOLT

ORBIT

An *Orbit* Book

First published in Great Britain in 1993 by Orbit
This paperback edition published by Orbit in 1993
Reprinted 1994 (twice)

A CIP catalogue record for this book
is available from the British Library.

ISBN 1 85723 126 0

Typeset in Plantin Medium
by Leaper & Gard Ltd, Bristol, England
Printed in England by Clays Ltd, St Ives plc

Orbit
A Division of
Little, Brown and Company (UK)
Brettenham House
Lancaster Place
London WC2E 7EN

For Natalie

Caen.

If it's half past four, that *must* be Caen. From up here, it could be Lisieux for all he knew, or Pont L'Evêque, or perhaps just an unusually large railway shunting yard, because geography wasn't exactly his strong point; but for once the map and the radio beacons and the big sprawling thing directly underneath him seemed to tally exactly. Prepared to stake good money that that's Caen. Nearly home. Good thing, too, what with the lack of petrol and everything.

It hadn't been the most restful of nights, even by his standards. Flak he could cope with; he didn't take it personally, it was like rain or turbulence, something that came at you out of the sky, a natural occurrence that had no innate malevolence. Fighters, on the other hand, were different. They frightened him. They were doing it on purpose. Furthermore, since Guy had no great confidence in his own abilities and attributed his survival in these circumstances to random or religious factors, he felt quite strongly that one of these days they were going to get him. Tonight was a good

1

example. Tonight they nearly had. Well, they'd got Peter.

'Didn't they, Peter?' Guy said. Peter didn't reply; his navigator in the seat next to him was dead, and in no position to comment. Mind you, he'd never exactly been the most riveting company, even at the best of times.

Guy wasn't sure when Peter had died, or even what had killed him. A fair number of bullets had hit the Mosquito at various times – it hadn't helped that Peter, not the world's greatest authority on navigation, had taken them directly over the night-fighter base at Aachen – or it could have been flak, or perhaps Peter just had a weak heart. He was definitely dead, though, and that was another good reason for getting home sharpish. One doesn't like to seem intolerant or anything, but Guy preferred not to spend too much of his time in the company of dead people. For all he knew, it might be catching.

Behind him, Guy was aware that there was a pretty sensational sunrise going on, which ought to be having some beneficial effect on his morale. Apparently not. A warm bath might do the trick, or fermented liquor or even a smoke, but not a sunrise. Guy tried to whistle the tune he'd thought up last evening, but his lips were too cold. Better be getting home. Rosy-fingered Dawn. Nuts.

'You can drop me off here if you like.'

Guy blinked. If this was going to turn out to be a ghost story, he really wasn't in the mood. He waited for a moment, then looked round. Not that there was a great deal to see, even with the early light of a new day, but Peter still looked remarkably dead; head lolling forward, that sort of thing. Perhaps he was confusing the intercom with the radio.

'Sorry?' he said tentatively.

'Here will do fine.'

'Ah,' Guy frowned. If this was really happening, then he felt he would be entirely within his rights if he baled out now, took his chances with the Germans, and the hell with the cost of the plane. The Government had lots of others, and this one had several holes in it. 'Did you say something?' he asked.

'Yes. Here will do fine. Thanks for the lift.'

'Are you all right, Peter?' Guy asked.

'I'm fine. Actually, my name's not Peter.'

There was a long silence. Not long now till they were out of France and over the Channel. Not much fun baling out over the Channel if you can't swim.

'I think it's terribly clever the way you people work these things.'

'Sorry?' Guy asked.

'Of course,' Peter's body said, 'you'll get much better at it soon. In twenty years or so, for instance, they'll work out how to fit heaters in these things and then it'll be much more comfortable. Do you intend to carry on flying after the War?'

'No,' Guy replied. 'Look, Peter, are you all —'

'My name's John,' Peter's body said. 'John de Nesle. To be honest with you, there's not a lot about this century of yours that appeals to me, but these aircraft things are really pretty impressive. If my old father could see this, he'd have a fit.'

'Peter . . .'

'You're lucky, though,' said Peter's body, 'that times have changed. I mean, when I was a lad they'd have

3

called this sort of thing witchcraft, and you'd have been tied to a stake and burnt so fast your feet wouldn't have touched. Very suspicious of technology they were, where I come from. Look, I hate to be a bore, but do you think you could just let me off here? I think we're getting pretty near the coast, and I don't want to be late.'

Guy could feel something uncomfortable happening to his insides. His mother had always declared that he had a nervous stomach. 'Peter,' he said sharply, 'will you please shut up? You're beginning to get on my nerves.'

'Sorry, sorry,' said Peter's body. 'I do chatter on, people tell me, but it's just my nature. Anywhere here will do.'

'Look . . .'

'You do know how to land one of these things, don't you?'

Guy turned his head and scowled. 'Of course I know how to . . . Look, who are you?'

The dead body didn't move. Thanks to the light of the spectacular sunrise, Guy could see that there was a large hole in Peter's head. Cannon-shell or something. The head was lolling forward. Extremely dead.

'John de Nesle,' said Peter's body. 'And will you please land this thing and let me out?'

'How can I let you out?' Guy said. 'You're dead.'

'Who's dead?' replied Peter's body huffily. 'If you can't do landings, just say and I'll do it. Which one of these things works the steering?'

I'll say this, Guy thought, going mad isn't nearly as bad as I thought it would be. I always imagined it hurt, but apparently not. I shall ignore the whole thing. I

4

shall switch the intercom off, and ...

'Here,' Guy shouted as the Mosquito suddenly lurched in the air, 'what do you think you're —?'

'Sorry,' said the voice in his ear, 'I think I pulled the tiller the wrong way. Which way is down?'

'You leave the controls alone!' Guy said. 'You could get us both killed. Me killed,' he corrected.

After a moment he felt control of the plane pass back to him. 'Fair enough,' said Peter's body. 'Just so long as you take us down.'

So Guy took them down. He found what looked like a reasonably flat field with no trees and headed for it. This was silly.

'Sorry if I startled you,' Peter's body said. 'I'm not really used to these old-fashioned planes, to be honest with you. The sort I'm used to, you can do it all just by pressing a few buttons. Shouldn't you lower your undercarriage, by the way?'

'I'm trying to,' Guy said.

'Ah. You think it's got stuck?'

'Yes.'

'Damaged, probably. Hit by flak or bullets or something. Want me to try?'

'No.'

'Be like that.'

The undercarriage definitely wasn't having anything to do with it, and Guy could understand its point of view, in the circumstances. Ah well, he said to himself, never mind, I wouldn't have enjoyed Life being off my rocker anyway.

'Are you praying?' said Peter's body after a while.

'Yes,' Guy said. 'Seems sensible, don't you think?'

'Oh, I don't mind,' said Peter's body. 'A man's

5

beliefs are his own affair and all that sort of thing. No, I was just wondering whether you shouldn't be trying to do something about those dratted wheels. I mean, we could crash, you know.'

Guy frowned. 'Is Death usually like this?' he asked.

'Gracious me, what a question!' replied Peter's body. 'How should I know?'

'Well ...' Guy looked at the ground. It didn't seem to be getting all that much closer. An illusion of time slowing up, he reckoned, probably quite normal. 'You *should* know,' he added.

'Why?'

'Because you're the Angel of Death, or whatever it is you call yourself,' Guy said. 'I'm going to die, and so I'm imagining you've come to life, or something like that. Hallucinating.'

'Are you feeling all right?'

'No, of course I'm not, I'm just about to die!'

Peter's body tutted disapprovingly. 'Here,' it said, 'you just relax; I'll see to things. I had an idea all along you weren't very good at landings. You should have said earlier, instead of going all to pieces.'

About thirty seconds later, there was a terrible jolt, and for a moment Guy imagined that the safety harness would break and he would be catapulted out through the perspex. But he wasn't. The plane stopped moving and sat there. On the ground.

'Right,' said the voice in his ear, 'I think we ought to get out now. Sorry.'

'Sorry?'

'I'm afraid I've damaged your aeroplane,' said the voice. 'As I think I said, I'm not terribly well up on these old-fashioned models. I have an idea I've ruptured the fuel-tanks. Shall we get out now?'

'Anything you say,' Guy replied. 'But I didn't think it mattered when you're dead.'

'It may well not,' said the voice. 'But I don't want to find out. Cheerio.'

The canopy was thrown back, and Guy saw someone jump out over the side. Interestingly enough, Peter's body was still there.

'Come *on*!' said a voice from outside the plane. Guy shrugged, took off his safety harness and clambered out. He was very stiff and his legs hurt. He nearly killed himself falling off the plane on to the ground, which was as hard as stone.

'Come *on*!' the voice said again. Guy picked himself up and ran clumsily in the direction of the voice. Not long afterwards, there was an explosion which landed him on his face.

He came round to find a tall young man standing over him. Odd chap. Dressed strangely.

'Are you all right?' said the odd chap. He sounded just like Peter's body.

'I think so.'

'Good. Here.' The odd chap reached out a hand and Guy pulled himself up to his feet. The odd chap smiled sheepishly.

'Very sorry about your aeroplane.'

Not far away, the Mosquito, or what was left of it, was burning merrily. Being made of wood it burnt well, and so there was plenty of light.

'That's all right,' Guy said. 'It wasn't actually mine. Belonged to His Majesty's Government.'

'Fair enough,' said the odd chap, 'but it's going to make it rather tricky for you to get home, isn't it?'

'How do you mean, home?' Guy replied, rubbing his eyes – odd; he could feel them itching. 'I'm dead, aren't I?'

'I wish you'd stop saying that,' said the odd chap. 'Makes me feel creepy, don't you know?' He looked around him, saw a church spire, and nodded. The sight of the spire had seemed to reassure him, Guy felt.

'We're about five miles from Banville,' the odd chap said. 'Can I offer you a drink?'

'A drink,' Guy repeated.

'Yes indeed,' said the odd chap. 'Don't know about you, but I feel a bit shaken. My place is only just round the corner.'

Guy thought about it. He thought very hard in a remarkably short space of time. It was probably the smell of burning flesh coming from the plane that decided him in the end. 'Thank you,' he said. 'I'm sorry,' he added, 'I don't think I caught your name.'

'John de Nesle,' said the odd chap. 'And you're ...?'

'Goodlet,' said Guy. 'Guy Goodlet.'

'Oh,' said John de Nesle. 'Where's Goodlet?'

'I'm sorry?'

John de Nesle shook his head. 'Tell me later,' he said. 'Come on. We need to find a town hall or something.'

'Here you are,' said the girl. 'I've brought you your tea.'

In the darkness of the cell the prisoner stirred and grunted. 'Don't want any tea,' he said in his characteristic muffled fashion. 'Go away.'

The girl frowned. 'Don't be silly,' she said. 'It's chicken broth. Your favourite,' she added.

The prisoner made an impatient gesture with one

manacled hand, startling a rat. 'Two points,' he said. 'First, it is *not* my favourite. Second, you put too much salt in it.'

'You should have said earlier.'

'When you put too much salt in it,' the prisoner continued, ignoring her, 'the drops that inevitably escape from the straw get in the fiddly bits of the mask and make it go all rusty. If there's one thing I can't be doing with, it's rust.'

'Sorry, I'm sure,' said the girl, nettled. The prisoner shook his head.

'It's me who should apologise,' he said. 'A bit grumpy, I'm afraid. What's the weather like outside?'

'Raining.'

'Really?' Although it was obviously impossible for the girl to see his face, she was sure the prisoner was smiling. 'I used to love rain,' he said.

'Did you?' The girl seemed surprised.

'Oh yes,' replied the prisoner. 'Everyone else in my family had this thing about sun, but I always preferred rain. What day is it today?'

'Thursday.'

'You don't say!' The prisoner sighed until the girl felt sure that his heart must break for pure nostalgia. 'Ah well. Chicken broth, you said? Yummy.'

She put the tray down. 'I'll put less salt in it next time,' she said.

'No, no,' said the prisoner, 'it's just fine the way it is. And what's for afters? Water? Oh good, I *do* like water.' Instinctively he reached for his belt; but there was nothing there. 'Sorry,' he said sheepishly and for about the ten thousandth time, 'I don't seem to have any money on me.'

9

The girl smiled. 'That's all right,' she said. 'Be seeing you.'

The prisoner nodded affably, and the door closed after her. With a soft moan, the prisoner sat down on the floor and stared at the wooden bowl, the earthenware cup and the straw. After a long time, he nerved himself to drink some of the broth, which was disgusting, as usual. Still, one had to keep one's strength up, apparently. Why, he was not quite sure; but it was a thing that one did, just as one always tried to be affable to the staff.

The rat scuttled up and sat on his knee, its sharp nose sniffing in the direction of the broth. The prisoner looked down.

'Hello, ratty,' he said, 'you want some? Well, help yourself, I disclaim all responsibility, mind.' He put the bowl on the floor and the rat scampered down his leg and hoisted its snout into the remaining broth. After a couple of sips, it looked up, shook its head and slunk away. From a far corner of the cell came the small, clear sound of a rat vomiting.

'Don't say I didn't warn you,' the prisoner said. Then he drank the water.

'It's all right,' said the odd chap. 'I've got a pass.'

Guy looked at him. By the full light of a summer's morning he had discovered that the odd chap was wearing: a pair of trousers with one red leg and one yellow leg; pointed red leather shoes with wiggly gold buckles; what looked suspiciously like a white silk long-sleeved vest; and a sort of cricket sweater made of tiny interlocking steel rings.

'Now hang on,' Guy whispered, but the odd chap

10

just smiled. He had an odd face too, very long, with a long, pointed nose, and his hair was cut strangely – all short at the sides and back, and thick and curly on top. It reminded Guy of something.

'You just leave this to me,' said the odd chap.

So saying, he walked round the corner, and Guy, to his amazement, found himself following. This was all extremely strange, but maybe being dead was like that.

The solid German soldier standing guard outside the Mairie of Benville looked up and started to unsling his rifle from his shoulder. Halfway through the operation, he stopped and appeared to relax.

'Morning,' said the odd chap. 'Let me show you my pass.' He reached inside the steel sweater and produced a scrap of folded parchment, which he opened up and showed to the guard. The guard read it, twice, thought about it, shrugged and saluted.

'Thanks awfully,' said the odd chap. 'The British airman is with me.'

The guard nodded. Guy followed the odd chap into the Mairie.

'Please don't get the wrong idea,' said the odd chap. 'I'm not German myself, if that's what you're thinking. It's a sort of all-purpose pass. Here, have a look.'

He handed Guy the scrap of parchment, on which was written:

THIS MAN IS A GERMAN GENERAL.

Guy thought about it. Then he started to reach for his revolver.

'No, no,' said the odd chap, stopping him. 'Sorry, I forgot you'd be convinced. Here, look again.'

Guy glanced down at the parchment in his hand, which now read:

THIS MAN IS *NOT* A GERMAN GENERAL.
HE IS JOHN DE NESLE.

'Sorry,' Guy said. 'It's just, you get suspicious, you know ...'

'That's all right.' De Nesle put the parchment away, and looked round. 'This way, I think,' he said.

He led the way up a flight of stairs to a small landing, off which opened a number of offices. It looked very much like a town hall anywhere. There was nobody about, but then, it was still early. De Nesle was reading what was written on the doors.

'You spoke to that guard in English,' Guy said, 'but he understood you.'

De Nesle shrugged. 'It's a gift I have,' he said. 'Ah, this looks like it might do the trick.'

He stopped in front of a door, on which was written *Privée: défense d'entrer.* He tried the handle, but it was locked.

'Yes, this'll do,' he said. He rapped sharply on the door three times, muttered something under his breath, and turned the door knob again. The door opened. He walked through the doorway and vanished.

For reasons best known to himself, Guy followed.

It is well known that if you are fortunate enough to have a large amount of money and don't feel like paying more tax than you can help, there are skilled professional men and women who will gladly assist you. What is less well known is that fiscal advice comes on four levels: the ordinary, or High Street level; the superior or specialist level; the de luxe or international consultancy level; and the *ne plus ultra* or 32A Beaumont Street level.

32A Beaumont Street, London does not demean itself by trading under a name or logo. It does not advertise; in fact, it does its best to conceal its existence from the public, since, despite the murderously high fee scale it operates, if its existence were to become common knowledge it would soon become inundated with enquiries to such an extent that it would no longer be able to function.

The criteria for selection as a potential client of 32A Beaumont Street are almost prohibitively stringent. Wealth beyond the dreams of avarice is certainly not enough. Neither is discretion. Birth, rank, political standing and other such ephemeral factors are of no account. What 32A Beaumont Street looks for in a potential client is compatibility of outlook. Prospective clients of the practice must love acquiring money and hate parting with it more than anything else in time or space.

Once you have been selected, you are secretly vetted and then directly approached by a member of the practice. If, after a rigorous catechism, you are found to be of the right calibre, you are invited to number 32A to hear what the practice has to offer.

A prospective client, who need not be named, was sitting in the inner office. To be precise, he was sitting on an upturned orange box drinking instant coffee out of a chipped mug. The practice has never vulgarised itself by putting on a gaudy front merely to impress the punters.

The three members of the practice were grouped round him on the floor. They were all peculiarly dressed and strange-looking, but the anonymous client hadn't become as rich as he had through judging by appearances.

'You are familiar,' said the senior partner – he spoke English as fluently as he spoke all the other languages in the world, but with a curious accent that was probably nearer Italian than anything else – 'with the concept of the tax haven?'

The client nodded.

'Liberia,' said the senior partner, 'the Isle of Man, that sort of thing?'

'Yes indeed.'

'Well,' said the senior partner, 'our basic investment and fiscal management strategy is largely based on the tax haven concept, but with a unique additional factor that we alone can offer. That's why,' he added with a smile, 'our fees are so utterly outrageous.'

The client smiled bleakly. 'Go on,' he said.

'Traditional tax haven strategies,' said the senior partner, 'rely on transferring sums of money from one fiscally privileged state to another. We call this the *lateral* approach, and we find that it has a great many imperfections. We prefer what we term the *vertical* approach. In our experience, which is considerable, it has no drawbacks whatsoever.' The senior partner smiled. 'Except our fees, of course. They're diabolical.'

'When you say vertical . . .'

'It's very simple, really,' said the senior partner. 'Whereas the traditional approach is to move money about from nation to nation, in other words to transfer money through *space*, we transfer money through *time*. Oh dear, you seem to have spilt your coffee.'

'Through —'

'Yes indeed,' said the senior partner, 'through time. Reflect. In Khazakstan in the third century BC, for example, there were no taxes whatsoever. On the other hand, there were no banks either, and nothing to invest in except yaks. We find that yaks offer a very low short-term yield. The Free World in the twentieth century, on the other hand, has a wealth of investment opportunities but insanely high levels of taxation. The obvious thing to do, therefore, is to find a time and a place which offers the golden mean between return on capital and fiscal intervention. We have found such a golden mean, and we can transfer your money there tomorrow, if you ask us to. For a fee, of course.' The senior partner chuckled. 'Oh yes.'

'Hang on a moment,' said the client warily. 'You mean you can actually send money back through time? Invest retrospectively or something?'

'Oh no,' said the senior partner, 'nothing as complicated as that. Let me put it this way.' He leaned forward and smiled pleasantly. 'You know what's meant by the Futures market, I expect. We trade in Pasts.'

'Pasts,' said the client. 'I see,' he lied.

'Because of – shall we say – a unique arrangement which we have with the central authorities,' the senior partner continued, 'we have access to time travel. We can take your money, travel back in time with it, deposit it in your name and arrange for the income to be mandated to you directly in whatever form – and at whatever time – you wish. We offer a return on capital of thirty-seven per cent.'

The client whistled. 'That's good,' he said.

'We can find better,' replied the senior partner airily. 'Much better. But,' he said, and leaned further forward still, 'we have chosen this particular location because of its unique fiscal advantages. The investment is entirely, one hundred per cent, tax-free.'

There was a silence – a complete, utter silence, born of reverence and awe. It was a bit like Sir Galahad's finding of the Holy Grail, except that, compared to the senior partner, Galahad exhibited a lack of due seriousness.

'Tax-free?' said the client at last.

'Absolutely,' said the senior partner. 'You see, the investment has charitable status.'

The client stared. 'You mean you've got hold of a charity that gives you money?'

'It isn't a charity,' the senior partner replied calmly. 'But it does have the status, as I just said. We invest all our clients' funds in the twelfth century AD, through the Knights Templar, for the purpose of financing the Second Crusade.'

A very long silence. 'I thought the Second Crusade was a war,' said the client.

'Strictly speaking,' replied the senior partner, 'yes. On the other hand, it's a very special war. God's war, and all that. As such, it qualifies as being for the purposes of the advancement of religion, which as you know is one of the fundamental heads of charity. At least,' said the senior partner, grinning, 'that's how they all regarded it at the time. And that, you'll agree, is all that matters.'

'Hold it just a moment,' said the client. 'I thought the Second Crusade was a gigantic flop.'

'Indeed it was,' the senior partner replied, and there might just have been a hint of sadness in his voice, 'indeed it was. A complete disaster. A shambles. A cock-up. The Crusader leaders Richard Coeur de Lion, Philip II of France and the Emperor Henry argued violently before they even got to the Near East, their armies were ultimately defeated, and the result was a net loss of territory in the Holy Land to the forces of Islam. As for the investors, most of them were wiped out. So it's just as well that we always withdraw our clients' funds at the very height of the crusade fever in 1189. We then reinvest it back in 1186. And so on. For ever.'

'I see,' said the client. 'Well, that's ... that's very clever.'

The senior partner smiled. 'Coming from you,' he said, 'if I may say so, that's a compliment of the highest order.'

Thus it was that a substantial sum changed hands, and another client was added to the already magnificent client base of 32A Beaumont Street – a client base which includes, or included, such figures as all the Rothschilds, Louis the Fourteenth, Elvis Presley and (interestingly) Julius Caesar.

It is, however, a fact of life that the really canny broker never shares the very best investments with the customers; he reserves them for himself. 32A Beaumont Street was no exception.

32A Beaumont Street might have a finger in the financial services pie, but its heart and soul were in the music business.

'Well,' said de Nesle, 'here we are at last. Make yourself at home.'

Guy looked about him. It was quite unlike any town hall interior that he had ever seen.

The roof was high – Guy had to tilt his head right back to see it – and constructed of great oak beams which were obviously carved, but too far away for Guy to make out what the carvings were. On the walls were long, gorgeously coloured tapestries, depicting scenes of hunting, warfare and gallantry in what Guy imagined (although he was no art historian) to be the High Middle Ages. Where a few square feet of naked wall peeped through the gaps between the hangings, it was bare yellow rock.

The floor on which he was standing was paved with stone flags strewn with what Guy took to be rushes. The furniture was sparse but magnificent; a massive table at one end of the room – the room was circular, incidentally – with benches on either side of it and at the two ends, two huge, high-backed gilded chairs with coats of arms carved and painted on them. A roaring fire in the middle of the room provided just about enough light to see by, and Guy realised that what was obscuring his view of the carved beams was smoke, billowing about round the ceiling trying to get out of a rather small and badly thought-out hole in the roof. Hung above the tapestries on the wall were about fifteen or twenty pear-shaped shields with heraldic devices painted on them; the colours looked bright and fresh, and the workmanship was of the highest order, but the paintwork was scratched and gouged, as if someone had been using the shields recently for actual fighting. Beside the shields hung a selection of helmets, coats of mail and enormous swords, all polished until they sparkled in the red light of the fire. There were three stuffed stag's heads, on the antlers of which someone had (inevitably) hung a selection of hats. Even the hats were peculiar, however; not a single homburg or derby to be seen. The firelight was supplemented by about twenty or thirty small earthenware oil-lamps, which seemed to Guy to be producing twice as much smoke as light, and which smelt rather awful. In fact, to be brutally honest, the whole place was distinctly niffy; and this had apparently not escaped the notice of the proprietor, who had recently been burning some sort of sweet, pungent incense, in Guy's opinion rather counter-productively. Apart from de Nesle and himself and three huge dogs sleeping heavily and noisily in front of the fire, the place was deserted.

'Be it never so humble,' de Nesle said. He had opened the lid of what looked like a large oak steamer trunk and produced a jug, which looked for all the world as if it were made of solid gold. He put this on a similarly golden-looking tray with two golden cups, closed the lid of the trunk, and put the tray on it. Then he took the jug and filled it from a barrel standing on a trestle like a sawing-horse in a dark corner of the room. He turned off the spigot, smelt the meniscus of the jug's contents, shrugged, and poured out two cups. The liquid that came out of the jug was brown and opaque, like cold tea.

De Nesle handed Guy one of the cups, and Guy nearly dropped it. It was quite remarkably heavy. He began to wonder if it really was made of gold.

'Here's health,' said de Nesle, and took a long drink from his cup. He made a face, which didn't reassure Guy very much.

'Er,' he said.

'Mead,' replied de Nesle. 'Would you just excuse me for a moment? I'm expecting a call any minute now.'

He pulled back the edge of one of the tapestries, revealing a small low open doorway. He vanished through it, and the tapestry slid back into place.

Guy stayed where he was, looking round slowly and trying to come to some sort of conclusion; but all he came up with was the thought that he hadn't realised that the Kingdom of Heaven had been designed and fitted out by D.W. Griffith. That wasn't very helpful. He looked into his cup, saw a dead wasp floating slowly round with one wing pointing up at him, and looked about him for a flowerpot. There wasn't one.

This is all very well, Guy said to himself at last, but I think I'd better be pushing along now. I could go and find that nice-looking German guard and give myself up. He turned and headed for the door he had come in by. It wasn't there any more. In its place was a tapestry depicting a fair damsel with no clothes on looking at her reflection in a rather stylised pool. When he lifted a corner of the tapestry, there was nothing to be seen but wall.

Guy Goodlet was not a hasty man; he preferred to think carefully before acting, and was generally happy to let his intelligence talk him out of things. On this occasion, however, his intelligence very wisely kept its mouth shut and its head down.

Guy put down the cup, unbuttoned the flap of his holster, and took out his revolver. Then he headed for the door through which de Nesle had disappeared.

It was a favourite saying of Pope Wayne XXIII (AD 2567–78) that about ninety-five per cent of a man's life is like mashed potato; he doesn't have to have it if he doesn't want to.

This is, of course, a gross simplification of a complex field of theochronology; but Wayne, like most of the other Australian popes of the twenty-sixth century, was selected more for his undoubted communication skills than for the clarity of his thinking.

What His Holiness was trying to encapsulate was one of the seminal arguments of theochronology, known since the twenty-third century as Bloomington's Effect. Bloomington observed that however much a man roams about in Time, it is inevitable, simply to maintain the continuity of history, for him sooner or later to return to the time and place from which he set out. Otherwise, people could simply disappear without trace and never come back; which would never do.

As a result of Bloomington's Effect, it follows that all time spent in time travel is Time Out – in other words, any period spent by an individual in wandering about in another century or centuries does not go towards filling up his allotted span of life. You can leave your own time on your twenty-fifth birthday, spend a hundred years in the past, the future, or both, and then come back to your own time, and you will still be exactly twenty-five years old. Your matter – the atoms and molecules making up your body – is thus preserved in the time and place where it rightly belongs, and you have not violated the fundamental laws of physics (because you have never been away). Your absence, in short, has about as much effect on the world about you as a dream.

It was very dark. There were more of those earthenware oil-lamps scattered about the place, but they gave out roughly as much light as the bedside lamp in a cheap boarding house, or a dying firefly. Guy bumped into at least three pillars before he found another doorway.

21

There was a thick, small door studded with large iron nails, very slightly ajar, and bright light was coming out from behind it in a long silver wedge. Guy pressed very gently on it and walked through. Contrary to his rather gloomy expectations, the hinges didn't creak.

He saw de Nesle, or rather his back, sitting at a long, low desk. There was a bright lamp beside him – a modern electric one – and on the desk were a collection of what appeared to be white boxes with glass windows in the front of them. Little green lights in the windows formed tiny letters, which changed as de Nesle touched what looked to Guy like a typewriter keyboard. It was all extremely odd and, Guy fervently hoped, nothing to do with him.

'Put your hands up,' he said.

He had hoped to say it rather more assertively; in fact, he squeaked the words rather than said them. But he did manage to cock the hammer of his revolver at the same time; and it was firepower rather than force of personality on which most of his hopes were pinned.

'Don't turn round,' he said.

'Why not?' said de Nesle to his glass window. Guy noticed that his hands were still on the keyboard.

'I told you, put your hands up,' Guy said. The voice was getting a bit better, but not much.

'What's the matter?' de Nesle said. 'Didn't you like the mead?' He raised his hands. 'Can I turn round now?' he asked.

'I suppose so,' Guy said. 'But remember, I'll shoot if I have to.' A thought struck him. 'I assume bullets can hurt you?' he added. He hoped, in vain, that it had sounded more like irony than a genuine request for information.

De Nesle was facing him now, still seated. 'That's a good question,' he said. 'Hurt, definitely yes, so I'd be awfully grateful if you were careful where you point that thing. I don't want to appear rude, but your hand is shaking rather a lot, and ...'

Guy tried looking stern. 'Never mind that,' he said. In retrospect, he felt, he could have done much better. Esprit d'escalier, and all that.

'As to whether bullets could actually kill me,' de Nesle went on, 'now there you have me, I'm afraid. Opinion, as they say, is divided. There's a school of thought that says that if I die, I come to life again immediately afterwards. There's another school of thought that agrees that I come to life again, but probably about five minutes before. They reckon five minutes because that gives me time to make sure that I stay well out of the way of whatever it was that killed me. The third school of thought, which includes my mother, feels that I probably stay dead. It's never actually been put to the test, thank goodness, and that's the way I like it. Was there something?'

'What?'

'The threat,' de Nesle explained. 'I generally find – don't you? – that when people wave weapons at you they want something. What can I do for you?'

'For a start,' said Guy, 'you can tell me how I get out of here.'

'Ah.' De Nesle made a sort of a sad face. 'That's tricky, I'm afraid. I'd have to come with you, and I *am* waiting for this *rather* important call. Do you think —'

'No.'

De Nesle considered for a moment. 'No, I imagine on balance that you probably don't. Sorry, that was very rude of me. But I do find being threatened puts me rather on edge, don't you know?'

Guy was beginning to feel bewildered. 'Look,' he said, 'exactly what is going on?'

De Nesle grinned. 'I must say,' he said, 'you do ask the most awkward questions. Might I suggest that you really wouldn't want to know?'

'All right,' Guy said. 'Just get me out of here and that's fine. I don't want you to come with me. Just show me the door.'

'I must advise —'

'The hell with your advice.'

De Nesle shrugged. 'Very well, then. To leave, go through that door behind you.'

Guy frowned, suspecting a ruse to make him turn his head. He felt that eye contact should be maintained at all times in these situations. He reached behind him with his free hand and found a door knob.

'This one?'

'That's the one. But really ...'

Guy opened the door, backed through it, and vanished. The door, which was marked *Private – Staff Only – No Admittance*, closed behind him.

'Oh *bother*!' said de Nesle.

He looked at his watch, a Rolex Oyster which he wore under the sleeve of this steel hauberk, frowned, and picked up the microphone of his answering machine.

'Hello,' he said into the microphone, in the slightly strained voice that people always use for that purpose, 'this is Jean de Nesle here. Sorry I'm not available to take your call. Speaking *after* the tone, please state the time at which you called and on my return I'll arrange to be here then. Thank you.'

He switched on the answering machine, took a sword from under his desk, and went through the door.

Guy was at a party.

More like a reception, actually. In the split second before his appearance, walking backwards brandishing a revolver and causing the seventy-four people in the room all to stop speaking at once, Guy thought he heard several languages and the characteristic hyena-like yowl of diplomats' wives laughing at the jokes of trade attachés.

He froze.

The men, he observed, were all wearing dinner jackets, the women posh frocks. They were holding wine glasses. Women in waitress outfits were holding trays of bits of minced-up fish and tiny impaled sausages. There was no band.

A woman screamed, in isolation. Being English and of the social class brought up to believe that being conspicuous is the one crime which even God cannot forgive, Guy began to feel distinctly uncomfortable. He tried to smile, found that he was having problems with his facial motor functions, and looked down at the revolver, which was pointing at the third waistcoat button of a tall, stout gentleman who Guy felt sure was a chargé d'affaires.

'Er,' he said.

'M'sieur,' said the chargé d'affaires. It was the way he said it that made Guy's bowels cringe; also the fact that he said it in French. Guy was no linguist, and the thought of trying to apologise, or say, 'Sorry, I thought this was the Wilkinson's fancy-dress ball' in a foreign tongue, was too much for him. His tongue clove to the roof of his mouth so effectively that he might as well have forgotten not only Jerusalem but Damascus and Joppa as well.

He was just about to shoot himself, as being the civilised way out of it all, when a familiar figure appeared behind him. A figure in red and yellow trousers and chain mail, holding a sword, handing a piece of tattered parchment to the toastmaster.

'*Monsieur le Président de la République*,' announced the toastmaster.

There was a brief, thrilled murmur from the distinguished guests, and Guy realised that they'd forgotten all about him. They were forming an orderly queue.

De Nesle, smiling brightly, stepped forward to start shaking hands. As he passed Guy, he hissed, 'Go back through the door you came in by, quickly,' out of the corner of his smile and passed on.

Guy needed no second invitation. Despite the fact that the door was marked *Défense d'entrer*, he pushed through it and found himself back in de Nesle's peculiar study. He sat down heavily in the chair and began to shake.

'I warned you.'

De Nesle was standing over him, a comforting grin on his face. A small part of Guy's mind toyed with the idea of pointing the revolver at him, but was howled down by the majority. He put the gun on the table and made a small, whimpering noise in lieu of speech.

'Don't worry,' de Nesle went on, 'I said that you were a new and rather over-zealous security guard.'

Guy found some words. They wouldn't have been his first choice, but they were there.

'Are you the president of the republic?' he asked.

'Good Lord, no,' said de Nesle. 'I don't go in for politics much, I'm afraid. Not deliberately, anyway. I think you'd better have another drink, don't you?'

This time, Guy felt, it would be churlish to refuse; and besides, he needed a drink, dead wasps or no dead wasps. To his surprise, however, de Nesle produced a bottle of brandy from a drawer of the desk and poured out a stiff measure into two balloon-shaped glasses.

'You must excuse my offering you mead just now,' de Nesle was saying. 'I forgot that you don't drink mead any more, and it can be something of an acquired taste. Cheers.'

He drank and Guy followed suit. It was very good brandy.

'Now then.' De Nesle sat down on the edge of the desk and stroked his thin moustache with the rim of his glass. He was grinning. 'I'm terribly sorry if I've put you out at all.'

'Don't mention it,' Guy heard himself saying. Pure reflex.

'Nonsense,' said de Nesle. 'If you hadn't been kind enough to give me that lift – oh yes, let's see if my call came through.' He pressed a knob on the box attached to his telephone, and then continued; 'No, not yet, what a nuisance. If you hadn't been kind enough to give me that lift, you wouldn't have been put to all this trouble. Actually,' de Nesle said, in a confidential whisper, 'I think you'd have crashed in the sea, because you were almost out of fuel. Can you swim?'

'No.'

'Oh well,' de Nesle said, 'I needn't feel quite so bad about it after all. Still, it was a bit of a liberty when all's said and done, particularly since your friend was, well, dead. A bit tasteless in the circumstances. Still, needs must, as they say.'

'Er,' said Guy.

'The main thing now,' said de Nesle, 'is to get you back where you want to be. Now I'm not sure I'm supposed to do that – they get awfully cross Upstairs when I go interfering with things that aren't really any of my concern – but if you can't help someone out of a jam, what's the point of any of it, that's what I always say. Where would you like to go?'

Guy took a deep breath. 'Would London be out of the question?' he said.

'By no means,' de Nesle replied. 'Anywhere in particular in London, or can I just drop you off at Trafalgar Square?'

'Yes,' said Guy. 'I mean, Trafalgar Square will do fine.'

'Splendid. Now then, when?'

'Sorry?'

'When would you like me to drop you off?'

Guy frowned slightly. 'Well, now, if that's no . . .'

De Nesle raised an eyebrow and pointed to the wall calendar. 'Are you sure?' he said.

Guy looked at the calendar. It was one of those mechanical perpetual-calendar things, and the little wheels with numbers on them to represent date, month and year were spinning like the tumblers of a fruit machine, turning so fast you couldn't read them.

'Now,' said de Nesle brightly, 'doesn't mean a lot here. We're in the Chastel des Temps Jadis, you see. Time here is very much what you make of it.'

A very silly thought made itself known in Guy's

28

mind, declaring to all who would listen that it might not be all that silly after all, if only it could get a fair hearing.

'Are you trying to tell me,' he said slowly, 'that this is a sort of, well, time machine?'

De Nesle grinned. 'Well,' he said, 'the strict answer to your question is No, but you're on the right lines. Now be honest; you'd really rather I didn't explain, right?'

Guy nodded.

'Good man.' De Nesle nodded approvingly. 'By *now*, I suppose you meant 6th July 1943?'

'Well, if that's all right . . .'

'Nothing simpler.' De Nesle stood up and pressed some keys on his typewriter keyboard. The green lights on the screen flashed and then went out. A moment later they read *6/7/43; #8765A7*.

De Nesle walked over to the door which, a few minutes earlier, had led to the diplomatic reception and pushed it open.

'Follow me,' he said.

Just then, the other door opened and a girl walked in. She put a cup of what looked like coffee down on the desk, picked up the two brandy glasses, smiled brightly at Guy, and walked out again.

'Er,' said Guy, 'just a moment.'

When Julian XXIII was installed as the hundred and ninth Anti-Pope, his unsuccessful rivals raised a number of objections, not least of which were the undisputed facts that he had previously been the Pope of Rome, and that he was now dead.

For his part, Julian treated these objections with the

contempt they deserved. Once established in his palace of the Chastel des Larmes Chaudes, he issued a bull pointing out that he wasn't dead at all, or else how come he could still do thirty lengths of the Anti-Papal swimming pool each morning, and that if he chose to travel to work each day from his home in the sixteenth century, how was that different, when you came right down to it, from the commonplace practice of millions of commuters all over the world? As to the other objection, the exact point in time he commuted from was a week before his election to the See of Rome, and thus he wasn't Pope yet, and it would be a fundamental breach of the rules of natural justice if the rules governing eligibility were to be applied retrospectively. He then had the bull pronounced by his Anti-Papal guard, who called on each of the disappointed candidates personally, usually at three o'clock in the morning and carrying big axes, and explained it carefully. As even his enemies had to admit, as a communicator Julian was hot stuff.

Once safely established in the Chastel des Larmes Chaudes, Julian set about the pressing task of clearing up the mess left over from the reign of his predecessor, the luckless Wayne XVII. Of the problems facing him, clearly the most urgent was that of Jean II de Nesle.

'I mean,' he observed to his chaplain, a timeless figure called Mountjoy King of Arms, 'the man's a menace. He's completely out of control. Zooming backwards and forwards between the centuries like the proverbial loose cannon. He just doesn't *think*.'

'Well,' said Mountjoy, 'it's not really his place to think, is it?'

'Be that as it may,' said Julian firmly. 'What gives

me sleepless nights is the thought that one of these days he might actually succeed. Find the wretched man. Then what? I don't suppose you've considered that.'

Mountjoy had the irritating habit of flickering at the edges when stuck for an answer. 'With all due respect,' he said, shimmering, 'that's not terribly likely, now is it?'

'Why not?' replied Julian gloomily. 'Stranger things have happened, you know that. I mean, by rights, none of us should be here at all.'

Mountjoy rematerialised completely. 'That,' he said stiffly, 'was an exceptional incident. Nothing like that could ever happen again.'

'You reckon?' Julian shook his head. 'Nothing like that could have happened in the first place, but it did. Now if I had my way, I'd go back and put a wet sponge down the back of his neck. That'd have woken the dozy so-and-so up right enough. Still, there we are. We're drifting away from the point. All this darting backwards and forwards has got to stop.'

'Well . . .'

Julian tried giving his chaplain a hard stare, but instead found himself staring at the wall through a vague and insubstantial silhouette. 'Go on then,' he said wearily. 'Spit it out.'

'With *all* due respect,' said Mountjoy, 'I would ask you to consider whether it's really up to you whether de Nesle is allowed to continue or not. Isn't that a decision for . . .?' Mountjoy made a gesture with his hands.

'Indeed it is,' said the Anti-Pope. 'And as his duly appointed agent, I take the view that I have full authority to . . . Stop fading when I'm talking to you, it makes me lose my thread. Thank you.'

'*Full* authority?'

Julian frowned. 'Yes, dammit, why not?' he said. 'Why can't I rub out Jean de Nesle?'

'The Seventy-Fourth Lateran Council —'

'Stuff the Seventy-Fourth Lateran Council.'

'The Bull *Non tibi soli* —' said a patch of glittering mist.

'Is neither here nor there,' snapped the Anti-Pope. 'And if you don't want to do it, then I quite understand. There'll always be a job for you in the Pensions department.'

Mountjoy rematerialised with an almost audible snap. 'I see,' he said. 'Right.'

'Not,' said Julian pleasantly, 'that I'm threatening you or anything.'

'No.'

'I mean,' Julian went on, 'I hear they've brightened up the decor down there quite a lot recently. Someone even cleaned the window, I think.'

'Nevertheless . . .'

'Good man,' said the Anti-Pope. 'Good Lord, is that the time? I must fly.'

'Um,' said Guy, as casually as he could. 'Who was that?'

'Sorry?' De Nesle was grinning.

'That, um, lady,' said Guy, 'who just came in.'

'Oh, *that*,' de Nesle replied. 'That was my sister, Isoud. Right, shall we be getting along?'

'Yes, yes, thank you,' said Guy, not moving. 'Your sister,' he repeated.

De Nesle sat down on the edge of the desk and picked up the coffee cup. He took a sip and grimaced. 'She's put sugar in it again,' he said. 'Yes, very much my sister. Makes a profoundly horrible cup of coffee, bless her, but otherwise she's better than having malaria. I take it you don't want to go home now.'

Guy lifted his head sharply, and saw that there was little point in lying. He nodded.

'You would prefer,' said de Nesle, with a certain degree of amusement in his voice, 'to spend the rest of your life as a knight of La Beale Isoud, doing deeds of note in her name and striving to be worthy of her?'

'Well,' said Guy, and then he nodded again. 'The

thought had crossed my mind, yes.'

De Nesle smiled. 'There's one born every minute,' he said, 'or at the outside, every ninety seconds. My sister has enough knights strewn across history to re-enact Agincourt. You may remember,' he added softly, 'what happened to the knights at Agincourt.'

'Oh.'

'Isoud,' de Nesle continued, 'is the plain one. My sister Mahaud, at the last count, had more admirers than there are Elks. Mahaud, by the way, isn't the pretty one. My sister Ysabel, *she's* the pretty one.'

'Um . . .'

'Fortunately,' de Nesle went on, 'Mahaud and Ysabel are both happily married and living back in time. Furthermore, they're both putting on weight. They do that. Not that Isoud's a slouch when it comes to putting away the carbohydrates; she may look like she'd get blown away by the downdraught from a closing door, but put her in front of a dish of roast pullets and you'll begin to believe what they say about how thin the dividing line is between humanity and the lower animals. The sight of Isoud eating corn on the cob . . . Sorry, I seem to have lost my thread.'

'I —'

De Nesle rested his chin on his hand and looked at Guy for a moment. 'When there's just one of them it's not so bad; it's when you've got three of them cluttering up the place that you've got problems. They gang up on you. They throw out shirts without telling you. They repaint bathrooms while you're out. Worse still, they repaint a third of the bathroom, get bored and leave the rest for you to do when you get back. They make funny remarks about you to visitors. They decide that they can't bear to live with the tapestries in the hall for another day, drag you round the fair looking at tapestries, moan at you for not taking an interest, and then sulk at you when you express an opinion. In my opinion, the idea of anyone wanting to fight knights and kill dragons just to prove themselves worthy of somebody's *sister* is so absurd as to be ludicrous.'

De Nesle finished his coffee and put the cup down. 'Anyway,' he said, 'that's all beside the point, isn't it? I take it that all my well-chosen words have been entirely wasted?'

Guy nearly said something but nodded instead. De Nesle shrugged.

'In that case,' he said, 'I suppose we'd better get down to business.'

Guy started. 'Business?' he said.

'Business.' De Nesle put a businesslike expression on his face. 'Terms and the like.'

'Terms?'

'Terms. I'd be only too glad for you to take La Beale Isoud off my hands – it wouldn't be losing a sister so much as gaining five hundred cubic metres of wardrobe space – but a man in my position has to make full use of all the resources at his disposal. So, terms.'

Guy swallowed. 'You mean,' he said, 'money?'

De Nesle scowled briefly, and then, as if remembering something, smiled again. 'Certainly not,' he said. 'My fault, should have made myself clear instead of trying to be delicate. Not money. Help.'

'Help?'

'Look,' de Nesle said, 'imitation may be the sincerest form of flattery and all that, but I wonder if you'd mind not repeating every single word I say? It makes one so self-conscious. Perhaps I'd better explain.'

'Yes,' said Guy.

'Right.' De Nesle stood up, walked round the room, and then sat down again. 'Yes,' he said. 'Cards on the table, and all that.'

Guy leaned forward slightly, to demonstrate attentiveness. This seemed to disconcert de Nesle somewhat, for he got up again and walked round the room the other way. Finally he sat down, scratched the back of his head and started making a chain out of paperclips.

'You see ...' he said.

'Yes?'

'Oh never mind,' de Nesle exclaimed. 'It's like this ...'

Once upon a time (said de Nesle) in a province of Greater France called England, there was a king; and his name was Richard. This king was so brave that people called him Richard the Lion-Heart; and at a time when most kings went down to posterity with names such as Charles the Bald and Louis the Fat, this must be taken as evidence that he was at least reasonably popular.

But then, King Richard wasn't like most of his fellow kings. For instance, when two peasants disagreed over who owned a particular pig and brought the matter to the King's court of justice for a ruling, Richard would usually end up giving the losing party a pig from the royal pigsties by way of a consolation prize. This was partly because Richard was not always fully capable of following the complexities of a fiercely contested legal argument, and so hedged his bets somewhat to avoid

36

injustice. On the other hand, his royal cousin King Philip Augustus of France, who was rather better at law, tended to resolve all such disputes by finding technical irregularities in the pleadings of both parties, dismissing the case and eating the pig.

What King Richard was best at was fighting; in fact, he was the finest swordsman and horseman of his age. The trouble was that he didn't enjoy it. War bothered him. It was, he felt, morally questionable, and if he had his way he would quietly phase it out and replace it with something rather less destructive, such as tennis or community singing (for Richard was extremely musical). Unfortunately, the times he lived in were primitive, to say the least, and warfare was in fact one of the milder and least hazardous pastimes available; besides, as the greatest knight in Christendom, Richard had appearances to keep up. If he suddenly turned pacifist and went about the place sniffing flowers, his adoring people would in all probability change his name to Richard the Fairy and burn him at the stake.

It was then that King Richard came up with a quite brilliant solution. He would organise a Crusade.

There had already been a Crusade, about a hundred years earlier. It was basically a joint-stock, limited-liability Crusade, organised by two astute French noblemen, and after deductions it paid a twenty-seven per cent dividend on capital invested, and was accordingly a success. It also recaptured Jerusalem, but the overheads proved unrealistic after a couple of years, and following a period of restructuring the Crusaders rationalised Jerusalem to the Saracens. Jerusalem, when all was said and done, hadn't really been the point.

Nor was it the point as far as King Richard was concerned. What interested him was the idea that he might, with a little low cunning and a great deal of luck, be able to induce the King of France, the Emperor of Byzantium and the Holy Roman Emperor, the triple pillars of Christendom, to stop beating the pulp out of each other for a while and direct their royal energies towards a common purpose. It troubled him that the common purpose, at least initially, would have to be beating the pulp out of Saladin; but Richard was a realist as well as a dreamer, and knew that there always has to be a loser somewhere. Besides, he had it on excellent authority that Saladin and his subjects were incurably bellicose and warlike, and as such were a serious obstacle in the way of world peace.

It was what would happen after Jerusalem was recaptured that Richard was most concerned about; for it occurred to him that the triple pillars, flushed with success and self-satisfaction after liberating the Holy Land, would be in a very good mood, and might be persuaded to sit round a table and discuss freedom, justice, tolerance, the pursuit of happiness and other such matters – particularly if Richard threatened to smack them round the head if they refused.

If there was one thing that Richard Coeur de Lion had, it was personality, and one by one the potentates of Christendom agreed to take part in the great adventure. Money to finance the project started pouring in – where from, Richard wasn't exactly sure; but there seemed to be plenty of it, which was all that mattered – and soon the preparations were complete. Amid unparalleled scenes of jubilation, the great expedition set off for the long journey to the Holy Land;

and if the main cause of the jubilation was the relief of the peasants of Europe at having got so many incorrigibly warlike knights out from under their feet, then that was yet another beneficial side-effect of the great venture.

And then Richard disappeared.

He was last seen, according to most reliable accounts, sitting under an olive tree on a beach in Cyprus with a footstool, a jug of mead and a book – Aristotle, or some such frivolous holiday reading. His fellow crusaders searched high and low for him, but found nothing apart from a footstool, an empty jug and an odd sock.

Not long afterwards, ugly rumours began to circulate. The French said that King Richard had been abducted by the Germans and was being held to ransom in a castle in Bavaria. The Germans declared that he had been imprisoned by the French king, who was demanding Aquitaine and ten million gold livres for his safe return. The Byzantines, who were a frivolous nation, suggested that the book, which Richard had borrowed from the world-famous library of the Abbey of Cluny, was three months overdue and the Abbot was holding Richard's person as security for unpaid fines. At any rate, the Crusade broke up, France and Germany declared war on Byzantium and burnt the Great Library of Constantinople, presumably by way of revenge for the Byzantine's tasteless remarks, and life in Christendom gradually returned to normal. After King Richard had been missing for a number of years he was declared officially dead and his brother John acceded to his throne. History, in its impartial and eclectic way, made a selection from the leading rumours to account for what had happened, and the world snuggled down to wait for the Black Death.

'Yes,' said Guy, 'that's really very interesting. Are you sure all this is —?'

'Yes,' said de Nesle.

'Ah,' Guy replied.

As already noted, de Nesle continued, King Richard was intensely musical, and one of his closest friends had been a French duke, Jean II de Nesle, known as Blondel —

'Relative of yours?' Guy asked.

You could say that, de Nesle replied; or at least, relativity does come into it. This Blondel was, among other things, the finest poet and musician of his age, and it was for this reason that he was so welcome at Richard's court. Before the Crusade drove all other concerns from his mind, the King's favourite occupation had been to sing duets with the Duke (Richard had a voice remarkably like a dying pig, but one does not mention such things to a feudal magnate who can split an anvil with one stroke of his sword) and one evening, probably after rather too much mead, the King had confided to Blondel his fear of being kidnapped. Holding kings to ransom was, after all, a substantial industry in the twelfth century; and King Richard, though not a collector's item like the Holy Roman Emperor, knew his own worth. He made Blondel promise that if ever he was abducted, Blondel would find him and help him escape; he was damned if his subjects' hard-earned money would be wasted paying ransoms, said the King (hiccoughing, probably), when a little courage and determination and forty feet of rope ladder could get him out of any castle in Christendom.

To this Blondel replied that that was all very well, but what if whoever had kidnapped him locked him up in a remote castle and refused to say where he was? Richard (we assume) smiled, and said that he'd thought of that, and that was where Blondel came in. Blondel could go round all the castles in Christendom (at the time, there were at least fifteen thousand castles in Christendom, give or take a few, but perhaps Richard didn't know that) and in each one he should sing one verse of that song they'd been singing just now, the one with Tristan in it. *L'Amours Dont Sui Epris*? Yes, that's the one. Good song, that. Anyway, Blondel should sing the first verse; and when Richard heard him singing it, he'd sing the second verse – he had a good loud voice, so Blondel should have no trouble hearing him. No indeed, no trouble at all – and then Blondel could sing the third verse, which would be a secret sign between them that Blondel would be waiting under the postern gate forty-eight hours later with a good, stout rope ladder and two horses. Blondel agreed that that was a perfectly splendid idea, and if it was all the same to his Majesty, Blondel wouldn't mind going and getting some sleep now, as it had got rather late.

Blondel was as good as his word. For years he wandered through France and the Empire, singing under the walls of castles, until at last his money was all spent and he had nothing left to sell or mortgage. He was sitting in abject despair in a small inn in Lombardy when he happened to get into conversation with a small group of travelling merchants. Pardon their asking, they said, but were they right in thinking that he was the celebrated Blondel?

Tired though he was, Blondel knew an artist's duty to his public and forced a smile on to his face. The merchants bought him a drink and said that they had long been admirers of his work. They thought he had originality and flair and what do you call it, that thing, relevance. They all thought he had a lot of relevance, and did he have an agent?

'What's an agent?'

The eldest merchant broke the silence first. He leaned ever so slightly forward, smiled in that way people do when they're appalled but fascinated, and said, 'It's like this . . .'

Blondel raised a polite eyebrow. He wasn't really all that interested, but it does no harm to listen.

'Look,' said the merchant, 'there's you, right, all creative, thinking high thoughts, goofing about humming and saying to yourself, Isn't the colour of my true love's hair just a dead ringer for a field of sun-ripened corn? That's great, absolutely. What you don't want to be bothered with is hiring a hall, getting your posters out, fiddling around with the popcorn concessions and getting the parking organised. That's where an agent comes in.'

Blondel thought for a moment. 'Like a steward or something?'

The merchant blinked. 'Well,' he said, 'yes. Sort of. Anyway, the main thing is, you'll be free to exercise your whatsit, artistic integrity, absolutely safe in the knowledge that the ticket office will be manned and the warm-up band'll be there on time.'

'How do you mean?' Blondel asked.

42

The merchants looked at each other.

'When you do your gigs,' one of them said. 'Concerts.'

'What's a concert?'

There was a long silence. It was as if God had said *Let there be light,* and the void had replied, *Sorry?*

'Um,' said the eldest merchant. 'It's like, lots of people gathered together in one place to listen to you singing.'

Blondel arched his brows. 'That sounds nice,' he said, uncertainly. 'Would they want to be paid, or do you think they'd make do with a cup of wine and something to eat?'

The youngest merchant said something very quietly under his breath, but the only word Blondel could catch was Idiot. 'I don't think so,' said the eldest, in a rather strained voice. 'In fact, they'd probably pay you ...'

'A token fee, of course,' one of the others added. 'Just a sort of little thank you, really ...'

'I don't know,' Blondel said. 'It sounds a bit, well, you know. Accepting money from strangers. Not quite the thing, really.'

'Covers expenses, though,' said the eldest merchant quickly. 'And a man as shrewd as you are, you'll see in a flash that that's got to be a good idea. I mean, you can get your message across to a wider audience, fulfil your destiny, all that sort of thing, and it won't cost you a penny. In fact, there might even be something in it at the end of the day, after expenses have been paid. You know, like ten per cent —'

'Five per cent,' said one of his brothers quickly.

'Five per cent of the net takings, all for you, to spend

on what you like. We'd take care of all the rest of it for you.'

'Really?'

'No worries,' said the eldest merchant. The middle partner, who had been writing something on the back of the wine list, nudged him and pointed at what he'd written. The merchant nodded. 'By the way,' he said, 'my partner here would like your, um, autograph. Not for himself, you understand, for his wife. She's a fan.'

Blondel frowned; it seemed a curious way to describe someone – flat, with crinkly edges, swaying backwards and forwards. Then the penny dropped and he realised that the man had meant a fan-*bearer*. One of those people who stood beside you and waved one of those big carpet-beater things. King Richard had had two of them in Cyprus, where it got very hot around midday.

'Certainly,' he said. 'Where shall I sign?' He squinted. 'Will underneath all this small writing do?'

The merchants assured him that that would do perfectly.

To his surprise, the Blondel Grand European Tour (as the merchants described it) was a tremendous success, and Blondel was able to carry on singing under the walls of all the castles in Christendom, frequently to audiences of well over ten thousand, without having to contribute a penny to expenses. For their part the merchants never seemed to grow tired of following him about and finding him castles to sing under, and if they insisted on him singing a lot of other songs as well as *L'Amours Dont Sui Epris*, Blondel didn't mind that in the least. He liked singing and was always making up new songs.

Eventually, however, Blondel found that he had sung under every castle in Christendom, and still he hadn't found the King. When he mentioned this to the merchants, they said that that was too bad, but they'd been thinking for some time now that the acoustics under castle walls didn't do him justice anyway, and what did he think to having a nice large arena built somewhere central with good parking facilities, proper acoustics and a seating capacity of, say, fifty to sixty thousand? It would, they said, take his mind off not being able to find King Richard.

And then, after Blondel had been singing to capacity crowds in the special arena for a month or so, a messenger came to see him. A great deal of detail can be omitted here; suffice to say that the messenger confirmed that Richard was alive and well, and was indeed being held captive in a castle. The problem was that the castle was very difficult to get to.

Blondel replied that he didn't care; he'd given his word to the King, and he wasn't going to give up now.

The messenger shrugged his shoulders and said that that was all laudable, but Richard hadn't been abducted by the King of France or the Holy Roman Emperor or any one of those small-time outfits. He was in the dungeons of the Chastel des Larmes Chaudes.

'So what?' Blondel asked. 'Where is the Chastel des Larmes Chaudes?'

'Good question,' said the messenger.

Blondel then requested the messenger to stop mucking about.

The Chastel des Larmes Chaudes, said the messenger, was hidden. Not only was it hidden in space, it was also hidden in time; it could be in the present, the past or even the future. Also, could Blondel please let go of his throat, as he was having difficulty breathing?

The messenger departed in search of witch hazel for his neck, leaving Blondel even more despondent than before. After all, time was time; nobody could travel to the past or the future. Nevertheless, he said to himself, he had come a long way and he wasn't going to let something like this stand in his way. The least he could do would be to put the problem to his agents (or rather his management company; they had incorporated under the name of the Beaumont Street Agency) and see if they could come up with anything.

'No problem,' they said ...

'And that,' Blondel said, 'is how it happened. More or less.'

'More or less,' Guy repeated. 'Are you saying that you're ...'

Blondel nodded. If his hand instinctively reached for something to sign his autograph on, his brain checked the impulse.

'You're telling me,' Guy went on, blundering through the words like a man in a darkened room, 'that you're nine hundred years old.'

To do him credit, Blondel simply nodded. Guy closed his eyes.

'Um,' he said. 'Mr ... Monsieur ...'

'Call me Blondel,' Blondel said.

'Thank you, yes,' Guy replied. 'Blondel, do you have a bathroom in this, er, castle?'

'Bathroom?'

'A privvy,' Guy said. 'A latrine. Er.'

Blondel raised an eyebrow. 'Not as such,' he said. 'After all, this is the twelfth century we're in now. Well, mostly. I get the electricity for the machines from the twenty-third century. By the time I reach there I'm going to have the most enormous bill. But the plumbing is, well, pretty medieval. Why do you ask?'

Guy thought hard, seeking to find the best possible form of words.

'I don't know about you,' he said at last, 'but I find physical discomfort is a great barrier to concentration, and just now I feel I ought to be concentrating on what you're saying.'

'Ah,' Blondel said, 'I see. Very sensible of you. We all use the channel that runs round the edge of the main hall. That's through the door immediately behind you.'

'Thank you.'

An empty bladder, Guy always felt, gives you a whole new perspective on things. Problems which had seemed insurmountable a few minutes before gradually begin to take on a new perspective. When he came back into the study a few minutes later, he was feeling much more able to cope.

'Well,' he said. 'Blondel, eh?'

'Yes indeed.'

'Pleased to, er, meet you.' Guy smiled weakly. 'Actually,' he said, 'I write songs too. That is, I, well, dabble a bit, you know.'

A very brief flicker of pain flashed across Blondel's eyes, and for a moment Guy wondered what he'd said; then he understood. It was the pain of a man who, for nine hundred years, probably more, has had strangers say to him, 'Let me just hum you a few bars, I expect it's the most awful rubbish really,' and has then had to perjure his soul by disagreeing. Guy changed the subject quickly.

'So,' he said, 'how do you do it? The time travelling, I mean. Does it just come naturally, or . . .?'

'Good Lord, no,' Blondel said, smiling. 'Not a bit of it. My agents fixed it for me. You see,' he said, standing up and opening a drawer of his filing cabinet, 'they originally come from the twenty-fifth century.'

Guy swallowed. 'Oh yes?'

'They do indeed.' From the drawer, Blondel produced a bottle of port. 'Have some?' he asked. '2740. It's going to be one of the best years on record, so they say. Mind you, it all tastes the same to me.'

Guy shook his head. The thought of drinking something that hadn't been grown yet did something unpleasant to his stomach lining.

'In the twenty-fifth century,' Blondel said, 'time travel will be as familiar as, say, air travel is to you. It'll be so commonplace that they'll need to advertise it on posters to persuade people to use it instead of other, more convenient methods. "Let the clock take the strain. We've already got there." That sort of thing. You sure you won't join me?'

Guy, who didn't wish to appear rude, accepted a glass.

'Now,' Blondel went on, 'orthodox time travel operates on a system called Bluchner's Loop. It's very technical and I really don't understand how it works, but it's something about the law of conservation of reality. The Fourth Law of Thermodynamics,' Blondel frowned, then shrugged. 'Something like that,' he said. 'I read an article about it once in *Scientific Oceanian* but it was all Greek to me. Anyway, it means that when a person travels in time, then time sort of heals up after him as soon as he's moved on; it means that whatever he does in the past, for example, the present and the future will be exactly the same as if he'd never been there. In other words, I couldn't stop the Napoleonic Wars by going back in time and poisoning Napoleon in his cot. No matter how many times I killed Napoleon in infancy, he'd still be there in 1799 overthrowing the Directorate. All right so far?'

'More or less,' said Guy. 'Very good port, this.'

'Like San Francisco,' Blondel agreed. 'That's orthodox time travel. My agents – the group of people who became my agents – found another way of travelling through time. It wasn't nearly as safe as the orthodox way, but it meant you could take things with you. The orthodox way, you see, only lets you take yourself; which can be awfully embarrassing, so they tell me. It means, for example, you run the risk of turning up at Queen Victoria's wedding with no clothes on. Another?'

'Thanks.'

'There's another bottle after we've finished this,' Blondel said. 'Plenty more where this is coming from. In fact, if you like, we can have the same bottle all over again.'

'No, really,' Guy said, 'a different bottle will do fine.'

'My agents,' Blondel said, 'saw at once that this new form of time travel had all sorts of possibilities. Commercial possibilities, I mean. The trouble was that if they told anybody about it, it'd be suppressed immediately; too dangerous. So they kept it to themselves. They used it for all sorts of clever financial deals, apparently. I've never been much of a money man myself so I don't really understand it all, but it seems they move money about throughout the centuries.'

'Why?'

Blondel shrugged. 'Tax reasons.'

'Ah,' Guy said. That, he felt, would account for it.

'What they used to do,' Blondel said, 'and please excuse me if I get the tenses wrong, was to take money from the future and invest it in the Second Crusade; you know, King Richard's crusade. Well, don't you see?'

'No.'

'Oh. Well, I'm not a hundred per cent sure myself. But it occurs to me that if you start bringing lots of things – you know, gold coins, that sort of thing – back through time and depositing them in another century, then that's going to make the century they end up in rather – what's the word? – unstable. Volatile, even. You run the risk of upsetting the balance of nature, or physics, or whatever. I think that because they made rather a mess of time at about that point, they made the next bit of history go all wrong. It couldn't happen the way it was supposed to happen, because of all these influences from the future upsetting it. On the other hand, it had already happened – because, well, it did – and as a result of it happening, history's what it is today. Or then,' Blondel scratched his ear, and continued. 'Anyway, I think that because of this imbalance or instability or whatever you like to call it, the whole thing sort of blew a fuse. Since the Crusade could neither happen nor not happen, history just washed its hands of the whole thing and left a great big gap. A

50

hole, if you like. And Richard fell into it.'

'My God.'

'Exactly,' Blondel finished his glass of port thoughtfully. 'Anyway,' he continued, 'that's beside the point. All I knew at the start was that my agents could take me about in time, so that's what I did. Instead of just going all round the world, I went all round time as well, looking for the King, like I'd promised I would. And that, basically, is what I'm still doing.'

'I see.'

Blondel lit a cigar and offered one to Guy. 'It's all right,' he said, 'we don't yet know how bad they are for you. After a while, I found out how to travel through time on my own, without any help from my agents, and it was about then that I started putting two and two together and wondering if perhaps Richard's disappearance might have been their fault. Once I'd come to that conclusion, of course, I didn't want anything more to do with them – well, you wouldn't, would you? – so I gave them the slip and set off on my own. I set up a sort of base here where I can slip back and keep a change of clothes and so on. A sort of *pied à temps*. Otherwise, I'm mostly on the move, I have to be,' Blondel added. 'You see, they're looking for me.'

Guy frowned. 'Who?'

'My agents,' Blondel replied. 'You see, they've got a contract. By the terms of it, I have to give two concerts a week for the rest of my life, and they get ninety-five per cent of the profits.'

Guy whistled.

'Not only that,' Blondel went on, grinning, 'but they've invested millions and millions of livres in setting up concerts – gigs, they call them – all through time and

51

now I'm not there to sing at them. No wonder they're worried. It's not their money they're investing.'

Guy grinned too. 'Awkward,' he said.

'Exactly,' said Blondel, tipping a little ash into a saucer. 'But the last thing I want to do is get pinned down by them again. I've got to find the King.'

'Er,' Guy said. 'Has it occurred to you that he might be, well ...'

'Might be what?'

'Well,' said Guy, 'that when he disappeared, or fell through time or whatever, that he might not actually be anywhere? I mean ...'

Blondel's face became very cold; then he relaxed.

'Perhaps,' he said. 'But I've got to keep looking. After all, I did give my word. Now then, another bottle.'

Blondel filled both glasses and they sat in silence for a while.

Guy said, 'So, er, where do your sisters fit in?'

'Sorry?'

'Your sisters,' Guy repeated. 'Mahaud and Ysabel and, er ...'

'Oh yes,' Blondel said. 'I forgot, do forgive me. They very sweetly agreed to help out, at least to begin with. But you know what women are like. After a bit, you see, they lost interest, got the urge to settle down, that sort of thing. Mahaud and Ysabel met men they rather liked, got married, settled down. Can't blame them, of course. I find that women have this terrible urge to be normal.'

'And Isoud?'

'Isoud's still with me,' Blondel said, 'but probably not for much longer. She's been getting terribly restless lately, I think she wants a change. I can recognise the symptoms. Once they start redecorating the place every five minutes, getting new curtains, you can be sure there's something in the air. Oh well, never mind.'

'So, er ...' Guy said.

'By all means,' Blondel said. 'You look a respectable enough sort of chap to me. You are, aren't you?'

'Oh yes.'

'Well then, that's fine,' said Blondel. 'I only ask because as head of the family I have to choose husbands for them, give my consent, dowry, all that sort of nonsense. We're a bit old-fashioned in our family, you see. Or as least,' he added, frowning, 'we will be.'

'So ...?'

'Absolutely,' Blondel said. 'Just so long as you do this one little thing for me.'

'Oh yes?' said Guy. 'And what's that?'

'Are you ready?'

'As I'll ever be.'

'Got everything?'

'Yes.'

'Right. If the horse gets restive, give him a lump of sugar.'

'Understood.'

'You're sure you checked the rope?'

'Positive.'

'Right then,' Blondel said. 'Here goes.'

A single shaft of moonlight cut through the thick clouds and, like a searchlight, picked out Blondel's hair and the silver mounts of his lute as he strolled up to the drawbridge of the castle. The drawbridge was raised, of course, but it was a narrow moat.

Guy looked round the trunk of the large oak tree he was standing behind and tried to work out how he had got there. There was something about the cold, the darkness and the rather ominous look of the castle that made him want to go away, but since he

hadn't the faintest idea of where – let alone when –
he was, he decided to stay and see what would
happen.

The horse, whose bridle he was holding, lifted its
head sharply and flicked its tail. Guy immediately
shovelled another sugar lump between its wet, smelly
lips. He disliked horses, and this one in particular.
He had an uneasy feeling that it was going to cause
trouble. It had been bad enough getting it here,
wherever and whenever that was; it had left mal-
odorous traces of its presence in the corridors and
had tried to pick a fight with the lift. He tried
thinking of the deep blue eyes of La Beale Isoud, but
somehow that didn't work.

The moon went behind a cloud, and Guy heard
Blondel clear his throat and touch the strings of his
lute. He was principally worried about dogs, but that
wasn't all, by a long way.

Then Blondel drew his hand across the lute
strings and began to sing:

    'L'amours dont sui epris
    Me semont de chanter;
    Si fais con hons sopris
    Qui ne puet endurer . . .'

A dog barked.

    'Et s'ai je tant conquis
    Que bien me puis venter . . .'

A light went on. Then another.

    'Que j'ai piec' a apris
    Leaument a amer . . .'

There was a flash of silver in the air, and a sound. A
sort of sploshing sound. Blondel stopped singing.

'And let that be a lesson to you,' came an angry

voice from the top of the wall. 'There's people up here trying to sleep.'

Blondel walked slowly back to the tree. He was very wet.

'Right,' he said, 'we can cross that one off the list. Well, don't just stand there. We've got a lot more to do tonight.'

Guy reached in the saddlebag and produced a towel. He'd wondered why Blondel had insisted on packing one; now he knew.

'Does that happen a lot?' he asked sympathetically.

'Quite a lot, yes,' said Blondel, drying vigorously. 'Some people, you see, have tin ears. However, that's beside the point. Ready?'

They walked in silence for a while. Guy, who wasn't used to walking about the countryside in the dark, was concentrating very hard on where he was going, while Blondel seemed to be wrapped up in his own thoughts.

'I liked the song,' Guy said at last.

'Sorry?'

'The song,' Guy repeated. 'I liked it.'

'Thank you.'

'Not at all.'

'Personally,' Blondel said, with a savagery that took Guy quite by surprise, 'I'm sick to the back teeth of it. If I never hear it again, I shall be extremely happy. After all,' he added, rather more calmly, 'I have been singing it now for longer than I can possibly hope to remember. No wonder I've had enough of it. In fact, all music makes me sick these days. If ever I do find the King, I'm going to spend the rest of my life not listening to music.'

That killed the conversation stone dead for the next ten minutes, during which they walked quietly along, Guy following Blondel and hoping that he knew where he was going. An owl hooted somewhere.

Guy was just starting to realise that he was feeling hungry when a large white shape appeared out of a bush beside the road, dashed across their path and disappeared into the darkness. As far as Guy was concerned it was one of those incidents which are best left shrouded in mystery, but Blondel suddenly seemed galvanised into action.

'Don't just stand there,' he said. 'After it.'

'After what?'

'The stag, silly. Quick, you get on the horse.'

Guy wanted to explain that he wasn't desperately efficient with horses, but by this stage Blondel was nowhere to be seen. With a despairing spurt of courage, Guy grabbed at one of the stirrups, put his foot in it and hauled himself up on to the horse. Thankfully, the horse took it quite well. He sorted out the reins, gave the horse a token kick, and was delighted to find that it seemed perfectly willing to accept that as a valid command to move. As he sped through the darkness, he tried to remember what his uncle in Norfolk had tried to teach him when he was ten about rising to the trot.

'Blondel,' he shouted, 'where are you?'

'Over here,' came a voice, a long way off. Blondel, it seemed, could run fast. Just as Guy had dragged out of his memory the recognised way of making a horse turn left, the horse pricked up its ears and set off towards the direction of its master's voice.

'He's in there,' Blondel hissed. Moonlight flashed on the blade of his sword, pointing (as far as Guy was concerned) in no particular direction at all.

'How do you stop this thing?' Guy asked.

'Pull on the reins,' Blondel replied. 'Get down and come and help.'

In the event, Guy found getting off the horse was quite simple, if not particularly dignified. He tied the reins to a handy bush and followed the sound of Blondel's voice. He longed for a torch.

'In the cave,' Blondel said.

'Which cave?'

'There is a cave,' Blondel explained, 'just over there. The white stag just went into it. You don't seem at home in the dark.'

'I'm not.'

'You should eat more carrots,' Blondel said absently. 'I think we should go in after it.'

Guy blinked. 'Do you?' he said.

'Absolutely,' Blondel replied. 'It had a gold collar round its neck, and the points of its antlers were gilded.'

'Escaped from a circus or something?' Guy hazarded.

'Something like that. Look, get the rope, we can use that as a halter. Then follow me.'

'Blondel . . .'

But Blondel had gone into the cave. As instructed, Guy fetched the rope. He took his time. No point in rushing these things.

'Hurry up with the damn rope,' came a voice from inside the cave. Against his better judgement, Guy followed. There was a silvery light coming from inside the cave. Perhaps someone in there had a torch.

As he entered, Guy saw that the light was coming from the antlers of the white stag; they were glowing, as if they were made of glass and had electric filaments inside them. The stag itself was milk-white, and it did indeed have a golden halter and some sort of gold leaf on the sharp bits of its antlers. It was eating sugar lumps from the palm of Blondel's hand.

'Tie the rope to its antlers,' Blondel whispered. 'Hurry up, man, we haven't got all night.'

Guy shrugged and edged forward, filled with the reckless courage of an elderly householder looking for burglars armed with his wife's umbrella. To his surprise and relief, the antlers were cold to the touch and the stag didn't try and stick them into him. He tied all the knots he could remember from his boy scout days and handed the other end of the rope to Blondel.

'Well,' Blondel said, 'this *is* a bit of luck, don't you think?'

Guy's eyebrows rose. 'Luck?' he said.

'Absolutely,' Blondel replied, patting the stag's muzzle. 'Not every day you run across an enchanted stag on Wandsworth Common, now is it?'

'Is that where we are?' Guy asked, stunned, 'Wandsworth Common?'

'We are indeed.'

'I've got an aunt who lives —'

'Will live,' Blondel interrupted. 'I make it the late fourteenth century, unless my calendar's stopped again.'

'Oh.' Guy felt suddenly wretched. 'I see.'

'Out there,' Blondel went on, 'they're having the Black Death and the Peasant's Revolt. Which makes having an enchanted stag a distinct advantage, don't you think?'

'Well yes,' Guy agreed. What he'd really like, he said to himself, in the circumstances stated, was a machine-gun and a gallon jar of penicillin, but he was prepared to accept any sort of edge he could get. 'Er, what do we do now?'

'Watch,' Blondel replied. 'Gee up there, boy,' he said to the stag. The stag turned its head and looked at him.

'My name,' said the stag, 'is Cerf le Blanc.' It said it coldly and without moving any part of its mouth. That, as far as Guy was concerned, put the tin lid on it.

'Where are you off to in such a hurry?' Blondel asked.

'Goodbye,' Guy explained. 'Thanks for everything.'

'Oh well,' Blondel called after him. 'Go carefully. Mind the wolves.'

Guy's head reappeared at the door of the cave. 'Wolves?' he enquired.

'Wolves,' Blondel replied, 'were still common in England in the fourteenth century, I think. I'm not sure, actually.'

'I think I'll come with you,' Guy said; then he whispered, 'Look, is that thing going to make a habit of talking?'

'I wouldn't worry about it,' Blondel said. 'I don't think it means to hurt us. Do you?'

'No.'

'There,' Blondel said, 'you see? Had it from its own lips.'

'I never *mean* to hurt anyone,' said Cerf le Blanc. 'Sometimes, though ... But it's always an accident. At least as far as I'm concerned, that is.'

Blondel gave the stag a reassuring pat. 'That's all right,' he said. 'Have some Turkish Delight and then let's be getting on.' He produced a pink cube from the purse at his belt. There were bits of fluff sticking to it, but the stag didn't seem to mind. When it had finished chewing, it lifted its head, and the light of its antlers dimmed to a discreet glow. It led the way.

Pursuivant rubbed his eyes and yawned.

At about this time, back at the Chastel des Larmes Chaudes, the lads would be opening a few cans, passing round the dry-roasted peanuts, getting on with the night shift. On Mondays, Wednesdays and Fridays they had a poker school. If the alarm rang, of course, they'd have to go and answer it, but somehow the alarm never seemed to ring any more. Not since Clarenceaux wedged a beer-mat between the bell and the clapper.

Although the regulation kagouls are supposed to be waterproof, it was Pursuivant's experience that there were a large number of vulnerable points through which rain could penetrate them, just as it had penetrated his sandwiches and his wellington boots. There was supposed to be an umbrella, but Mordaunt Dragon of Arms had snitched it for when he went fishing. The only waxed cotton jacket in the department belonged to White Herald; and given his personal habits, nobody in

61

his right mind would want to wear it even if White Herald was inclined to offer, which he wasn't.

Pursuivant shivered and wiped the rain off his nose. They'd hired a video for tonight, too.

He peeled back his sleeve and looked at his watch, first wiping away the moisture that obscured the dial. He was due to be relieved at six, but there was a long way to go before then. Plenty long enough to catch pneumonia. There were few crimes he wouldn't commit for a nice hot mug of tea.

Out in the darkness, a long way off, a pale white light was glowing. Pursuivant rubbed his eyes again and stared. This was more like it, he thought. He reached for the night-glass, wiped the lenses and peered out. The light wasn't there any more. Seeing things.

No, he wasn't. Clear as anything, a pale white light. Fumbling with numb hands, Pursuivant adjusted the glass and saw two men, very wet, leading a horse and a white stag, whose antlers were producing the light. They were a long way off still, but heading this way. Pursuivant chuckled and wound the handle of the field telephone. It rang, and rang, and rang. Nobody answered it, and no wonder. Some clown had wedged a beer-mat between the bell and the clapper.

'Oh *shit*,' Pursuivant muttered under his breath.

Still, there it was. Nothing for it but to do it himself. Thinking very bitter thoughts about the rest of the department, he groped for his shield (a mitre argent on a sable field, a bend cross keys reversed gules, attired of the second) and his pickaxe handle with big rusty nails driven through it. Chivalry was a concept familiar to the staff of the Chastel des Larmes Chaudes, but they didn't make a big thing about it.

★

Feeling extremely foolish, Guy put his revolver away and came out from behind the horse.

'Is he all right?' he said.

Blondel looked at the body at his feet. 'Well,' he said, 'if he is then I've just been wasting my time. Thanks for your help, by the way. You meant well.' He stuck a finger through the bullet hole in his hat and spun the hat round a couple of times.

'Like I said,' Guy muttered defensively, 'I don't see terribly well in the —'

'Yes, well,' Blondel said, 'it's the thought that counts.' He put up his sword, gave the body a kick, and put his hat back on. 'Don't worry about him,' he said. 'He'll be right as rain in the morning.' He glanced up at the sky. 'Well, better, anyway.'

'Footpads?' Guy asked.

'Footpads be blowed,' Blondel replied. 'See that shield? Mitre argent on a sable field and bunches of upside-down keys? No, if it was footpads I'd be inclined to worry.' He turned round and stood in front of the stag, hands on hips.

'Now then,' Blondel said, 'I think you and I should have a little talk.'

The stag gave him a blank look, as if to say that deer are not capable of human speech. Their larynxes are the wrong shape, said the stag's eyes.

'Unless,' Blondel continued, 'you don't want to talk, of course, in which case it's venison rissoles for my friend here and myself. *Capisce?*'

The stag breathed heavily through its nose.

'I'll count,' said Blondel sweetly. 'Up to five. One.'

'All right,' said the stag, without moving its lips (the

larynxes of stags are totally incapable of forming human speech), 'there's no need to come over all unnecessary. I was only doing my job.'

Blondel smiled. 'And what might that be?' he said. In the background, Guy coughed.

'Excuse me,' he said.

Blondel turned his head. 'What?' he asked.

'Do you mind if I have a cigarette?' Guy said. 'All this excitement ...'

'Go ahead,' Blondel replied. He turned back to the stag. 'Your job,' he said.

'I serve His Excellency Julian XXIII,' mumbled the stag. 'All right?'

'Yes, I know that,' said Blondel. 'A mitre argent on a sable field and all that nonsense. You were told to come here?'

The stag nodded. The movement of its antlers jerked Guy's hand, sending his cigarette arcing through the air like a flying glow-worm. He said something under his breath and lit another.

'And when we turned up, you were to lead us towards where the idiot there was lying in wait?'

The stag nodded again but Guy was ready this time.

'Thought so,' Blondel said. 'Now then. Who said we'd be coming this way tonight?'

The stag gave him a blank look.

'Come on,' Blondel said. 'Someone must have said.'

The stag shrugged.

'Oh, be like that, then,' said Blondel. 'Now then, where did you come from?'

Silence. It wasn't (Guy felt) that the stag didn't want to say; more like it didn't actually know. Probably it didn't understand the question. Blondel rephrased it.

'Where,' he asked, 'do you live?'

Silence.

'You know what?' Blondel said to Guy. 'I think we're wasting our time. Just because the dratted thing can speak doesn't necessarily mean it's intelligent.'

'Here,' said the stag, affronted, 'just you mind what you're —'

'In fact,' Blondel went on, 'I think that if we look carefully . . .' He went across and started to feel the fur between the stag's ears. 'Ah yes,' he said. 'Here we are.' He pulled, and something came away in his hands. The light went suddenly out.

'Blondel,' Guy complained, 'what are you doing?'

'See this?'

'No,' Guy replied. 'Somebody put the lights out.'

Blondel showed him a little grey box, with wires coming out of it. 'This,' he said, 'is a radio transmitter-cum-microphone-cum-hologram projector. It also sends electrical impulses into this poor mutt's brains to control its actions. Cerf le Blanc,' he said, patting the stag's nose, 'is just an ordinary white deer, aren't you, boy?'

'Oh,' Guy said. 'I see.' To a certain extent, he felt, he ought to be relieved. Somehow he wasn't.

'All those magical effects,' Blondel went on, 'were produced by this little box of tricks here. That's where the voice came from. I expect it's also transmitting what we say back to Head Office, wherever that is. Is that right, boys?' he said.

'Yes, that's . . .' said the voice of Cerf le Blanc. Another voice said something rude and there was an audible click. Blondel chuckled softly and then put the box on the ground and jumped on it.

'All right,' he said, 'you can turn the deer loose now. We'd better be going.'

Cerf le Blanc, freed from the rope, picked up his hooves and ran for it. Blondel took back the rope, coiled it up neatly and stowed it in the saddlebag. 'Time we weren't here,' he said. 'Now, our best bet will be a corn exchange or something like that.'

Guy, who had just started to feel he could cope, on a purely superficial level at least, felt his jaw drop. 'A corn exchange,' he repeated.

'Or a yarn market will do,' Blondel replied. 'We can make do with a guildhall at a pinch, I suppose, but there may well be people about. Somehow I don't feel a church would be a good idea. They may be idiots, but they aren't fools. Coming?'

It was about two hours before dawn when they reached the town. Fourteenth-century Wandsworth was waking up, deciding it could have another ten minutes, and turning over in its warm straw. Blondel quickened his step.

'In the 1480s,' he whispered as they crept past a sleeping beggar, 'there was a corn exchange in the town square, but they may not have built it yet. Looked a bit perpendicular when I saw it. Hang on, this'll do.'

They were standing under a bell-tower. Blondel was looking at a small, low door, which Guy hadn't even noticed. It wasn't the sort of door that you do notice. Over its lintel were letters cut into the stone.

NOLI INTRARE, they said, AD VSVM CANONI-CORVM RESERVATA.

'That's the Latin,' Blondel explained, 'for No entry, staff only. This'll do fine. We'll have to leave the horse, but never mind.'

He knocked three times on the door and pushed. It opened.

'So?'

'He hit me,' Pursuivant explained.

'I gathered that. What else?'

Meanwhile the doctor's assistant was up a ladder in the stockroom, looking at the labels on the backs of what looked like shoe-boxes. 'We've only got a 36E,' he called out. 'Will that do?'

'Have to,' the doctor said. 'Means he'll get bronchitis from time to time, but so what?'

Pursuivant sat up on the operating table. 'Hold on, doc,' he said. The doctor pushed him down again.

'You never heard of the cuts?' he said. 'You're lucky we've got a 36E. There's been a run on lungs lately.'

'Yes, but . . .'

'Don't be such an old woman,' said the doctor. 'We should have some 42s when you have your next thirty-year service. Until then, you'll have to make do.'

Mountjoy, who had been standing fiddling with his signet ring all this time, was getting impatient. 'He hit you,' he repeated. 'Then what?'

'Then I fell over,' Pursuivant replied. 'Look, boss, in the contract it plainly states that all damage will be made good, and —'

'Shut up,' said Mountjoy. 'You fell over. Go on.'

'But boss —'

'Look,' the chaplain snapped, 'I should be at an important meeting. Get on with it.'

In actual fact, Mountjoy was at the meeting – in fact, he'd been three minutes early – but there was no need to mention that. He flickered irritably.

'I fell over,' Pursuivant said. 'Then there was a bang and the bloke's hat came off.'

'What?'

'His hat,' Pursuivant explained. 'He was wearing a hat and it came off. Don't ask me why.'

'I see,' Mountjoy said. 'And what happened next?'

'I died.'

'I see,' Mountjoy said. 'And that was all you saw?'

'Well,' said Pursuivant, 'my whole life flashed in front of me, but I don't suppose you want to hear about that.'

'Not particularly, no. What was this other man like?'

Pursuivant furrowed his brows, thinking hard. 'Odd bloke,' he said. 'About my height, dark hair, wearing a sort of sheepskin coat, no sword. If you ask me, he didn't seem to have much idea of what was happening.'

'That,' said Mountjoy unkindly, 'would have made two of you.' He put away his notebook and turned to the doctor. 'Right,' he said, 'how long before this one's up and about again?'

'Let's see,' said the doctor. 'Neck partially severed, multiple wounds to lungs, stomach and shoulders, compound fracture of the left leg. I'll need to keep him in for observation, too. Say about twenty minutes.'

'Oh for pity's sake,' snapped Mountjoy petulantly. 'Doctor, you are aware of the staffing shortages?'

'Not my problem,' the doctor replied. 'All right, nurse, close him up.'

The staff nurse put down her visor and lit up the welding torch.

'Blondel,' said Guy, 'can I ask you something?'

The tunnel was damp and smelly. The ceiling was

low and the light from the torches in the wall-sconces wasn't quite bright enough. On a number of occasions, Guy had trodden in something. He was glad that he didn't know what it had been.

'Fire away.'

'How do you do that?'

'What?'

'Go through doors,' Guy said, 'that lead to ... well, this.'

Blondel laughed. 'This is how we travel through time,' he said. 'My agents taught me.'

'I see.' Guy walked along in silence for a while. He was getting a crick in the neck from keeping his head ducked. 'Er, how does it work?' he asked.

'On the principle of Bureauspace,' Blondel replied. 'Are you all right with the saddlebags or shall I carry them for a bit?'

'No, no, that's fine,' Guy said. 'What's Bureauspace?'

Blondel stopped under a torch and looked at a little book. He was actually rather shorter than he looked, Guy noticed, and didn't have to lower his head to avoid the ceiling. 'This way,' he said at last. 'I thought we'd taken a wrong turning back there, but it's all right. Now then, the proper name for it is the Bureaucratic Spatio-Temporal Effect, but we call it Bureauspace for short. It's really very simple, once you grasp the fundamental concept.'

'Oh good,' said Guy. He had the awful feeling that this was going to be one of those questions you regret asking.

'It's like this,' Blondel said. 'Oh, left here, by the way. Mind your head.'

'Ouch.'

'At the heart of all bureaucratic organisations,' Blondel said, 'there's a huge lesion in the fabric of space and time. It's like a sort of ...' Blondel thought hard. 'It's like the gap between the sofa-cushions of time and space. Things fall into it, get lost and then get washed out again. In the meantime, they've been whirled round all through time and space until they end up more or less where they started. That's how the system works. They're all well aware of it in the public services, only they call it going through channels. However, it has its advantages.'

Guy stopped just in time to avoid walking into a pillar. 'Oh yes?' he said.

'Yes indeed.' Blondel had halted again and was screwing up his eyes to read small print by the light of a very dim torch. 'You see,' he said, 'all bureaucracies are one bureaucracy. The British Ministry of Works is in fact the same organisation as the Turkish Home Office, the Tresor Royale of Louis XIV and the Roman Senate's sub-committee on Drains and Sewers. They had different notepaper for each department, but they're all basically the same thing. And all bureaucracies are built over this lesion in the fabric of space and time, what Marcus Aurelius would have called the Great Chesterfield. This is why, sometimes, when the system breaks down, you get an income tax demand that should have been sent to the Shah of Persia, while the Archbishop of Verona gets your electricity bill.'

'I thought so.'

'Sorry?'

'Never mind,' Guy said. 'Go on, please.'

'Well then,' said Blondel, 'once you've realised that

fact, you can make use of it. We are presently in a duct in the bowels of the Civil Service. What they call the Usual Channels. Or, if you prefer, we've fallen down behind the back of God's filing cabinet. Right now we're directly underneath the Finance and General Purpose Committee of the Anglo-Saxon Folkmoot. Over there somewhere is the National Bank of the Soviet Union, and that corridor on your right leads under the commissariat division of the grand council of Genghis Khan. You soon find your way about down here. It's a bit like the Phantom of the Opera.'

'But how did we get here?' Guy asked.

'Easy.' Blondel stopped and rubbed his eyes. 'You'll have noticed how, in every public building ever constructed, from the Ziggurat of Ur to the Coliseum to Chichester Cathedral to Broadcasting House, there are always lots and lots of doors marked *Private, staff only, do not enter.* Yes?'

'Yes,' said Guy.

'Well then,' Blondel said, grinning, 'haven't you ever wondered where they lead to?'

'No,' Guy admitted.

'Of course not,' Blondel said. 'You're brought up not to. Nobody knows, that's the whole point. I mean, you've never actually seen anyone going in or out of them, have you?'

'Guy shook his head.

'Well,' said Blondel, 'now you know. They all lead down here. Which means,' he yawned, closing his little book and putting it away in his purse, 'that wherever there's a public building of any description – library, town hall, railway station, government ministry, kennel for the King's Wolfhounds –' Blondel sniffed and

71

pointed upwards '– sewage farm, manhole cover, orbiting space station, anything like that – there's a gateway to the whole of time and space, and all you have to do is knock three times and enter. It's as simple as that. It certainly beats all that mucking about with transmat beams. Ah,' he said, 'I think we've arrived.'

In front of them was a door.

'For a while,' Blondel was saying, 'I thought they might have King Richard down here. You know, filed away in the archives, bound hand and foot with red tape. But they haven't, I've looked.'

'Where are we?' Guy asked.

'You'll see,' Blondel smiled. 'Ready?'

'Usher,' said Oliver Cromwell, 'take away that bauble.'

Behind the Speaker's chair, a door opened. Not many people had ever noticed it was there, probably because it had *staffe onlie* painted on it in gold leaf.

Slowly, and with infinite misgivings, the usher rose to his feet and walked towards the table on which the Great Mace lay. Cromwell's face remained implacable.

'It's his warts,' explained a colonel to the Member for Ashburton. 'When they're playing him up he can be that difficult . . .'

On the back benches a solitary figure rose. The usher stopped dead in his tracks. He knew that history was being made; he was also acute enough to guess that the production of history, like coal-mining, is a highly hazardous occupation.

'Mr Protector,' said the solitary figure, 'by what right . . .?'

Behind the Speaker's chair, Guy froze. He had a horrible feeling – not unlike the sensation of discovering that the large bowl of water one has just upset all over one's host's carpet had originally contained one's host's goldfish – that he knew exactly where he was, and when.

'Come on,' Blondel hissed, 'you're dawdling again.'

'Yes, but . . .'

But Blondel wasn't there. Instead he was standing in front of the Speaker, showing him a raggedly little scrap of paper. The Speaker, having read it, nodded and called upon Blondel to speak. Apparently he was under the impression that Blondel was the Member for Saffron Walden.

Actually, Blondel didn't so much speak as sing; he sang *L'Amours Dont Sui Epris*, and had got as far as *Remembrance dou vis* before the big spotty man who'd been talking when they came in shouted to a couple of guards to take this something-or-other and throw him in the river.

It was, Guy realised, a time for swift and positive action. He started trying to back through the door he'd just come through on his hands and knees.

Blondel had turned round and was glaring at Cromwell with a sort of paint-stripping fury in his eyes.

'Who are you calling a —' Then he noticed that a halberdier was trying to annex his collar, kicked the man neatly in the groin and jumped up on the table with the mace on it, his sword in his hand.

'Oh *hell* . . .' said Guy to himself.

If he'd had time to analyse his reluctance to get involved, he would have said to himself that this was a crucial moment in the development of English Parliamentary democracy, and that if he loused it up he would probably be responsible for a new Dark Age of royal supremacy and baronial repression. As it was, time was short. Very tentatively, he stood up and drew his revolver.

'Excuse me,' he said.

The Lord Protector, the Long Parliament and an assortment of officials and soldiers turned and looked at him. In a brief instant of total perception, Guy realised that he hadn't shaved, his fingernails were dirty, his left sock had a hole in it, he was probably going to die very soon, his jacket was too big and his hair badly needed combing. He said 'Er.'

Blondel, meanwhile, had jumped down from the table, sheathed his sword, picked up the mace and clobbered two halberdiers with it. Then he swatted Black Rod across the kneecaps, stunned the Member for Kings Langley, caught the usher a savage blow on the funny bone and fell over. The guard who had felled him, rather unsportingly from behind, with a bound copy of Bracton, drew back his arm for another blow . . .

'Freeze!' shouted Guy.

Of all the peculiar situations he had found himself in recently, Guy felt, this had to be the loopiest. Here he was, Flight Lieutenant Guy Goodlet, bachelor, twenty-six, until the outbreak of war a respectable bank official, standing on the floor of the House of Commons pointing a loaded revolver at Oliver Cromwell. However, despite the ludicrous nature of what he was doing, it had to be admitted that he seemed to be having the desired effect. Nobody seemed terribly interested in doing anything just at that moment. The entire House was frozen, like a group of statues assembled by a dangerously eccentric collector.

What eventually happened was Blondel made a jump for it, a halberdier standing to his immediate right – not the one with the copy of Bracton, a different one – took a mighty slash at his head with a large sword, and Guy, more by way of a nervous twitch than with malice aforethought, pulled the trigger. There was a loud bang (the acoustics of the House are excellent) and everybody started yelling at once. Oddly enough, the only thought passing through Guy's mind was 'Oh fuck, I've shot Cromwell, Mr Ashton will never forgive me.' Mr Ashton had been Guy's history teacher, and was a great advocate of Cromwell and the seventeenth-century republican movement as a whole. In fact he had once lent Guy a copy of the collected works of John Lilburne, which Guy had always intended to read.

That was it, actionwise, as far as Guy was concerned, and the guard who had been stalking him for the last five minutes would have had no difficulty in grabbing and disarming him if he hadn't been hit over the head with the Great Mace of England first.

'Come *on*,' Blondel shouted in his ear. 'This way.'

A moment later the door marked *Staffe onlie* had closed behind them and three guards were unsuccessfully trying to lever it open with their halberds. Cromwell, meanwhile, picked up his hat and dusted it off. There was a hole in it. Pity. New hat, too.

'Order!' he shouted.

The halberdiers stood up, looked at their bent spearheads, shrugged and returned to their posts. The Long Parliament sat down. Cromwell resumed his seat.

'Well anyway,' he said, 'that's got rid of the mace.'

★

The negotiations had reached a critical stage.

With a practised hand the senior partner motioned a waiter to bring a fresh pot of coffee and five more pipes of tobacco.

'But if we withdraw all our clients' money from the South Sea Company,' the broker was saying, 'isn't that going to cause a crisis of confidence?'

'Maybe,' said the senior partner. 'So what?'

'But ...' The broker, lost for words, waved his hands about. His colleague took up the argument.

'If the public get the idea that there's something wrong with the South Sea Company,' he said, 'the effects could be catastrophic. There would be an immediate collapse. The economy of the nation – of Europe even – would —'

The senior partner cut him short with a wave of his hand. 'Listen,' he said, 'Mr, er ...'

'Smith,' said the broker's friend, 'Adam Smith.'

'Mr Smith,' the senior partner went on, 'you haven't answered my question. So what? All your funds will be safely invested in Second Crusade 67% Unsecured Loan Stock. What possible difference will it make to you if the whole British economy crumbles away into dust?'

Mr Smith's lower lip quivered slightly. 'But that's —' he started to say.

'In fact,' the senior partner went on, 'what could be better, from your point of view? Sell now, reinvest, buy back at the bottom of the market, make a double killing. The wonderful part of it is that, thanks to the unique facilities offered by our Simultaneous Equities Managed Fund, your money can be invested in both the Second Crusade and the slow but steady regrowth of the British economy at the same time. Well, concurrently, anyway. There is a technical difference, but I don't want to blind you with science.'

'I ...' Mr Smith stuttered, but his friend the broker stopped him.

'Actually,' he was saying, 'I rather like the sound of that.'

The senior partner smiled. 'That's the spirit,' he said. 'Now, if we can move on to the topic of life assurance, we offer a wide range of tailor-made retrospective endowment policies which —'

'Hold on,' Mr Smith interrupted, 'hold on just a moment.'

The partners turned and looked at him. 'Well?' they said.

'Gentlemen.' Mr Smith calmed himself down into an effort. 'You may not be aware of this,' he said, 'but I am by profession a student of economic theory; in fact, I pride myself on being on the verge of a breakthrough in monetary analysis which will, I sincerely believe, revolutionise the practice of economic planning in Europe, and my view is —'

'You mean,' said the senior partner slowly, '*The Wealth of Nations*?'

Smith's jaw dropped. 'You've heard of my book?'

'Naturally.'

'But that's impossible,' Smith replied. 'Why, I only completed the final draft today. In fact, I have it with me now. I'm taking it to my publisher.'

The senior partner smiled politely. 'You have the actual manuscript with you?' he said.

Smith, in spite of himself, could feel a glow of pride creeping over his face. It had been a long time since anyone had taken him seriously, since he'd been shown the proper respect his genius merited. 'I do indeed,' he said.

'Really!' The senior partner's manner changed; he became deferential. 'I have indeed heard of your work, Mr Smith,' he said. 'The word "seminal" would not be an overstatement.' Smith blushed. 'In fact, I would go further and say that your book brings the Dark Ages of economics to an end. May I see?'

After a very brief moment's hesitation, Smith dived into his battered brown bag and produced a manuscript. It was thick, dog-eared and bound up in red string. He handed it to the senior partner, who threw it on the fire.

'Now then,' he said, 'we offer a wide range of tailor-made retrospective endowment policies which ...'

'You really must learn,' Blondel said, 'to be more careful with that thing.'

'I wasn't —'

'I mean,' Blondel said, 'it's a nice trick if you can do it, but there are some people who have very pointy tops to their heads. You could injure somebody that way, you know.'

'It wasn't —'

'Anyway,' Blondel leaned against the wall and caught his breath. 'I don't think they're following us, do you?' he panted.

'No.'

'Splendid. Now, where are we, do you think?' He produced his little book and began to study it. Guy, who had got out of the habit of running shortly after leaving school, leaned with his hands on his knees and gasped for air.

'Blondel,' he said, 'I nearly killed Oliver Cromwell.'

'I know,' Blondel replied. 'Now, I make that the Un-American Activities archive over there, so if we head due south ...'

'I nearly changed the history of the world.'

'Then we can take a short cut through the New Deal, which ought to bring us out where we want to be. Sorry, you were saying?'

'History,' Guy repeated. 'I could have really messed it up, you know?'

'Exactly,' Blondel replied. 'Very volatile stuff, history. Give you an example. You tread on a fly. The fly is therefore not available to walk all over your great-great-great-great-grandfather's breakfast, and so he fails to die of food poisoning. Your family therefore does not sell up and move from Cheshire to Norfolk, with the result that your great-grandfather doesn't meet your great-grandmother at a whist drive, and you don't get born. That means you never existed, so you can't travel back through time and squash that fly in the first place. Result: your great-great-great-great-grandfather gets food poisoning, the family moves from Norfolk to Cheshire ...'

'Um.'

'And you,' Blondel went on, 'become a temporal anomaly, zipping in and out of existence like the picture on a television screen, thousands of times a second. Then you start to cause real problems, because of the knock-on effect and Ziegler's Mouse, and you end up with the Time Wardens after you.'

'Time Wardens.'

'Like game wardens,' Blondel explained, 'only with even more sweepingly wide powers. They won't be appointed for a hundred years or so yet, but when they are they'll travel back and start rounding up all the Loose Cannons.'

'Loose Canons,' Guy repeated. 'Is that some kind of religious order?'

'Not quite,' Blondel replied. 'You're thinking of the Giggling Friars, which is odd enough in its way, because they were all wiped out by the Time Wardens in about six hundred years' time. The Wardens have been looking for me since before I was born,' he added, 'or at least they will be. Actually, they're not a problem. It's the bounty hunters you've got to be wary of. Now, I think that if we go along this passage here, we'll come to a sharp left bend which should . . . ah, here we are.'

As far as Guy was concerned it was just another tunnel, but Blondel seemed to recognise it at once. He said, 'Nearly there,' several times, and whistled a number of tunes, including *Stardust* and *The Girl I Left Behind Me*.

'History,' he was saying, 'is fluid: you've got to remember that. It's changing all the time, what with the Loose Cannons and the Time Wardens and the Editeurs Saunce Pitie. Now then, if I press this lever here . . .'

A door opened, and Blondel walked through it.

Experience, the psychologists say, is like a man who walks into a lamppost, knocking himself out. When he comes round, the blow has caused a partial memory loss, which means that the victim forgets, inter alia, that colliding with lampposts causes injury. He therefore continues walking into lampposts for the rest of his unnaturally short life.

'Blondel,' said Guy, but Blondel wasn't there any more. He shrugged and followed.

'*L'amours dont sui epris
Me semont de chanter,*'
Blondel sang. A few passers-by threw small coins into

his hat, but otherwise nobody took a great deal of notice.

'Oh well,' he said at last, 'he doesn't seem to be here. Right, what about a drink?'

Guy had tried to explain to Blondel that there wasn't in fact a castle at the Elephant and Castle; that it was, to the best of his recollection, something to do with a mispronunciation of the Infanta of Castile; that even if there ever had been a castle here, there was highly unlikely to be one still here in 1987; and that even if there was one in 1987 they'd come up in the tube station instead. He'd done his best to convey all these things, and he didn't believe that 'That's what you think' was a satisfactory rejoinder. On the other hand, the idea of a drink sounded splendid, and he said as much.

'You're on, then,' Blondel said. 'Watch this.'

He laid his hat down beside him, produced his lute and sang some more songs, ones that Guy hadn't heard before and which he didn't like much. His view was not, however, shared by the passers-by, and they soon had a hatful of coins which Blondel judged to be adequate for the purpose in hand.

'There used to be a rather nice little Young's pub just round the corner from here,' he said. 'Nice beer, but the only way you could ever get on the pool table was to nip back through time and get your money down before the previous game started. Let's give it a try, shall we?'

'Used to be,' Guy repeated. 'When was that?'

'When I was last here.'

'1364?' Guy asked. '1570?'

Blondel grinned. '1997, actually. Like I always say, doesn't time fly when you're having fun?'

They wrapped Blondel's sword and Guy's revolver in a blanket to avoid being arrested and walked round the corner to the *Nine Bells*. As they sat down and tasted their beer, Blondel smiled.

'That's one of the advantages of my lifestyle,' he said. 'You get a better angle on progress.'

Guy wiped some froth from his lips. 'Come again?' he said.

'You know what I mean,' Blondel replied. 'You know how, as you get older, the beer never tastes as good, the policemen get younger every year, that sort of thing. Now I do my return visits in reverse chronological order whenever I can, so I get the opposite effect; yummy beer, geriatric policemen, and the last time I was here it was thirty pence a pint more expensive. Drink up.'

Guy drank up. It made him feel very slightly better.

'I suppose,' he said, 'I must be in my seventies by now. That's if I survive the War.'

'Quite so,' Blondel replied. 'There's an outside chance you might meet yourself, you never know. That's why it's so important not to get chatting about the War with old men in pubs.'

Guy nodded. 'Unless,' he said, 'I remember I was here before, of course. Then I'd know, I suppose.'

'Don't count on it,' Blondel said. 'I knew a chap once who met himself. Actually – he was a terribly clumsy sort of fellow, you see – he accidentally pushed himself under a train. It was his future self that got killed, of course, not his time-travelling self. Tragic.'

Guy looked up from his beer. 'What happened?'

'Poor chap,' Blondel said, 'went all to pieces. I said to him, Listen, George, it's no use living in the past.

83

But Jack, he said, I haven't really got any bloody choice in the matter, have I? In the end, the Editeurs came for him. It was the only thing to do.'

'Who are the —'

'Never you mind,' Blondel said. 'It'd only worry you. I think we have time for another.'

He went to the bar and returned with more beer.

'Blondel,' Guy asked, 'is that where ghosts come from?'

'Sorry?'

'Ghosts,' Guy said. 'Are they people who've got — well, lost in time? I mean, it sounds as if they could be people who've —'

'Nice idea,' said Blondel, 'but not really, no. Ghosts are something quite different. I'll tell you all about that some other time. Now then let's have a look at the schedule.'

He produced a tattered envelope, on the back of which was a long list written in minuscule handwriting. About a fifth of the entries were crossed off. Blondel deleted another three, and Guy noticed that three more added themselves automatically at the end. He asked about it.

'Automatic diary input,' Blondel explained. 'When I go to a place/time, it doesn't mean I've dealt with it once and for all. It just means that it goes to the back of the queue. However, I'm pleased to say we're more or less on —'

'Is this seat taken?'

A shadow had fallen across the table. Guy looked up and saw three men. They were dressed in smart charcoal grey suits and had dark grey hair. It was hard to tell them apart. They could easily have been brothers; triplets, even.

Blondel glanced up, smiled and said, 'Hello there, Giovanni, fancy meeting you here. Yes, by all means, take a pew. What'll you have?'

Guy stared. For some reason which he couldn't quite grasp, he could feel his hand walking along the seat on its fingertips towards the blanket.

'That's all right,' said Giovanni, 'Iachimo will get them. Same again?' He sat down, strategically placed between Guy and the blanket. Guy had the feeling that he'd done that on purpose.

'That'll be fine,' Blondel was saying. 'Guy, how about you?'

Guy said yes, that was very kind. One of the three went to the bar; the other one sat down next to Blondel and produced a cigar.

'We just missed you last time you were here,' Giovanni said. 'Marco, offer these gentlemen a cigar.'

'Your local, is it?' Blondel asked.

'Not really,' Giovanni replied. 'But we look in from time to time. Handy for the office, you know, meeting clients, that sort of thing.'

Blondel nodded. 'That's right,' he said, 'I forgot. Beaumont Street's just across the way, isn't it?'

Giovanni smiled. 'Well then,' he said, 'it's been a long time, hasn't it?'

'Quite,' Blondel replied. 'It must be —'

'Eight hundred years, exactly,' said Giovanni. 'To the day, in fact.'

'Is it really? Doesn't time —'

'Eight hundred years,' Giovanni went on, 'since you skipped out on us. Welched on your contract. Left us in a most unfortunate position.'

Blondel smiled. 'I don't think you've met my

colleague, Mr Goodlet,' he said. 'Guy Goodlet, the Galeazzo brothers; Giovanni, Iachimo, Marco. They're in the ...', Blondel considered for a moment, '... the timeshare business. And other things too, of course.'

The Galeazzo brothers turned and looked at Guy. Then they turned back and looked at Blondel, who was still smiling.

'Mr Goodlet,' he said, 'is a historian. In fact, he's with the History Warden's Office. Something to do with the fiscal division, aren't you, Guy?'

Some last vestige of native wit prompted Guy to sit still, say nothing and try and look very much indeed like a souvenir from Mount Rushmore.

'I see,' Giovanni said. 'No doubt he's got some means of identification.'

'Indeed I do,' Guy said. 'Would you like to see it?'

'If you don't mind.'

Guy nodded. 'I'll just get it,' he said. 'It's in that blanket over there, so if you'll just excuse me ...' He leaned across Marco, fumbled in the blanket, found his revolver and pressed it into Marco's side, discreetly below table level. Blondel thought for a moment, and then put his hat on Marco's head. Marco didn't move.

'Believe me,' Blondel said, 'you're much safer that way.'

After a long and slightly uncomfortable silence, Giovanni sighed and said, 'That's all very clever and impressive, but it doesn't really get us anywhere, does it?'

Blondel shrugged.

'I take it,' Giovanni went on, 'that your friend isn't actually a historian?'

'Correct,' Blondel smiled. 'Nor is he a top-notch marksman. At this range, however —'

'Yes, all right, I think you've made that point,' Giovanni scowled. 'Violence really isn't our way, you know,' he said. 'The last resort of the incompetent, and all that.'

'In which case, gentlemen,' Blondel replied, 'I think you probably qualify. Good Lord, is that the time?'

'All right,' Giovanni said, 'point taken. We have an offer.'

'I know all about your offers,' Blondel replied. 'Please don't try and stop us. I'm very fond of that hat, and another hole in it will leave it fit only for the dustbin. Thanks for the drink.'

He stood up and took hold of the blanket. Giovanni shook his head.

'We can help you find what you're looking for,' he said. 'That is, provided you're prepared to help us.'

Blondel raised one eyebrow. Then he sat down again, the blanket across his knees. To a certain limited extent, he looked like Whistler's Mother.

'The last time I listened to you gentlemen,' he said, 'I ended up with my face all over thirty thousand imitation satin surcoats.' He frowned. 'It's taken me eight hundred years to get over that,' he said.

Giovanni shrugged. 'So maybe we overdid the merchandising,' he said. 'You're an artist. Deep down, you need to perform. You need to communicate to vast audiences. You have a duty to your public.'

'I haven't got a public,' Blondel replied. 'And I am decidedly not an artist. Artists wear berets and smocks and cut their ears off. Messire Galeazzo, you are talking through your hat, and that is a very risky thing to do while Mr Goodlet's anywhere in the vicinity. Good day to you.'

Giovanni shrugged. 'It's up to you,' he said. 'But if you do actually want to find the King...'

Blondel closed his eyes for a moment and then sighed deeply.

'All right, then,' he said. 'Let's hear it.'

'Well —'

Before Giovanni was able to say anything else, however, the side door of the pub flew open and three men burst in. They were wearing dark green anoraks and holding big wooden clubs. Having entered, they stopped still and looked around them. Nobody seemed particularly bothered by their presence.

'Oh, how *tiresome*,' Blondel said. 'You just wait there.'

He got up, pulled his sword out from under the blankets, rushed at the three men and cut their heads off. A head rolled across the floor, was deflected off the leg of a chair, and ended up with its nose against Guy's foot. He looked down, feeling sick, terrified and, above all, horribly conspicuous. He needn't have worried, however; nobody was looking at him, particularly.

Someone behind the bar started to scream. Blondel frowned.

'Right,' he said, 'I think we ought to be getting along.'

There is a wide dichotomy between actual truth and perceived truth; and if the actual truth about the history of the world is that it was just one of those things, that is not necessarily important or even relevant to the people responsible for making sure that it doesn't happen again. Of this latter group, a considerable number have offices at the Chastel des Larmes

Chaudes; and one of them in particular, having just had a report from his senior operations manager, was not happy at all.

'Idiot,' he said.

Mountjoy King of Arms was far too spiritual, in the widest sense of the term, to be upset by vulgar abuse. He flickered for an instant, like a table lamp in a thunderstorm, and carried on with what he'd been saying.

'After that,' he said, 'they gathered up the bits and came back.'

Julian II snarled and stabbed the arm of his chair with a pencil, snapping it.

'Sack the lot of them,' he said. 'I ask you, what is this world coming to? You send out your top men – supposedly your top men – and what do you get? Unseemly brawls in public houses. I want them all back in the filing department by this time tomorrow, do you hear?'

Mountjoy nodded. His Unholiness' outbursts of temper rarely lasted long, and he never remembered what he'd said afterwards.

'And meanwhile?' he asked.

'Good question.' Julian's face calmed down slightly – the act of thinking always had that effect on him – and he stroked his beard gently. Small flashes of blue fire crackled away into the air.

'So where are they headed now, do you think?'

'We don't know,' Mountjoy replied. 'However, we have at last got some information on the men who were with him.'

Julian lifted his head and nodded approvingly. 'That's rather more like it,' he said. 'What have you got?'

Mountjoy took out his notebook. 'One of them,' he said, 'is a British citizen by the name of Guy Goodlet.'

'Yes?'

'From the mid-twentieth century,' Mountjoy went on. 'Some sort of professional warrior. His family held land in Norfolk at the time of the Domesday Book, but they've always been what you might call small to middling yeomen. No particular antecedents.'

'That doesn't sound very promising.'

'No indeed. The other three men are in fact the Beaumont Street Syndicate.'

Julian looked up. 'Are they indeed?'

Mountjoy nodded. He had decided that there was no point in trying to cover it up. After all, he really had nothing to hide. When he'd invested his small savings in the Beaumont Street Renaissance Income Fund, he'd had no idea that they were mixed up in anything untoward.

'The Beaumont Street Syndicate,' Julian repeated. 'Well, well. How deeply do you think they're involved?'

'Too early to say,' Mountjoy replied. 'It might be,' he added cautiously, 'that their involvement is entirely innocent.'

'Well quite,' Julian replied, nodding. 'In fact, I expect we'll find that that's it, entirely. I mean, everybody's got to have a financial adviser, even Jean de Nesle. No law against it.'

'No indeed.'

'Just common sense, really.'

'Quite so.'

'Well, there you are, then,' Julian said. 'Nevertheless,' he added, 'we'd better keep an eye on them. Discreetly, of course. Wouldn't want to start a scare on the Exchanges, would we?' He laughed brightly. 'Right, you get that in hand straight away. Put Pursuivant on to it, why don't you? He's got more brains than the others. I've even known him switch on a light without blowing all the fuses. Oh, and Mountjoy . . .'

'Yes?'

'I wonder if you'd mind just sending a fax for me. To my broker, you know,' Julian said. 'Just a little bit of personal business.'

'Blondel.'

'Testing, testing, one, two, three,' said Blondel. 'Yes?'

Guy frowned. He didn't want to appear faint-hearted or anything like that, but he felt he had a right to know. 'Those people,' he said. 'You know, in that pub?'

Blondel thought for a moment. 'Oh,' he said, 'you mean in that pub in the Elephant and Castle?'

'That's right,' Guy said. 'After we'd been sorting things out with the Lombards; the men who came in and . . .'

'Got you, yes,' Blondel said. He peered at the microphone and blew into it, giving rise to a sound like God coughing. 'What about them?'

'It's nothing, really,' Guy replied. 'It's just . . . well, does that sort of thing happen very often? Because first there was the fight we had with the man when we followed the stag, and then that business in the Houses of Parliament, and now this . . .'

'The Houses of Parliament thing was different,' Blondel said. He adjusted the microphone stand slightly and tightened up the little clips. 'They were just

91

ordinary guards. Must be an awful job, I always think, being a guard. Complete strangers forever hitting you and so forth.'

'But the other ones,' Guy persisted. 'What about them?'

Blondel shrugged. 'I don't really know all that much about them myself. They just keep turning up and trying to attack me. They're not very good at it, as you'll have seen for yourself. Their arms and legs don't seem to ... well, to work properly, if you know what I mean. They've been doing it for as long as I can remember.'

'How can you tell?' Guy asked. 'That it's the same lot, I mean.'

'Easy,' Blondel replied. 'It's always the same people. They never seem to get a day older, you know. Been jumping out on me for years, some of them have.'

'Have you tried finding out who they are?'

'What, from them, you mean? No point.'

'Why not?' Guy asked. 'Do they refuse to talk, or something?'

Blondel scratched his ear. 'It's not that,' he said, 'far from it. It's just that when you try questioning them, they go all to pieces.'

'Perhaps if you tried, I don't know, being a bit less intimidating ...'

'No, you don't understand,' Blondel said. 'When I say they go all to pieces, I mean all to pieces. If you don't duck pretty sharpish, bits of them hit you. Legs, kidneys, that sort of thing.'

Guy stared. 'You mean they ...?'

'Blow up, yes. Now, where does this wire go?' He traced the course of the wire to the back of a huge amplifier and pulled it out. 'There,' he said, 'that's better. Never could be doing with all this gadgetry.' He picked up the microphone and tapped it. Silence. 'I always reckon that if you can't make them hear you at the back of the hall then you shouldn't call yourself a singer. Why they blow up, of course, I haven't the faintest idea, but they do. The odd thing is that it can't do them much harm, because a month or so later they come bouncing back, club in hand ...'

'You're telling me,' Guy said, 'that the same men who blow up ...'

'That's right,' Blondel said. 'Anyway, that's all I know about them. Except, of course, that they're something to do with the Chastel des Larmes Chaudes. They've got the Chastel livery, you see.'

'Fine,' Guy said. 'So what's the ...?'

But Blondel had gone off to disconnect the boom mikes, and Guy thought it was best to leave it at that. The hell with La Beale Isoud, he had decided. If there was any way he could get back to his own time, he'd do it. If not, well, he'd have to settle down here (wherever here was) and get a job. But no more of this being jumped on by strange exploding assassins. Not his cup of tea at all.

'Now where's he gone?' said a voice behind him. It was Giovanni, the senior partner.

'He went off to look at something,' Guy replied. 'Something technical, after my time. Look, can I ask you something?'

Giovanni raised an eyebrow. 'What can I do for you?' he asked.

'It's like this,' Guy said. 'Have you known Blondel long?'

93

Giovanni grinned. 'Yes,' he said.

Guy nodded. 'All this stuff, about time travel and the civil service and Richard the Lion-Heart. It's not for real, is it?'

'I'm sorry?'

'I mean,' Guy said, 'it's not actually true, is it? None of this is actually happening, or about to happen or whatever; it's all just ...'

Giovanni had both eyebrows raised. 'Of course it's *true*,' he said. 'What a very peculiar thing to suggest. After all, here you are experiencing it; it must be true, don't you think?'

'I ...' Guy rallied his thoughts. 'I just find it hard to accept,' he said, looking out over the auditorium, 'that I'm here with the court poet of Richard the First, who's about to give a concert in a specially built auditorium somewhere in the middle of the Hundred Years War. With a public address system,' he added, 'which makes the sort of thing we have back in my own century look like two cocoa tins and a length of string. I mean, you'll understand my being a bit confused.'

'Indeed I do,' Giovanni said. 'And I think I can help.'

'You can?'

Giovanni smiled. 'I believe so,' he said. 'What you're really saying is that you're worried.'

'Extremely worried.'

'Perfectly understandable,' Giovanni said. 'After all, you can't be expected to know what's going to happen next. You've absolutely no way of knowing, from one moment to the next, what the future, immediate or long-term, has in store for you.'

'Exactly,' Guy said. 'So perhaps ...'

'What you need,' Giovanni said, 'is your own personal pension scheme. Now it so happens . . .'

It had taken a long time.

Well, it would, wouldn't it, if all you had to dig with was the handle of a broken spoon, and the wall was thirteen feet thick and made of a particularly hard sort of toughened silicon.

And then there was the problem of disposing of the dust and the rubble; you can't just leave it there, or the guards will notice and get suspicious. You have to stash it somewhere out of sight. The prisoner had eventually hit on the idea of stuffing it into bags and hanging them from the roof, where it was so dark that nobody could see them. But the only materials he had for making bags from was spiders' webs – it takes literally hundreds of miles of spiders' web to weave three inches of reasonably strong thread – and the skins of rats. He had, over many years, found out that his cell produced only enough food for one spider and one rat to live on at any one time. But one thing that the prisoner had plenty of was time; and while he was waiting for the spiders to spin another few inches of gossamer and for the rats to die of old age, he could always get on with the digging.

And now he was almost through. Another half inch, no more, stood between him and whatever it was that lay on the other side of the wall. If he really got stuck in and put his back into it, he'd be through in five years, or six at the very latest. He was virtually free already . . .

He was just about to set to work when he heard footsteps in the corridor outside. Hurriedly the prisoner dropped the spoon-handle back into the hole he'd gouged in the floor for a hiding-place, and sat on it. The door opened.

'Afternoon,' said the jailer.

'Afternoon,' replied the prisoner affably. He was always careful to be as pleasant as he could with the staff. After all, it couldn't be a wonderfully exciting and fulfilling job working in a place like this, and the prisoner was the sort of man who thought about such things.

'I've got some good news for you,' said the jailer. 'The bloke in the cell next to you's just died.'

The prisoner went as white as a sheet. Since he hadn't seen daylight for a very, very long time now, this wasn't immediately apparent to the jailer.

'Which side?' the prisoner asked.

'Sorry?'

'On which side was his cell?'

'That one,' the jailer replied, and pointed. The prisoner's heart started to beat again. Not the side he was digging on, thank goodness!

'Got to be that side,' the jailer continued, ''cos there isn't a cell the other side. The other side's the exterior wall of the castle. Anyway,' he went on, 'your neighbour's just snuffed it.'

'Ah,' said the prisoner. This was supposed to be good news, and the prisoner could see nothing pleasant in the news that a man had just died, even if it was a man he'd never even heard of before.

'And the good news,' the jailer went on, 'is that that means his cell's now empty. We can move you in there straight away.'

'But ...'

'You'll like it,' the jailer said. 'It's got a lovely south-facing aspect,' he went on. 'Bigger than this one, too; you'd have – oh, six inches at least more living area. Open plan. The door doesn't squeak, either, and it's ever so quiet and peaceful. It's even got a window.'

'I —'

'Well,' said the jailer, 'maybe that's a bit of an exaggeration. What I mean is, the door isn't exactly flush, and so when there's a lamp lit out in the corridor, that means that a little crack of light gets in under the door. Now isn't that something?'

'Yes, but I —'

'Kept it lovely, he did,' the jailer went on blithely. 'The bloke who's just died, I mean. He did this nice sort of mural thing all over the walls with chalk. Sort of pattern of bunches of six lines down and one line through them. Simple, if you know what I mean, but sort of striking.'

'Yes, but I can't —'

The jailer smiled. 'That's all right,' he said. 'I know what you're going to say, but really, no problem. You've never been any trouble, you haven't, not like some of them, and you've always had a cheerful word for me and the kids of a morning. We appreciate that sort of thing in the prison service, believe you me. So this is my way of saying thank you. I mean, if we can't help people out sometimes, what sort of a world is this, anyway?'

'But ...' The prisoner couldn't help turning and looking into the darkness at where his tunnel, which had occupied his waking and sleeping thoughts for so long now that he couldn't remember a time when ...

On the other hand, a voice said at the back of his

mind, this gentleman is being extremely kind and generous, doing his best to be helpful, and even when people do things for you and give you things that you don't actually want, you must always remember that it's the thought that counts. Anything else would be sheer ingratitude.

'Thank you,' said the prisoner. 'Thank you ever so much.' He looked round for the last time. 'I'll just say goodbye to my rat and I'll be right with you.'

The concert had been a success.

Nominally, it was a charity gig, with all the proceeds going to finance a last-ditch attempt to turn back the tide of Islam and recapture Jerusalem; hence the name of the organisation – CrusAid – and the stalls at the entrances to the auditorium selling a wide range of official souvenir missals, holy relics and I-Forcibly-Converted-The-World surcoats. In reality, CrusAid was a wholly-owned subsidiary of Clairvaux Holdings, the property arm of the United Lombard Group of Companies, which in turn was a satellite corporation of the Second Crusade Investment Trust (established 1187) into which the Beaumont Street Syndicate funnelled the accumulated capital of the centuries. By the time the proceeds reached SCIT, however, the money had been not so much laundered as washed in the blood of the Lamb.

In spite of all that, however, they came in their thousands from all over Christendom, and when Blondel sang *O Fortuna Velut Luna*, *Imperator Rex Graecorum*, *Aestuans Intrinsecus* and other numbers from his 1186 hit missal *Carmina Burana*, they had to be forcibly restrained by the Templar security guards from ripping up the seats and setting fire to them.

Afterwards, Giovanni came backstage. He looked exhausted and his hands were black with silver oxide from helping his brothers count the takings. They had had to hire fifteen mules and three hundred Knights Templar to transport the money to Paris to be banked.

'Blondel,' he said wearily, 'that was great. I mean really great. Stupendous.' He sat down heavily on a chest and massaged his wrists.

'Good,' said Blondel absently, towelling his damp hair. 'Can we be getting on now, please?'

'I'm sorry?' Giovanni said.

'Well,' Blondel replied, 'there's no point in hanging about here, is there? I thought you said you wanted me to do several concerts.'

'Yes,' said Giovanni, 'but not now, surely. I mean ...'

'No time like the present,' Blondel said, 'if you'll pardon the expression. When to?'

'Now hang on a minute ...'

Blondel shook his head. 'We had a deal,' he said. 'I was to do a certain number of concerts, and then you'd tell me what you know about the Chastel des Larmes Chaudes. You didn't say anything about intervals between the concerts. I just want to get all this fooling about over and done with and then get back to work.'

Giovanni shuddered. 'Fair enough,' he said, 'but –'

'But nothing,' Blondel replied firmly. 'Where's the next venue?'

Just then the door of the dressing room burst open, and in tumbled three large men in armour, all with that air of complete discomfort that comes from charging a door with their shoulders without first ascertaining whether or not it's actually locked. They grabbed at a table to try and stop themselves, succeeded only in turning it over, skidded across the flagstones, collided with the wall and fell over, stunned. On their surcoats they bore a coat of arms comprising a mitre argent on a sable field, a bend cross keys reversed gules, attired of the second. Blondel blinked, stood motionless for a second as if rapt in thought, and then grabbed a fire extinguisher and hosed them down until they were all thoroughly drenched in white foam.

'Now try it,' he said. 'Go on.'

The three men made various gestures. Their reactions suggested that what they'd expected would happen hadn't.

'Thought so,' Blondel said. 'I thought you wouldn't be able to blow up if you were all wet. Now, I think it's time we had a chat, don't you?'

'We're saying nothing.'

'All right, then,' Blondel replied grimly. 'Guy, shoot their hats off.'

'But they aren't wearing ...'

Blondel scowled, and then grabbed the headgear from the Lombard brothers and rammed it down over the ears of the prisoners. 'They are now,' he said.

Guy reached, rather hesitantly, for his revolver. One of the prisoners let out a howl of anguish and asked Blondel rather urgently what it was that he wanted to know.

'You could start,' Blondel said, 'by telling me where the Chastel des Larmes Chaudes is.'

The prisoner thought for a moment and then said 'Pursuivant, Sergeant at Arms, 87658765.'

'Come again?' said Blondel. 'Was that supposed to

be a map reference or something?'

'Name, rank and number,' Guy interrupted. 'It's all a prisoner of war has to tell you, under the Geneva Convention.'

'Which hasn't been signed yet,' Blondel replied. 'Mr Pursuivant, if you will insist on talking through your hat, perhaps you'll find it easier with a hole to talk through.'

'Pursuivant, Sergeant at Arms, 8765 —'

'Oh for pity's sake,' Blondel said. 'Go and make some custard, somebody.'

There was a baffled silence for a moment. 'Custard?' Giovanni eventually enquired.

'That's right,' Blondel said, 'custard.' He folded his arms, smiled, and leaned against the table.

'What's going on?' Pursuivant demanded querulously. 'What are you playing at?'

'You'll see,' Blondel replied. 'Now then, while we're waiting for the custard, would either of you two gentlemen care to tell me anything?'

'Clarenceaux, Sergeant at Arms, 987665723,' mumbled the shorter of the other two prisoners. His companion said nothing.

'Fine,' Blondel sighed. 'We'll do it the hard way if you wish. Anybody got any peanuts out there?'

'Here,' said Clarenceaux, but his companion told him to shut up. Blondel's smile widened into a wicked grin.

Giovanni came back with a large pudding-basin. 'You're in luck,' he said. 'Just by chance I found some in the kitchens of the Burger Knight stall. It's cold, I'm afraid, but . . .'

'Oh that's all right,' Blondel said. 'Cold's fine. Now

101

then, one last chance. Any offers?'

Clarenceaux would have said something if his companion hadn't stamped viciously on his foot. Blondel made a sort of tutting sound and lifted Clarenceaux up by the collar of his kagoul.

'Sorry about this,' he said, 'but that's how it is. To a certain extent, of course, I admire your courage.'

'Courage?' Clarenceaux whimpered.

'Sorry,' Blondel replied. 'I should have said heroism. You see,' he went on, as he lifted the borrowed hat off the prisoner's head, 'when you're dealing with people who, every time they get beaten up, mutilated or killed, are somehow magically restored to life and health by their bosses, there's clearly not much mileage in conventional torture. But,' he said, tipping a copious amount of custard out on to the top of Clarenceaux's head, 'pain and death aren't the only things we're afraid of in this life. Oh no. There's also,' he said, flexing his fingers and massaging the custard into Clarenceaux's scalp, 'humiliation, embarrassment and being made to look a right nana. I mean – anybody got any jam? – I expect your comrades in arms are a right little bunch of humorists, aren't they? Once they get hold of something they can be funny about, you'll never – blackcurrant'll do fine, thanks – hear the last of it. And correct me if I'm wrong, but since you're effectively immortal, and stuck doing the same job with the same bunch of people for effectively the rest of time – that ought to do it; now, I'll need some flour, some eggs, some feathers and, of course, the peanuts and a razor – the very worst thing I could do to you would be send you back to Headquarters all covered in horrible sticky mess with half your beard shaved off and a packet of peanuts down the back of your neck. Oh, I forgot the shoe polish.'

'All right,' Clarenceaux squeaked, 'all right, I give up.' His companion tried to jump at him but Guy hit him with the fire extinguisher and he sat down again. 'Just let me wash all this off and I'll talk.'

'After you've talked,' Blondel said. 'And any mucking about and it's the honey and feathers treatment for you. No, not honey,' he added. 'Treacle.'

Clarenceaux made a sort of rattling noise in the back of his throat. 'You wouldn't do that,' he gargled. 'That's ... that's not *fair*.'

Blondel grinned and shook his head. 'Let's have it,' he said. 'Where's the Chastel des Larmes Chaudes?'

'I —'

'Yes?'

Clarenceaux gagged, spat out a mouthful of custard which had dripped down his nose into his mouth and said, 'I don't know.'

'You don't know?'

'Really I don't.'

Blondel paused for a moment, while the prisoner watched him with big, round eyes.

'Have you thought,' Blondel said at last, 'what your so-called mates are going to do to you when you turn up later on this evening all covered in rice pudding and with a banana shoved right up your —'

'I don't *know*,' Clarenceaux screamed. 'We aren't allowed to know, just in case we're caught, see? There's this sort of bus thing picks us up and takes us to where we got to go, and then takes us back when we finish. They put paper bags over our heads while it's moving. Honest, I'm telling the truth.'

Blondel stroked his chin with the custard-free back of his hand. 'I don't believe you,' he said. 'Guy, see if you can find some rice pudding. Lots of rice pudding, there's a good chap.'

'Look, mister . . .'

'And a banana, of course. Mustn't forget the banana.'

Clarenceaux started to sob, but Blondel's face remained unchanged. 'The Chastel,' he said. 'Where is it?'

'I don't . . .'

'Got that rice pudding yet, Guy?' Blondel asked. Guy stood up. Where, he asked himself, was he expected to get rice pudding from at this . . .?

'Leave him alone,' Pursuivant interrupted suddenly. 'Can't you see he's telling the truth?'

Blondel turned slowly round and looked Pursuivant in the eye. '*Lots* of rice pudding,' he said.

'It's the truth, I tell you,' Pursuivant whined. 'We don't know nothing, any of us. The bus just comes, and then it takes us away again after. It's a big grey thing,' he added desperately, 'with a duff exhaust.'

Blondel nodded and folded his arms, inadvertently getting custard on himself. 'Go on,' he said.

'What do you want to know?' Pursuivant asked.

'Well,' said Blondel, 'you could start with the number plate.'

'That's easy,' Pursuivant said. 'It's Z —'

Then something happened which Guy didn't expect. Giovanni, who'd been standing behind Blondel holding the pudding-basin full of custard, suddenly lifted it up, turned it over, and shoved it down on top of Blondel's head. As Guy moved to strike him, one of the others –

Iachimo, probably – threw the flour in his face and squirted an aerosol of whipped cream, which he apparently happened to have by him, in his eyes, leaving him momentarily blinded. The third brother, meanwhile, bundled the three prisoners to their feet and towards the door. Guy wiped cream furiously out of his eyes, gave Iachimo a shove that sent him reeling, pulled out his revolver and fired a shot at the retreating prisoners. There was a crash of splintering china, and the pudding-basin over Blondel's head split exactly in two and slid down over his shoulders to the floor. Giovanni was hit on the ear by a fragment of ceramic shrapnel, yelped and sat down heavily on a plate of mince pies. Iachimo had fallen into a laundry basket. The third brother, Marco, had jumped out of his skin when Guy fired his revolver, slipped on a patch of custard and collided with a standard-lamp, the shade of which fell down over his shoulders like a jousting-helm. The door closed with a bang, and from the corridor outside came the sound of hurried squelching, fading away into silence.

Blondel found a towel and wiped the custard out of his eyes and ears. 'Right,' he said, 'that's quite enough of that for one evening. Now then.'

He turned towards Giovanni, who cringed slightly, and Guy instinctively realised that, for all his dexterity with a pudding basin, the eldest Lombard was not primarily a man of action.

'It's all right,' said Blondel wearily. 'But what the devil possessed you to do that? The so-and-so was just about to ...' He checked himself, flicked a fragment of custard-skin irritably out of the corner of his eye, and sighed. 'I think I see. It's because that ... he was just

105

about to tell me the bit of information you lot know. And if he'd told me, you lot wouldn't have had any way of making me do those other confounded concerts.'

Giovanni had the grace not to meet Blondel's eye. He nodded. 'After all,' he said, 'it's not our money we put up to arrange those gigs. We've got a duty to ...'

Blondel held up his hand. 'Please,' he said, 'spare me all that. The important thing now is to get on with it. You lot get all this mess cleared up and ready to go. I think I'd better wash my hair.'

He shook his head once more and started to walk towards the bathroom. Then he turned to Guy, who was standing holding his revolver as if it was a dead fish and gave him a very significant look.

'Practise a lot, do you?' he said, and left the room.

'Are you *sure* we're going the right way?' Giovanni asked.

'Positive,' Blondel replied. 'If you'd rather navigate . . .'

Giovanni shrugged. Ever since the slight misunderstanding in the dressing room at the auditorium, there had been a slight coolness between Blondel and his agents, which the perennial map-reading debate wasn't helping. 'Not at all,' he said. 'Leave it entirely up to you. That way, if we end up in the Second Ice Age and get frozen to death, it won't be my fault.'

After that they went on in silence for a while, until they came to a quite indisputably dead end. The tunnel stopped leading anywhere, and there was just a wall.

'Well?' Giovanni said.

'Yes,' Blondel replied. 'Yes, on balance, I think you may have a point. Pity about that.'

They sat down and Giovanni produced a cigarette-lighter, by whose light Blondel studied his little book.

'I see,' he said after a while. 'What I thought was the Quattrocento was in fact the Enlightenment. One's marked blue on the map, you see, and the other's a sort of dark mauve. Easy to get them muddled up.'

Giovanni made a faintly contemptuous noise. 'So where are we, then?' he said.

'Well,' Blondel replied, 'if I'm right about where we went astray before, that wall is the Fall of Constantinople, so really we want to go back the way we came, turn left at the next interchange and keep on till we come out into the European Monetary System. How does that sound?'

There was a little muted grumbling, and Iachimo said something about next time it being easier just to go the long way round. They picked up their luggage and set off back down the tunnel. They had gone no more than a quarter of a mile when they came to another dead end.

'Oh, that's marvellous,' Giovanni said. 'Now what's happened?'

Blondel walked forwards and examined the obstruction. 'There's been a timeslip,' he said. 'We'll have to go back and find a way round.'

Guy asked what a timeslip was.

'Like a landslip,' Blondel explained, 'only more awkward if you're in a hurry. All that's happened is that the roof of the tunnel's caved in, and a slice of some other period has fallen through and is blocking the way. Someone from the Work of the Clerks' office'll be along sooner or later to patch it all up. Meanwhile —'

'Don't you mean Clerk of the Works?' Guy asked.

'I mean what I said,' Blondel replied, nettled. 'This whole network, you'll recall, is the work of generations and generations of government clerks. They have an unofficial agreement that when something goes wrong with the fabric, they take it in turns to fix it. Just as well, really. If nobody looked after it and it all started falling to pieces, you'd have massive timeslips all over the shop – it'd be chaos. Luckily they keep it all in quite good order. Now ...'

He broke off and stared at the obstruction in front of him. 'Hello,' he said, 'I don't like the sound of that.' He turned to Giovanni. 'What do you think?' he said.

'What?'

'Listen,' Blondel replied. 'Oh, how aggravating!'

Guy pushed his way past Iachimo and asked what was going on.

'I don't want to alarm you,' Blondel said, 'but I think this lot may be unstable. Listen.'

Guy listened. It was just as well, he told himself, that he had a firm grip on reality, because otherwise he might have believed that he was hearing little faint voices coming out of the wall of rubble in front of him.

'Hear them?' Blondel asked. Guy nodded. 'That's that, then,' he said firmly. 'Back the way we came, quick.'

They started to walk fast down the tunnel. The voices followed them, gradually getting louder; then, not so gradually, getting louder still. It was rather disturbing, in fact.

'Run!'

As he ran, Guy tried to hear what the voices were saying. Most of them were talking languages he couldn't understand – there was French, and a lot of Latin, and probably Spanish; just occasionally, though, someone said something in English. None of it sounded particularly cheerful, whatever it was. Guy ran faster.

'Come on,' Blondel was shouting, 'for pity's sake get a move on.' Guy looked up, but in the darkness of the tunnel he couldn't see where the others had gone. Meanwhile the voices were getting louder all the time. They seemed to fill up space behind him. He stumbled over something and nearly lost his footing, and as he staggered along he distinctly felt something fly over his head, shrieking in French as it went. After it came some Italian, and some Latin, and what sounded like Turkish. Guy kept his head bent low and tried to run faster, but there was a limit to what his muscles could achieve.

'*Dear Sir,*' something was yapping behind him, '*Dear Sir, Dear Sir.*' He could almost feel it, close on his heels. There were others with it, all saying the same thing, but in many different voices, high and low, old and young, male and female, friendly, unfriendly and very, very hostile.

'*G. Goodlet Esquire,*' they screamed, '*37 Mayflower Avenue Sutton Surrey Our reference Jay Oblique Three Seven Nine Dee Four Six Thirteenth October Nineteen Seventy One Dear Sir ...*' Guy put his hands over his ears but it didn't seem to make any difference. Some of it was coming from over his head anyway. Something inside him told him that if they once managed to get in front of him, that would be it. He somehow managed to run faster.

'*It has come to our attention,*' they screamed, '*that you have failed to complete an annual return for any fiscal year since Nineteen Forty Two.*' Guy started to howl, but he couldn't hear himself, only a lot of voices, very cold voices, saying '*You are reminded that interest at the statutory rate runs on all tax due and unpaid*

within thirty days of the date of the respective assess-
ments.' Something was holding on to the lobe of his ear
now, bending it back, and shouting directly at him,
'*Unless the prescribed forms are completed and returned
to this office within the next seven working days, we shall
have no alternative but to ...*' Then he lost his balance,
crashed into the wall of the tunnel, lurched hopelessly
and fell. A great wave of sound rolled over him, in
every language ever heard or read, physically crushing
him. He tried to move ...

Further up the tunnel, Blondel stopped and collapsed,
gasping, against the bulkhead door he had just managed
to slam shut. It was beautifully quiet here ...

'That was close,' he said.

Giovanni, huddled on the ground at his feet, interrupted his panting to make an indeterminate noise and
then rolled over onto his back. Iachimo and Marco had
fainted.

'Never mind,' Blondel said, 'all's that well that ...
Hello, where's Guy got to?'

Giovanni looked up. 'Who?'

'Guy Goodlet,' Blondel replied. 'You know, English-
man, doesn't like hats.'

'Oh,' Giovanni said, 'him. Lord knows. Fell over his
feet, I think.'

Blondel sighed deeply and slid down the door to the
ground. 'Oh *bother*,' he said. 'What a confounded
nuisance.'

'Well,' Giovanni replied, 'there's no point getting all
emotional about it. These things happen in time, you
know that.' He shrugged his shoulders. 'Just as well he
didn't take out any life cover after all,' he added.

111

Blondel gave him a disapproving look. 'What's that supposed to mean?' he asked.

Giovanni shrugged again. 'Look,' he said, 'the man's popped it. Got drowned in a timeburst. All very sad but there it is. There's absolutely nothing any of us can do about it.'

'You reckon?'

'Yes,' Giovanni said, 'I do. It's just one of those things. Look, shouldn't we be . . .?'

But Blondel wasn't listening. He was very gingerly lifting the bar on the bulkhead door. Before Giovanni could stop him, he'd opened it. There was a sudden deafening roar of voices, and then the door slammed again, with Blondel on the other side of it.

'Hey . . .' Iachimo had come round just in time to see. He tried to get to the door before it shut, but he was too late.

'Forget it,' Giovanni said. He was very white in the face, and shaking slightly.

'Giovanni,' Iachimo said, 'did you just see that? He deliberately —'

'I said,' Giovanni interrupted, 'forget about it.'

'Yes, but —'

Giovanni slapped his brother across the face. It worked; Iachimo calmed down a little. 'He's had it, too,' Giovanni said. 'Pity, after all that trouble we've been to, but there it is. Gone. That's it. No more Blondel.'

The three brothers sat there for some time, not saying a word, until at last Giovanni got to his feet and pulled the others to theirs.

'Come on,' he said, 'we've got work to do.'

'Work?' Iachimo looked at him with empty eyes.

'Giovanni, it was horrible, he just —'

'Work,' Giovanni repeated. 'Now.' His mouth quivered slightly. 'Or had you forgotten?'

'Forgotten what?'

Giovanni was grinning now. 'Forgotten that we've insured the bastard's life for fifty billion livres. Come on, let's find a notary.'

They got up and walked slowly down the tunnel. After a while, they all started whistling.

La Beale Isoud, having washed her hair and done her nails, wandered down into the Great Hall of the Chastel de Nesle and plugged in the hyperfax.

There have been many inventions that might have revolutionised the world if only someone had had the vision to invest in them at the crucial moment; one thinks automatically of the frictionless wheel, the solar-powered night storage heater (stores up warm summer evenings for winter use) and the Wilkinson-Geary hingeless door. The hyperfax was no less remarkable, technologically speaking, than any of these; but it differed from them in never having had a chance to be neglected. The prototype and all the blueprints and design specifications had vanished mysteriously from an office in the Central Technology Department of the Oceanian Ministry of Science back in 2987, and the design team were so dispirited by this setback that they forgot all about the project and went back to designing sentient sleeping policemen for the Road Traffic Department. The only working hyperfaxes now in existence are the original prototype, installed in the Chastel de Nesle, and the Mark IIb. Nobody has ever been able to find out what happened to the Mark IIb.

La Beale Isoud sat down and pressed the necessary keys. The screen flickered for a few moments and bleeped. The word

READY?

appeared. La Beale Isoud rubbed her palms together and nodded.

CAN WE START NOW?

La Beale Isoud shook her head. 'Let me just have a think, will you?' she said. 'I'm not sure what I want to send yet.'

YOU SHOULD HAVE THOUGHT OF THAT BEFORE

'Oh, nuts to you,' replied La Beale Isoud. 'Don't fluster me, or I'll never be ready. If you want something to keep you busy, you can print me out all the towns in Europe with a population of over ten thousand.'

There was a high-pitched screaming noise, and a stream of paper flew out of the side of the machine. It took about three seconds.

FINISHED

It is impossible for eight illuminated green letters to look smug, but somehow the word FINISHED managed it. The hyperfax was, after all, very good at faffing about with the laws of possibility.

'In alphabetical order?' Isoud asked sweetly.

NATURALLY

'Oh.' Isoud frowned slightly. 'Well done. Now do me

the same for every year between 1066 and 2065.

The machine beeped, and then started screaming again. Meanwhile, Isoud scratched her nose and tried to think of something that would be fun to do, but which wouldn't irritate the machine, which was inclined to be touchy.

FINISHED AGAIN

'Well aren't you clever!' Isoud said. 'Right, I'm all ready to start. Receive mode, please. Bring me ...' She made a random sweep of her subconscious mind '... a tail-feather from the Golden Phoenix of the Caucasus Moun —'

A bell rang, and a silver plate popped out of a door in the front of the machine. On it was a single green feather.

'Oh,' said Isoud. 'You might let me finish my sentence.'

SORRY, I'M SURE

Isoud picked up the feather, looked at it closely, sniffed it, sneezed and asked, 'Are you sure this is from —' The machine beeped at her. 'Sorry,' she said, 'sorry. It's just it's not, well, very special looking, is it?'

TOUGH

'I didn't mean to imply —'

DIDN'T YOU, THOUGH?

'No,' Isoud said patiently, 'I didn't. I just thought —'

READY?

'Oh don't sulk!'

'Now I've offended you,' Isoud said. 'I'm really very sorry and it's a lovely feather, really. Look, it just goes nicely with my scarf!'

YOU'RE JUST SAYING THAT

'No I'm not,' said Isoud, through gritted teeth. 'Now, why don't we forget all about it and you bring me something nice.'

SUCH AS?

'Oh,' said Isoud, 'I don't know. Strawberries. An ice cream. Violets. Anything. Use your bloody imagination.'

TOGETHER OR SEPARATELY

Isoud's fingernails dug into her fine lawn handkerchief. 'Separately, please.'

WRAPPED?

'If you like, yes.'

The bell rang, the door opened, and a little spring began firing strawberries, individually wrapped in silver foil and ribbon, straight at Isoud, who ducked. Then came the ice cream, which fortunately she was able to avoid, followed by a bombardment of violets, which burst on hitting the opposite wall and went everywhere.

'Thanks,' Isoud said grimly when it was all over. 'Now can I have a vacuum cleaner, please?'

The bell rang, and a beautiful chrome-plated Electrolux rolled out and sat at her feet. It too was festooned in ribbon, which managed to get tangled up with the lead.

Isoud sighed. The hyperfax was all very well in its way, but she could see now why they'd said it needed working on before it was ready for mass market release. 'All right,' she said. 'Switch from receive mode to transmit mode, please. I want to send all this lot back.'

SUIT YOURSELF

The door opened, and a great wind blew through the hall. A few moments later, the feather, the strawberries, the ice cream, the violets and the hoover had all gone. So had two cushions and the heel of one of Isoud's shoes, but she knew better than to try and make something of it. She thanked the machine, decided that she would far rather get on with her embroidery instead, and stood up to switch it off at the mains.

Then the little bell rang again, and a man fell out of the door, rolled round on the carpet a couple of times and came to rest under the sideboard. He lay there very still. The screen read:

STILL RECEIVING

'Really!' Isoud said, irritably. 'Please prepare to transmit immediately!'

The screen flickered – a sort of digital shrug – and the man was dragged slowly back the way he had come. As his head collided with the leg of the table he let out a pitiful howl and Isoud, on impulse, pressed the Pause button. The screen went insufferably blank.

'Ouch,' said the man.

Isoud looked down at him. 'Mr Goodlet, isn't it?' she said. 'Would you care for some tea?'

117

★

Blondel woke up, hauled himself painfully to his feet, and looked at the notice. It said:

THIS WAY

That didn't seem to make a great deal of sense. From what little he could see of his surroundings, he was in the middle of a huge empty space, and the only light was a sort of pale glow around the notice; there was no sign of any roof, sky, walls or anything helpful like that, and there was nothing in the notice itself to suggest which way was the way referred to. On the other hand, he instinctively felt, this wasn't the time to start making difficulties. He had just, as far as he could judge, drowned in time, and the best thing to do was probably keep a low profile, just in case he was really supposed to be dead.

The scabbard by his side was empty, and a quick survey revealed that he had lost all the cherished little artefacts which he had collected over a very long life of time-travel: the map of the tunnel network, for example; the mirror which showed demons in their true shape; his all-purpose combined season ticket, identity card, passport, museum pass and phonecard; even his calculator watch and his comb. On the other hand, apart from a number of bruises and a nagging pain in his left wrist, he was reasonably undamaged, so the odds were still on his side. *Dum spiro spero*, and all that.

He decided to walk; in which direction he neither knew nor cared, now that he'd lost his matchbox with the compass in the lid. He set out brightly, on past the notice, into pitch darkness. He started to whistle; then

it occurred to him that, since he had never been this
way before he might just as well give it a shot, and he
sang *L'Amours Dont Sui Epris*.

Another notice loomed up at him out of the darkness. It too seemed to be self-lit, and it said:

MAXIMUM HEADROOM 4′ 7″

Since it was at least ten feet high, it was obviously
lying, and Blondel ignored it. If any of this was
supposed to impress him, it wasn't going to work. He'd
been in places that made this seem boringly normal.

A noise behind him – a sort of soft creaking – made
him look round, and he saw a ship sailing past, about a
hundred yards or so away. He had no reason to suppose
that there was any water over there, or certainly not
enough water to float a fifteenth-century Flemish
merchantman, and so he put it out of his mind. Sure
enough, the ship veered slowly away and vanished.
Kids' stuff. If someone was doing this deliberately, they
hadn't got beyond Grade II yet.

The gradient changed to a fairly steep descent, and
Blondel realised that what he was walking on was
waves; invisible, bone-dry, rock-solid waves. If he stood
still, he could feel them rising and falling very slowly.
An English privateer bobbed through the shadows at
extreme range, but too far away for him to be able to
pick out any identifying marks. He could, however, just
make out what they were singing.

*'Por li maintaindrai l'us
D'Eneas et Paris
Tristan et Pyramus
Qui amerent jadis.'*

With an effort, Blondel closed his mouth, which had

fallen open, and then picked up his feet and started to run. The crew were singing:

'*Or serai ses amis*
Or pri Deu de la sus
Qu'a lor fin soie pris . . .'

. . . a bit he'd never been particularly fond of. He could make out the ship properly now; a heavy twin-castled long-distance flying the pennant of the Cinque Ports and the arms of Winchelsea. And they were singing:

'*L'amours dont sui epris*
Me semont de chanter.'

Blondel filled his lungs and shouted, 'Ahoy!' Well, why not? He waited. The ship was still going. Then it changed tack, slewing around slightly. There was a sort of flat-bottomed thud and he looked up to see that they had launched a boat. He stood up and waited.

'Are you all right?' The man in the boat was talking to him.

'Fine,' he shouted back. 'Why were you singing that particular song?'

'I'll throw you a line,' said the man. 'Tread water till I get to you.'

Blondel was about to comment but he thought No, why bother? He yelled back his thanks and stayed where he was. After a while, the boat came close enough for the man to throw him a length of rope, which he caught. Then he walked across to the boat and climbed in.

'Ahoy,' he said affably.

The man in the boat looked at him for a moment. He seemed very worried. 'Where are we?' he said.

Blondel smiled. The man didn't look like he was ready for this; but then, people who can't handle heavy

120

answers shouldn't ask heavy questions. He decided to put it as gently as he possibly could.

'I can't say for sure,' he said, 'but I have a feeling that we're in the Archives.'

'The Archives,' the man repeated.

'That's right,' Blondel replied.

'You don't mean the Maldives?'

'No, not the Maldives,' Blondel answered. 'The Archives are quite different. Not that I'm sure, like I said. Did you sail off the edge of the world?'

The man nodded.

'I thought so,' Blondel said. 'Somebody told you the world was round, and that if you kept sailing due west you'd end up in India. A man in a pub, right?'

The man nodded again.

'And you thought about it, and you reckoned Yes, it must be, else the sea would all fall off the edge, and so you set out and you got to the edge and you fell off. Yes.'

'Yes.'

Blondel sighed. 'And all these other ships must have done the same, I suppose. That settles it. We're definitely in the Archives.' He thought about it for a moment. 'Pity, that,' he added.

The man gave him a long, deliberate stare. 'So where are we? I mean, is there any chance of getting back?'

'Your guess,' Blondel replied, 'is as good as mine. I got here another way, so maybe there is. On the other hand maybe there isn't, that's the trouble with this lot here. Nobody knows anything about it. Except that it exists, of course. Everyone's pretty definite about that.'

The man's two friends who had been rowing the

boat were beginning to get restless. 'I'm sorry,' Blondel said, 'maybe you'd prefer it if I left.'

'For God's sake, man,' said the man, 'tell me where the hell we are and stop fooling about.'

'You may not like it.'

'For God's sake ...'

'Oh,' said Blondel. 'All right, then.'

History, as has been observed before, is constantly changing. This is partly due to the activities of irresponsible time-travellers; but mostly the changes are quite natural.

Consider leaves. For a while they hang about on trees; then they die, fall off and lie about on the ground. If nobody happens along to sweep them up, they rot down into a compacted mass and stay there until geological forces put heavy weights on top of them and turn them into coal. Later still, they become diamonds.

Just as the strata of the earth have faults in them, so does history; chunks of it get pushed out of shape, deformed or misplaced. In the same way that some leaves become coal and some become diamonds, so not all events decay in the same way. Some of them, in fact, go wrong. Badly wrong. In due course, they can become extremely unstable and accordingly hazardous.

The Archives are where events are stored which shouldn't have happened but did. It is impossible to be exact, but recent estimates suggest that they now occupy a much larger area of SpaceTime than the Orthodox or Correct course of history, and the number of reported leaks of excluded matter from the Archives into the Topside (as the Orthodoxy is called in theo-chronological jargon) increases alarmingly each year. To a certain extent this is due to the irresponsible and highly illegal exploitation of the mineral resources of the Archives by pirate chemical companies – most areas of Archive time predate the commercial use of fossil fuels, and so there are enormous untapped reserves of oil, coal and natural gas down there, but of course it is incredibly hazardous to bring it back – and the Time Wardens have recently been awarded Draconian powers to prevent the traffic. Unfortunately, their efforts so far have been less than successful, and the conclusion of their latest report – 'Whether it is possible to eradicate this menace, time alone can tell' – has been widely criticised as extremely unhelpful.

'You're having me on,' the man said.

'I didn't think you'd like it,' Blondel replied. 'Why were your crew singing that song?'

'Which song?'

'*L'Amours Dont Sui Epris*,' Blondel said.

'Is that what it's called?' the man said. 'Because it's a good song, I suppose; everybody knows the words and when you've got a ship full of men all on the point of complete and utter panic, I always find the best thing to do is sing something, terribly loudly. Look, does it matter?'

'You haven't,' Blondel persevered, 'seen Richard the Lion-Heart anywhere, by any chance?'

'Who?'

'Never mind,' Blondel said. 'It was only a thought. Look, I mustn't keep you. Thanks for everything.' He stood up and climbed out of the boat.

'Look ...'

'Cheers, then!' Blondel waved, and started to walk.

'Come back!' the man yelled. 'Look, how do we get out of here?'

Blondel turned round and looked at him sadly. 'You don't,' he said. 'You never happened. Ciao.'

He walked on for a while, thinking deeply. It was logical, after all, that by stepping out into a timeslip as he had done, he would be swept into the Archives; presumably Guy was down here too somewhere, although quite possibly not in the same Archive. For all he knew, the poor chap was swanning around somewhere in the Trojan War, shooting the hats off Greek heroes. Blondel groaned; the last thing he needed was somebody else to look for. How, Blondel now asked himself, am I going to get out of here?

For a while he gave that some serious thought, but nothing brilliant occurred to him, and he decided not to let it worry him. At least he knew where he was, and he always found that that was the main thing. Once you'd got that sussed, in his experience, everything else fell into place somehow or another. He remembered the time he'd accidentally come up on the wrong side of the Day of Judgement. That had been a bit hairy, for a while, but he'd got away without any difficulty in the end, with the aid of a sheepskin rug and a great deal of charm. Whatever else he was, Blondel wasn't a worrier.

Far away in the distance he saw a light, and he started to walk towards it. As he approached it, the non-existent waves under his feet became clammy and smelt unpleasantly of chemicals. Strange.

He walked on, squelching now, and quite soon came to another notice. Whoever set up this Archive had been pretty conscientious about keeping people informed.

EXTREME DANGER

it said, and a little bit further down, in tiny little letters:

MEN AT WORK

Well indeed. Blondel stopped and scratched his head. Logic told him that it was highly unlikely that anyone could be bothered to do anything in an Archive; once you were here you were here, and either you found a way out or you got used to it. Anything in the way of industrial activity was counter-intuitive, to say the least. However, in the circumstances EXTREME DANGER probably wasn't to be taken at face value. When you have just been edited out of history and thus caused to cease to have existed, it's hard to think of anything that could actually make things worse.

About a hundred yards further on, he came to another notice. This one said:

HARD HAT AREA: NO ADMITTANCE

Blondel grinned; then he took off his belt and wrapped it round his right hand. When people didn't want you to go in somewhere, it usually meant there was something worth taking a look at.

He stepped forward, stopped suddenly, and rubbed his nose. He'd bumped into an invisible brick wall. More promising still.

Very cautiously, he felt his way along the wall until his sense of touch suggested that he'd come to a gateway; then he crouched down and waited. About a quarter of an hour later, a door opened and a man in a boiler-suit and a yellow hard hat came out and started to light a cigarette. Whatever it was they did in there, they weren't allowed to smoke while they were doing it.

Something dropped into place in Blondel's mind. He edged forward, tapped the smoker gently on the shoulder, and punched him.

Fortunately, the man's clothes fitted Blondel pretty well. He carefully stubbed out the cigarette, opened the door and walked in.

Inside, things were very different. There was light, for one thing; lots of it, coming from a battery of big white arc-lamps on a scaffolding tower, which loomed over a collection of huts and big machines. There was also a tall flame, rather like the flare from an oil well, rising up from a hole in what one could probably call the ground, although Flaubert would have found a more apt word for it. An illicit drilling station, of the sort that was causing all those headaches in the Time Warden's department. How very convenient.

There were a lot of men in boiler-suits and yellow hats scurrying about, and Blondel found no difficulty in blending in. He found a clipboard and wandered around for a while pretending to be bored. After the first half-hour, he didn't have to pretend very hard.

It was the tannoy that put the idea into his head; and once it was there it made quite a nuisance of itself. Left to himself, Blondel would have bided his time, slipped aboard the bus or whatever it was that took the workers back Topside when their shift was over, and gone on his way singing. As it was, the Idea insisted that he locate the site office, find the man with the microphone who worked the tannoy, stun him with the fire extinguisher and start singing *L'Amours Dont Sui Epris* into the PA system. And, under normal circumstances, he'd probably have found a way of getting away with it. He'd been in worse scrapes than this before now and still been back home in time for *Cagney and Lacey*.

As it was, something happened which he hadn't bargained for.

Someone began to sing the second verse.

'Thank you,' Guy said.

'Milk?'

Guy nodded. La Beale Isoud picked up a little bone-china jug and fiddled about with it.

'Sugar?'

'Thanks, yes. Look ...'

'How many?'

'I'm sorry?'

'How many lumps? One? Two?'

Guy wrenched his mind back to where it should be. 'Two,' he said, 'thanks. Look, I hate to be a nuisance, but ...'

Isoud looked at him, and he realised that she was going to offer him something to eat. If he refused the biscuits she would offer him cake. Best not to fight it, said his discretion, just get it over with.

'Would you like a biscuit?' said La Beale Isoud. Guy nodded, and was issued with a rather hard ginger-nut. That seemed to be that.

'The weather,' La Beale Isoud said, 'continues to improve.'

'Good,' said Guy. He noticed that he was sitting in a low, straight-backed chair and wondered how the hell he'd got there. Instinct, probably.

'Are you interested in gardens, Mr Goodlet?'

enquired La Beale Isoud. Guy shook his head. 'A pity,' La Beale Isoud went on. 'We have rather a nice show of chrysanthemums this year.'

'What's happening?' Guy asked.

'We're having tea,' Isoud replied. 'Please do not make any sudden movements.'

'Oh, quite,' Guy said quickly, 'certainly not. My mother likes chrysanthemums,' he added. It was a lie, of course, but with luck she wouldn't notice.

'Another biscuit?'

'Yes, thank you.' Guy leaned slowly forward, picked up a ginger-nut and put it on his knee with the other one. He hadn't eaten anything for a very long time, he remembered. He fiddled with his teacup.

'I don't know how long my brother is likely to be,' said La Beale Isoud. 'He's terribly unpunctual, I'm afraid. Still, he's usually back around this time, if you'd care to wait a little longer.'

'If you don't mind,' Guy said. 'How did I get here?'

'I don't know,' said La Beale Isoud politely. 'I thought you might be able to tell me that.'

'Ah.' Guy stirred his tea for a moment and then raised the cup to his lips, without actually going so far as to drink anything. 'I fell over,' he said.

'Did you really, Mr Goodlet? How intriguing.'

'In a tunnel,' Guy went on. 'I was running away from a lot of voices which kept trying to ask me things about income tax, and I must have tripped over my feet and fallen over. And the next thing I knew, I was here. Something seemed to pick me up and ...'

'I see,' Isoud said. 'In that case, the fax must have brought you. What a curious coincidence, don't you think?'

'Er,' said Guy. He looked up over his teacup and smiled. La Beale Isoud pursed her lips, as if trying to reach a decision, and then smiled back.

'Would you care to see some photographs?' she said.

Drink generally made Iachimo rather maudlin. Usually that was no bad thing; he was, Giovanni had long since realised, one of Nature's accountants, and anything which let his long-repressed emotions out of their cage and let them walk around and stretch their legs was to be encouraged, in moderation, so long as he didn't actually start to sing.

'I mean,' Iachimo said, 'we shouldn't just have left him like that. Really nice bloke, he was. Do anything for you. Lovely voice. Generous.'

'Gullible,' Giovanni said. 'Very, very gullible.'

'The most gullible bloke,' Iachimo agreed, 'you could ever hope to meet. Could have sold him anything. Anything.' He sighed. 'And now it's too late. Poor Blondel.' He reached for his drink and drank it.

'Never mind,' Giovanni said firmly. 'We've got to think of the future. I'm sure that's what he'd have wanted.'

Iachimo looked up unsteadily. 'You think so?'

'Absolutely,' Giovanni said. 'Blondel,' he went on, fixing his brother with a businesslike look, 'was an artist ...'

'Can you say that again?'

'An artist,' Giovanni repeated, 'and what do artists really want? They want —'

'Twenty-five per cent guaranteed return on capital,' said Marco. He was the dozy one, and they had had to teach him little set phrases, of which *twenty-five per cent guaranteed return on capital* was the longest by some way.

'No,' Giovanni said, 'that's where artists are different from you and me. Artists don't care about things like that, or at least,' Giovanni added, thinking of Andrew Lloyd Webber, 'most artists don't. What they care about is posterity, the opinion of future generations, their place in the gallery of fame.'

'Go on!'

'They do,' Giovanni said, 'and Blondel was an artist to his fingertips. Absolutely zilch use as a businessman, but give him a rebec and a mass audience, and there was nobody to touch him.'

'Too right,' Iachimo said. 'Bloody genius, that's what he was.'

'Exactly,' Giovanni replied, 'a genius, which is why we have a duty to continue marketing his material just exactly the way we did while he was alive. In fact,' he added, thinking of Blondel's lapsed five per cent share of royalties, 'even more so. With a genius, you see, the real appreciation comes after they die.'

'Really?'

'You bet.' Giovanni rubbed his hands together involuntarily. 'It's only when they die that you can be absolutely sure there isn't going to be any more. When you get to that point, you're in a controlled supply marketing environment, and if you've been clever enough to get sole distribution rights —'

'Have we got sole distribution rights?'

'Yes, Iachimo, we have indeed.' Giovanni grinned. 'Go and get another jug of this stuff, will you, Marco? I think a modest celebration is in order.'

The Beaumont Street Partnership had long ago

sorted out the problem of management role co-ordination. Giovanni did the thinking, Iachimo kept the books, Marco went to the bar. Usually, too, Marco paid.

'What it boils down to,' Giovanni said, when his cup was once more full, 'is that the only thing better than a sucker, from an investment management point of view, is a dead sucker. Cheers.'

'Pity he's dead, though,' said Iachimo with a sigh. 'Wrote some lovely songs, he did.'

'He did indeed,' Giovanni replied. 'And there's no reason why he shouldn't write plenty more.'

'But he's ...'

'I know, Marco,' Giovanni said patiently. 'But he wasn't dead this morning, was he? All we have to do is go back to when he wasn't dead, get him to hum something, and there we go. No reason why we can't go on indefinitely. And no royalties, either.'

Marco looked up from his drink, most of which he'd managed to spill on his tie. 'No,' he said, 'you're wrong there.'

His brothers looked at him. 'Come again?' Iachimo said.

'He fell into a timeslip, right?' Marco said. The other two nodded. 'Well then,' he continued, 'stands to reason, doesn't it?'

'Ignore him,' Giovanni said. 'He still hasn't worked out what a Thursday is.'

'No, listen,' Marco protested. 'Look, if he fell into a timeslip, right, then it stands to reason he'll have drowned in time. Loose Cannons. Time Wardens.' Marco made an effort and marshalled his thoughts, which was a bit like trying to produce *Die Frau Ohne*

Schatten with a cast of five-year-olds. 'What's a time-slip made of?' he asked.

Giovanni was about to interrupt, but he didn't. 'Unstable time,' he said. 'Like lava from a volcano, you might say. What of it?'

'Anything that gets trapped in a timeslip,' Marco ground on, 'gets taken away to the Archives, right?' He looked up, waiting for someone to interrupt him, but for once they were both listening. He smiled happily. This was good fun. 'And anything that gets taken to the Archives, right, it's like it never existed. So if Blondel's gone there, it's like he never existed.'

'Jesus Christ,' Giovanni said quietly.

'And if he never existed,' Marco continued – it was like watching a woodlouse climbing a wall, listening to Marco doing joined-up speaking – 'then he couldn't have made up any of those songs. Which means his songs don't exist any more. Which means they never existed to start with. Which means – where are you going, Giovanni?'

'Get your coat.'

'But Giovanni ...'

'I said get your coat.'

Marco pulled a face, but it was no good; they weren't listening to him any more. He got his coat.

'And this one,' said La Beale Isoud, 'is Blondel, my sister Mahaud and me at Deauville.' She squinted at the picture. 'Summer, 1438,' she added. 'It's changed a lot since then, of course.'

'Yes,' said Guy. He was beginning to have second thoughts about being in love with La Beale Isoud. She seemed to have enough photograph albums to fill up at least seventy years of matrimony. 'Er . . .'

'And this one,' she continued, 'is Blondel, my sister Mahaud, my sister Ysabel and me in Venice. You can't see Ysabel terribly well, I'm afraid, because she moved just before the picture was taken. That's her, look, behind the prow of the gondola.'

'Ah yes. Would you mind terribly if —'

'And this one . . .' La Beale Isoud stared at the album for a moment. 'No,' she said, 'that one hasn't been taken yet. It's too bad of Blondel, he keeps getting them muddled up and out of order. Oh look,' she said, 'it's got you in it.'

Guy blinked. 'Me?'

'That is you, isn't it?' Isoud said. 'Standing there on the steps of the church with a bouquet of flowers in your hand. And who's that beside you?'

Guy examined the photograph. 'That's my friend George,' he said. 'Who's that?'

'That's my aunt Gunhilde,' Isoud replied. 'She's dead now, of course, but she comes back occasionally for visits. Christmas, you know, and weddings. That's the good thing about having all this time travel in the family, it means one can keep in touch.'

Guy was still examining the photograph. 'Whose wedding is this?' he asked.

'No idea,' Isoud replied. 'Oh look, I think that's Mahaud there, in the blue. She never did suit blue, but you couldn't tell her.'

Guy could feel his hand shaking. 'It looks,' he said, 'rather like I'm meant to be the bridegroom.'

'Yes,' Isoud replied, nodding, 'it does rather, doesn't it? Now this one here . . .'

'So who,' Guy said, 'is the bride?'

'You can't see,' Isoud replied. 'She doesn't seem to be in the photo. Oh look, there's Mummy. What a big hat she's wearing.'

Guy stood up. 'Well,' he said, 'thank you ever so much for the tea. I don't think I'll wait for Blondel if you don't mind.' He could feel the sweat running off his forehead. 'So if you'll just tell me where the time tunnel is ...'

'Are you leaving?' Isoud said.

'Better had,' Guy said firmly. He had always previously believed that he was too young to die, but now he was absolutely positive that he was too young to get married. 'This door here, isn't it?' He opened it and walked through. A moment later he came back again, immediately followed by three raincoats, a hat and an umbrella.

'No,' said Isoud, 'that's the coat cupboard.'

'I rather thought so,' Guy said. 'Which door leads to the time tunnel, then?'

Isoud looked at him. '*I* don't know,' she said. 'Blondel deals with all that sort of thing.'

'But you must know ...'

Isoud smiled grimly. 'It keeps changing,' she explained. 'One day it's one door and the next day it's a different one. Terribly difficult to know where to put your coat sometimes.'

'Ah,' said Guy.

'Not to mention,' Isoud went on, 'the empty milk bottles. I expect there's a doorstep in the future or the past somewhere with hundreds and hundreds of our milk bottles on it. The milkman must wonder what we do with them all.'

'Quite probably.' Guy could feel the hairs on the

134

back of his neck rising. 'You don't mind if I just, sort of, investigate, do you? Only . . .'

'Oh look,' Isoud said, 'here's another one of the same wedding. Oh *look*!' She lifted her head and stared at him. 'Mr *Goodlet*!' she said.

'Goodbye,' Guy said firmly. He opened a door, saw with great relief that there was nothing on the other side of it, and stepped through.

'Mr Goodlet,' Isoud said, a few moments later. 'You seem to have fallen into the coal cellar.'

'Yes,' Giovanni said, 'but can you do it?'

The man scratched the back of his head doubtfully, and then made a few rough sketches on the back of an envelope, ending up with something that looked perilously like the Albert Memorial. Then he played with a calculator for a while, looked some things up in a price list which seemed to have an awful lot of noughts to each digit, and spat on the floor.

'Dunno,' he said. 'It's the stresses, see. Could tear the wings off, the stresses we're talking here. Then there's your frame. Got to be titanium.'

'Is that expensive?' Iachimo interrupted. He was making a parallel set of notes on the back of another envelope. In fact, the place was beginning to look like a sorting office.

'Ignore him,' Giovanni said. 'Look, I don't care what it costs. Can you do it?'

'And then there's your PCVs,' the man said. 'I can put you in Bergsons, no difficulty there, mind, Bergsons, but what's that going to do to your lateral stability? You put too much stress on your laterals, you're going to be really stuffed up. Mind you . . .'

The man seemed to pass into a sort of coma or trance, from which it would probably be dangerous to arouse him. Any minute now, Giovanni said to himself, he'll be asking if there's anybody here called Vera.

'Mind you,' said the man, recovering, 'if you use titanium alloy *throughout*' – he made the word throughout sound so expensive that Iachimo winced, as if something had bitten him – 'then you might get away with it. Hard to say. Wouldn't want to be responsible, really, I mean titanium alloy B-joints could pack up on you just like that. Real dodgy.'

Giovanni breathed out heavily through his nose. 'Look . . .' he said.

'All right,' replied the man severely, 'all right, hold your water a minute. Let the dog see the rabbit.' He bent down and started to leaf through a huge pile of dusty, cobwebby magazines on the floor. 'Saw something like what you're after in one of these once,' he said, 'twenty, twenty-five years ago now, mind. One of them big mining companies did it, only they used carbon fibre. Can't use carbon fibre now, of course.'

Giovanni asked why not but the question was obviously beneath contempt. 'Now then,' the man said. The three brothers leaned forward to look. 'See that?' the man said, pointing to a picture of something or other, 'that was one of mine, that was. Nothing to do with what you're after,' he added. He threw the magazine to one side and went on looking.

'Look,' Giovanni said, 'all we need to know is —'

'Magnesium,' the man said suddenly. 'You just wouldn't believe what some people do with magnesium. No,' he added.

'No what?'

136

'No, I can't do it. Impossible,' he explained. 'Bloody silly idea to start with.'

'Thank you so much,' Giovanni replied through gritted teeth.

'I mean,' the man went on, 'drill a probe through the Archive walls, absolutely out of the question. What do you want to do that for, anyway?'

'Pleasure to have met you,' Giovanni said, putting on his hat and pocketing the card he had put on the table at the beginning of the interview. 'Send us your invoice.'

'What invoice?'

'Any bloody invoice,' Giovanni said, and closed the door quickly.

'Overtime,' said White Herald, suddenly.

The others looked at him as if he'd just gone mad. The bus went over a patch of turbulence, jolting them about. The sort of turbulence you get in time travel makes a little bit of rogue cumulonimbus over the Alps seem like a feather bed.

'We could all claim overtime,' White Herald continued. 'Dunno why I didn't think of it before.'

Nobody said anything. Pursuivant looked at Clarenceaux and then nudged Mordaunt, who giggled. Clarenceaux glared at them both, as if challenging them to make something of it. They beamed at him. Just when he thought he was safe, Mordaunt turned to Pursuivant and said, 'If we went around asking for overtime, we'd end up with egg on our faces all right, eh?'

'Look ...' Clarenceaux said angrily. They smiled at him.

'Sorry?' Pursuivant enquired sweetly.

'Just watch it,' Clarenceaux replied. 'That's all.'

'Sure thing,' Mordaunt replied, and turned back to his companion. 'No, the yolk would be on us then, wouldn't it?'

'Did you say something?'

Mordaunt shook his head innocently. Clarenceaux dragged a sigh up from his socks and let it go. Blondel's horrible prophecy had come horribly true, starting with the moment of their return to the Chastel, when Mountjoy King of Arms had seen him squelching up the drive covered all over in custard, jam and cream and had observed, somewhat inevitably, that Clarenceaux was clearly not a man to be trifled with. Since then, if anything, it had got worse.

'Other people get overtime,' White Herald continued, 'so why not us? Time and a half, even.'

'Do you mind?' Clarenceaux said irritably. 'We got enough trouble travelling through it without claiming it as well. Where are we going this time, anyway? Anybody know?'

Silence. Three blank faces. At least nobody said anything about eggs, or custard, or bananas. If ever he saw that sodding Blondel again, he'd give him bananas all right ...

The bus slowed down, jolted violently, and stopped. After a moment the automatic doors opened, and the crew climbed out. White Herald, whose turn it was to be Sergeant, took out the sealed envelope and opened it.

'Orders of the day,' he said. 'Er ...'

'Give it here,' said Clarenceaux testily. 'You got it upside down,' he pointed out.

'Reading isn't everything,' White Herald replied.

'Cretin.' Clarenceaux ran his finger along the lines. '*You have arrived at the South-Western Main Archive,*' he read. 'Here, what's an Archive?' he asked. Nobody knew. '*Proceed to the oil well which you will find approximately half a mile due east of your arrival point and arrest Jean de Nesle, also known as Blondel. You are authorised to use maximum force if necessary.* Then there's a big blob of red wax with a picture on it. Ouch!' The paper had burst into flames, and soon Clarenceaux was holding only the corner. '*PS,*' he read, '*this message will self-destruct in thirty (30) seconds.*'

'Nice of him to tell you,' Mordaunt commented. 'Anybody got a compass?'

It isn't all fun and games commanding an illicit oil rig in the middle of an insubstantial sea, and unauthorised visitors don't help. To make matters worse, Commander Moorhen was only too aware that he was running about a fortnight behind schedule, as a result of the Mistral Chronologique arriving a month earlier than forecast and the diamond-molybdenum drill-bit breaking, and that there were reports of Warden patrols not a million years away. He was not a happy man.

'Music while you work,' he said, 'I can handle. But aliens breaking in and coshing the staff just so's they can sing to them is another matter. Take him away and chuck him off the derrick.'

Sergeant Peewit looked at him and didn't move. The prisoner, for his part, smiled.

'Come on,' Moorhen shouted. 'Jump to it.'

'No sir,' said Peewit, back straight as the proverbial ramrod.

'You what?'

'With respect, sir.'

Moorhen stared. 'And why the hell not, sergeant?'

'Because, sir,' Peewit replied, 'with respect, sir, this here is Blondel de Nesle, and the lads won't stand for it.'

The biro in Moorhen's hands snapped, apparently of its own accord. 'What did you say?'

'No, sir.'

Moorhen hesitated for a split second. They'd done mutinies at training school, naturally, but it had clashed with his violin lessons and so he'd pretended to have a cold. To the best of his recollection, you had people shot, but he couldn't swear to it. Besides, there weren't any guns on the rig.

'Do you know,' he said quietly, 'what happens to NCOs who disobey a direct order?'

'Yes, sir,' Peewit replied. 'Regulation 46, subsection (b), sir.'

'Oh. Yes, thank you. Here, stand back, I'll do it myself.'

Peewit placed a piano-sized fist on Moorhen's chest. 'With respect, sir,' he said, 'Blondel de Nesle is the greatest all-round entertainer the world has ever known, and the lads said to tell you that if you hurt one hair of his head, like, they'll chuck you down the main shaft, sir.'

Moorhen was about to say something extremely pertinent and germane when the alarms went off. A second bombardier, very much out of breath, came clattering up the stairs to report that four armed intruders had broken in via the main gateway. Then a grenade exploded somewhere below them, and life began to get extremely complicated.

'Are you trying to say,' said the Chief Warden, 'that you're attempting to bribe me to let you into the Archives?'

'Yes,' Giovanni said.

The Chief Warden stroked his beard. 'How much?' he asked.

'How much do you want?'

'No.' The Chief Warden smiled. 'I admit I was tempted, but no. And now I think we'd better have a word with Security.'

Giovanni was about to simper appealingly when he noticed the CD player and the stack of discs in the corner of the office. 'Of course,' he said, 'the bribe wouldn't necessarily have to be money, would it?'

The Chief Warden paused, his hand over the buzzer. 'I beg your pardon?' he said.

Giovanni walked over to the CD player. 'You're a Blondel fan, I see,' he said.

'What's that got to —'

'Very impressive collection you've got here.'

'Complete,' the Chief Warden said involuntarily. 'Look —'

'I could get you tickets,' Giovanni said.

The Chief Warden's hand moved away from the buzzer. 'Tickets?' he asked.

'Tickets,' Giovanni repeated. 'St Peter's Square, 1173.'

'Out of the question. I —'

'Constantinople, 1201.'

'You don't seem to realise that —'

Giovanni shrugged his shoulders. 'Whatever you say,' he replied. 'Of course, if two tickets for the Piazza

San Marco gig of '98 made any difference ...'

There was a very long pause.

'Near the band?'

'You could reach out,' Giovanni said, 'and pinch the second flautist.'

'If anybody found out ...'

Giovanni shrugged again. 'You're right,' he said. 'If I were you I'd call Security and have us thrown in jail.' He picked up a framed photograph of a very pretty girl in an official Blondel European Tour wimple from the Warden's desk. 'Your wife?' he asked.

'No,' said the Chief Warden. 'My, er, niece.' He leaned forward conspiratorially. 'There wouldn't be any chance,' he whispered, 'of, well, going backstage after the show ...?'

Having been blown to smithereens by the explosion of the oil storage tanks (caused by one of their own ineptly-placed grenades) the identifiable fragments of Clarenceaux, Mordaunt, Pursuivant and White Herald were collected by a relief team sent from the Chastel des Larmes Chaudes, packed in dry ice and taken directly to the central works depot, where a team of highly qualified and extremely resentful mechanics were ready to begin work.

'I mean,' said the Chief Footwright, taking a handful of toes from a cardboard box and sorting through them for a reasonable match, 'what the hell is the point of it all? You spend half an hour getting the right and left legs all nicely balanced, the cornering and the foot wear all sorted out, and then a few days later back it comes, all mangled to cock and fit for nothing but the breakers.'

'Hoy!' said Pursuivant. The Lead Vocalist, who had just reconnected his vocal chords, disconnected them again.

The Master Armerer frowned savagely. 'You think

you got problems,' he replied, 'you want to try it from this end.' He looked at the mess on the bench in front of him and shook his head sadly. 'The really daft thing about it is the way they try and patch 'em up themselves in the field units.' He placed a spatula under a limp forearm and pointed to it with disgust. 'Just look at that, will you?' he said. 'Talk about a Friday afternoon job. Dunno who fitted that, but he didn't know his elbow from —'

'You can talk,' broke in the Head Technician. 'All you've got to do is get the bits out of a box and bolt them on. Me, I've got to wire the whole lot in. Look at *that*, for Christ's sake.' He pointed at Clarenceaux's trepanned skull, which lifted its eyes and scowled at him. 'You don't want a nerve specialist for that lot, you want a bleeding plumber. I ask you! Great big lumps of loose solder everywhere, bits held on with crocodile clips, contacts twisted round rusty old nails – it's a wonder the whole lot didn't short out. And they expect the perishing things to be able to read.' He sighed, adjusted his torque wrench, and went to work on the cervical joint.

'Right,' he continued after a while, 'that'll have to do for now. So long as they don't use it for competition stuff or expect it to win any Nobel prizes, should be OK for another fifty thousand. Expect it'll get blown up before then, anyway. Close it up, George.'

Fully restored and operational, Clarenceaux had his permitted cup of tea – more to test the hydraulic lines than to restore him after his ordeal; at any rate, they never put sugar in it – donned his regulation fatigues and went to report to his superior.

'Well?' Mountjoy said.

'Well ...' Clarenceaux reported. Mountjoy invited him to expand on that. 'Well, sir,' Clarenceaux continued, choosing his words with care, and (bearing in mind that the portion of his brain that handled such matters had been in a cardboard box in the stockroom half an hour ago) doing better than he expected, 'you could say it was a qualified success. On balance, like.'

'Oh yes?' replied Mountjoy ominously. 'Go on.'

'Well,' Clarenceaux said – his new sweat glands were working fine, he noticed – 'we got there all right —'

'Hardly surprising, considering you had nothing to do with it.'

Since his self-respect had not been replaced (shortage at the supply depot), Clarenceaux ignored that. 'And then,' he went on, 'we found the oil rig, no trouble at all. There was a guard on the gate so we had to use all reasonable and necessary force to get in, and then some other guards came up and tried to grab us, so we, er ...'

'Yes?'

'White Herald,' said Clarenceaux – peer-group loyalty is an optional extra on the Popular range – 'had got hold of this hand grenade thing from somewhere, and he chucked it at them.'

'Really.'

'Oh yes,' Clarenceaux confirmed. 'Worked a treat so far as reasonable and necessary force was concerned. Trouble was, it blew the rig up. And that's where we, sort of ...'

'Yes,' said Mountjoy, 'I think I get the picture. Do you think there were any survivors?'

Clarenceaux thought for a moment. 'Well, not us,

for a start,' he said firmly. 'We copped it. Hell of a bang, it was.'

'So I gathered,' Mountjoy replied. 'But do you think it likely that de Nesle could have survived the explosion? If he was on the rig, I mean?'

Clarenceaux shook his head, an unwise move considering that the bearings were still stiff. 'Can't see how he could have, sir,' he said. 'Like, we'd heard him singing, right, over the tannoy, when we were approaching the rig?'

'So?'

'So,' Clarenceaux continued, 'stands to reason that if he was singing into the tannoy, he must have been in the office building, or near it. And the office building was next to the storage tank. In fact, I seem to remember it was a bloody great chunk of the office building took my head off. Don't see how anyone could have survived in there when the tank went up.'

'I see.' Mountjoy nodded. 'That's pretty good deduction, Clarenceaux. You thought that up all by yourself, did you?'

Praise was something that Clarenceaux had heard about, even vaguely believed in, like telepathy, but had never previously experienced in the flesh. He glowed slightly. 'Yes, sir,' he replied.

'Thought so,' said Mountjoy. 'That fool of an engineer's gone and fitted you with a Mark IVB instead of a Mark III. Go back to the sick bay and tell him to take it out again at once. Hasn't he heard about the cut-backs?'

As Clarenceaux wandered sadly away, Mountjoy turned himself back up to full illumination and considered the position. If Blondel really had been blown to bits ... But that was a very big if. The wretched man seemed to have the knack of getting out of certain death, the way a really dedicated twelve-year-old always gets out of Sports Day. Personally, he wasn't going to believe it until they brought him Blondel's head on a dish; and even then he'd want indemnity insurance. In short, he wasn't sure, and would institute further enquiries. He reached across and switched on the intercom.

'Get me Intelligence,' he said.

A luminous white Land Rover was bumping across the insubstantial waves of the Great North Archive. The passengers were not enjoying the experience much.

'If,' grumbled the Chief Warden, 'after all this, he doesn't sing *Ma Joie Me Semont*, I'll have your guts for braces.'

'He'll sing it,' Giovanni assured him, taking his hand briefly away from in front of his mouth. 'I was there, I know.'

'He'd better, that's all,' the Warden snarled. 'All right, we're here. Now, what exactly are you looking for?'

'Well,' Giovanni said. 'Actually, we aren't quite sure.'

The Warden stared at him. 'You commit the biggest crime in the Universe, corrupting a Time Warden, and you aren't sure what you're looking for. What are you, tourists?'

'We're looking for someone,' Marco started to say, but Giovanni trod on his foot. Too late.

'Oh yes?' asked the Warden suspiciously. 'Who?'

'Oh, nobody you know,' Giovanni said. 'What's that over there?'

147

The Warden raised his field glasses. 'Looks like a column of smoke,' he said. 'That's odd, this is all water.'

'Water?' Marco looked out of the window nervously. 'Then why aren't we . . .?'

'Deactivated water,' the Warden told him. 'It's got all the hydrogen and oxygen taken out. Keeps better,' he explained. 'If you gentlemen wouldn't mind, I think I'd better take a look.'

'That's fine,' Giovanni said.

They drove on until they came to the ruins of a stockade. The surface of the immaterial sea was littered with mangled scraps of iron; the place looked like a battlefield, or the Hayward Gallery. Here and there lay yellow plastic helmets, boots, fragments of office furniture. No corpses, needless to say; anyone who dies in the Archives was never born in the first place.

'It's one of those pirate rigs I was telling you about,' the Warden said. 'Looks like someone got careless.'

'There's somebody over there, look,' Iachimo said, pointing. 'In that rowing boat.'

They drove over, climbed out and stopped the boat with their hands. Inside was a very frightened-looking man in the remains of a pair of overalls. After a while, they were able to get some sense out of him.

'These men,' he said, 'soldiers, guards, something like that. I was on sentry duty. They hit me.'

'Were they Wardens' officers?' the Warden asked.

'No idea,' the sentry replied.

The Chief Warden turned to the Galeazzo brothers. 'My men have orders to destroy these places on sight, no questions asked,' he explained. 'I know it seems hard, but you've got no idea the damage they can do.'

He turned back to the sentry. 'They knocked you out, did they?'

The sentry nodded. 'Bloody lucky they did, I guess,' he went on. 'I'd just come round when the whole lot blew up. No survivors, except me. I was lucky; a bit of the fence fell on me and shielded me from the blast, I suppose. About half an hour later a van turned up, more like an ambulance; they took the bodies of the soldiers away. Our blokes just sort of —'

'Yes,' said the Warden, who wasn't a cruel man. 'Yes, I wouldn't worry about that. No survivors, then?'

The sentry shook his head. 'None of our lot,' he said. 'No sign of the other one, either.'

The Warden raised an eyebrow. 'What other one?' he said.

'Blondel,' said the sentry.

There was a silence. It probably seemed longer than it actually was.

'Did you say Blondel?' the Chief Warden asked. 'Blondel the singer?'

The sentry nodded. 'That's right,' he said. 'I recognised the face when he thumped me.'

'He thumped you ...'

'When he broke into the rig,' the sentry explained. 'That was, oh, fifteen minutes before your blokes.'

Giovanni pushed his way past the Chief Warden. 'You can't be sure it was him,' he said. 'Just a quick glance ...'

'But I heard him,' replied the sentry. 'He sang, over the tannoy. I'd know that voice anywhere. He sang that big number from the 1189 White Album. You know, goes like —' He hummed a few bars.

'*L'Amours Dont Sui Epris?*' the Chief Warden

149

whispered. He had gone very pale all of a sudden.

'That's it,' the sentry said. 'Dead good, that, especially that bit where ...'

Nobody was listening. The Chief Warden turned to the Galeazzo brothers.

'Did you know,' he said softly, 'that Blondel was in the Archives?'

By a feat of great dexterity, Giovanni stood on the toes of both his brothers at once. 'I had no idea,' he said. 'That's awful.'

The Warden gave him an extremely unpleasant look. 'You're sure, are you?' he said. 'Well, what a coincidence. Because if you'd known he was here, and there had been a chance of saving him ... You realise that now none of his songs were ever written?'

'Really?' Giovanni raised both eyebrows. 'What a tragedy.'

'Well ...' The Warden shrugged his shoulders. 'You'd better help me get this man in the car. We'll need him for questioning.'

Together they lifted the sentry into the Land Rover. It wasn't till he was safely installed on the back seat and propped up on two cushions that the Chief Warden produced a gun and ordered the brothers out of the car. Once they were out of it, but while they were still reacting strongly and making a variety of protests and appeals to his better nature, he slammed the door and told the driver to drive on.

The choice between being forcibly married to a beautiful but incompatible girl and remaining indefinitely in a coal cellar is not one that many people have to confront. Even Aristotle, whose works cover a wide range of possible moral dilemmas, glosses over it in a very perfunctory manner; and Guy wasn't exactly one of Aristotle's greatest fans in any event. He decided to rely on instinct.

'If it's all the same to you,' he shouted through the door, 'I'll stay where I am, thanks.'

'Mr Goodlet . . .'

'Thank you,' Guy repeated, politely but firmly. To reinforce the point, he piled coal against the door.

'You're being rather childish, Mr Goodlet.'

Maybe, Guy thought. So what's wrong with children all of a sudden? Clever people, children. Don't have to go to work.

'I'm sure that if we discussed this in a sensible manner,' said La Beale Isoud, 'we could easily sort matters out.'

'No, really,' Guy said, 'I like it here. So, if it's all the same to you . . .'

'It is *not* all the same to me,' retorted La Beale Isoud, and there was something in her tone of voice when suggested that her previously inexhaustible-seeming reservoir of ladylike behaviour might be running a trifle low. 'Mr Goodlet,' she went on, 'whether you like it or not – whether either of us likes it or not, come to that – it would seem that at some time in the future we are to become man and wife. I really think that we should be trying to establish the ground-work for a mature and meaningful relationship, and I don't really see how that can be achieved with you in the coal cellar.'

Guy said nothing. Something or other ran lightly over his foot and up his leg as far as his knee. He shuddered slightly.

'Mr Goodlet. Guy,' said La Beale Isoud, 'I'm not going to plead with you indefinitely, you know. What will be, will be, and if you want to start off our relationship on this sort of note, then I for one will not be answerable for the consequences.'

Guy considered this for a moment; then, having reflected maturely on what Isoud had said, and also the way in which she had said it, scrabbled around for some more coal to pile against the door. The woman sounded exactly like his cousin Flora.

There was a long silence, but Guy wasn't going to be fooled. She might have gone away; on the other hand, she might be waiting outside the door, holding her breath and with an attendant clergyman and two bridesmaids standing behind her fingering sacrificial implements.

'Are you there, Mr Goodlet?'

'Yes.'

'It may interest you to know,' said La Beale Isoud, 'that I am none too happy about this idea myself. However, instead of shouting at each other through the door, perhaps we should be considering how we can prevent this thing happening?' A long pause. 'Mr Goodlet?'

'Still here.'

'Mr Goodlet, I'm rapidly running out of patience. Would you at least have the good manners to answer me when I speak to you?'

'Look,' Guy said, 'I really don't want to seem rude, but if there's a photograph of us on our wedding day, then I'm afraid I'm just going to stay put. The way I see it, we can't get married if I stay here. If you want to get on and do something else, please don't mind me.'

'Oh, for heaven's sake ...'

Guy heard the sound of bad-tempered heels clacking away across flagstones, and relaxed slightly. It might be that she'd gone to fetch a crowbar, but as far as he could remember it had seemed like a good, solid door, opening inwards. He lay back on the heap of coal and considered his situation in some detail.

He tried to puzzle out, from what Blondel had told him, how time worked. On the one hand, it seemed, you could whizz back and forwards through time as easily as catching a train. On the other hand, it stood to reason that if a photograph of him on his wedding day had been taken, then he'd had a wedding day at some time or other – some time in the *future*, of course – and in that case, the thing had already happened and there was absolutely nothing he could do about it. Except, of course, that it was in the future, so it couldn't already have happened. He could stop it happening by taking his revolver and shooting himself here and now – assuming he didn't miss, which seemed on recent experience to be quite a large assumption – but since he wasn't seriously proposing to put it to the test, that one could be shelved for the time being.

Meanwhile, what he needed most of all, he decided, was a smoke; and to this end he produced from his pockets his last remaining cigarette, his last two matches and the remains of his matchbox, which had not been improved structurally by having been fallen on several times recently. He struck a match.

No Entry. Authorised Personnel Only.

The match went out and he struck another, which flared up, managed to find a gust of wind in the entirely draught-free environment of the cellar and blew out. Guy stretched out a hand and felt for the door he'd just seen.

As Aristotle said, when caught between a ravening tiger and a process-server bearing a legal document, it's always worth looking for the fire escape.

The Chief Warden returned to his office tired, worried and upset. In the space of a single day he had broken all the laws and regulations of his vocation, only to discover that his aiders and abettors were responsible for the annihilation of (in his opinion) the greatest musical genius who had ever lived, who had perished in one of his own Archives. As if that wasn't bad enough, he remembered, his wife had told him they had people coming to dinner and he was on no account to be late. As he unlocked the office door, he toyed briefly with the idea of nipping back through time to half past six and thus at least saving himself a degree of aggravation. It would be a flagrant breach, of course, but compared with what he'd done, it was a mere parking ticket on the windscreen of his honour. Still, perhaps not. Now, all he had to do was open the safe, put the key back in it for the night, and think of a reasonable excuse on the way home ...

There were people in his office. They had been sitting in the dark, because the light was off when he walked in; almost as if they were waiting to catch him unawares.

'Good evening, Chief Warden.'

Even if he'd contemplated turning and trying to make a run for it, there wouldn't have been any point; a very substantial security officer had filled up the doorway. The Chief Warden relaxed. After all, since it was all such a foregone conclusion, there was no point in getting all tense about it.

'Come in and take a seat, please.' Although it was – what, two hundred years? About that – since the selection committee meeting when he'd received his appointment, he recognised the voice instantly; and when the speaker swivelled round in the chair and faced him, he was ready for it. But he still couldn't help making a sort of mouse-in-a-blender noise and turning his head away. The Chief Warden was, after all, human, and no human being, however cool or laid back, can hope to face a man split down the middle with equanimity.

'That's all right,' said the half-man, pre-empting the apology. 'I'm used to it by now, Lord knows. I won't be offended if you look the other way.'

'Thank you, sir,' the Chief Warden said, to the opposite wall. He sat down.

'Now then,' the half-man continued, 'you can't see them, but sitting on my right is His Holiness Anti-Pope Julian II, whom I believe you've met. Yes? And on my left,' the half-man continued, with a chuckle, 'is His Holiness Pope Julian XXIII. Before you say anything, yes, they are one and the same person; as you know, Julian was Pope of Rome, died, and now commutes from the sixteenth century to be Anti-Pope. Well, he's kindly agreed to make two simultaneous trips, one in each capacity. Apparently it's the first time it's been done, so he asks you to make allowances. For a start, it means he can't speak.'

The Chief Warden's curiosity got the better of him. 'May I ask . . .?'

'For fear,' replied the half-man, 'of contradicting

155

himself. Since he is speaking *ex cathedra* in both capacities, the results might be extremely unfortunate. He will therefore communicate with me by means of sign language, which does not qualify as a medium for Infallible statements, and I will relay his points to you myself. Since you cannot, understandably enough, bear to look at me, you'll have to trust me to interpret accurately. Are you agreeable to that?'

'Perfectly,' said the Chief Warden.

'Splendid,' said the half-man. 'Finally, as these are judicial proceedings, we have a shorthand writer present who will take a transcript for the record. You have no objection?'

'None whatsoever.'

The half-man nodded to Pursuivant, who was sitting at the end of the desk. Pursuivant sharpened his pencil, opened his notebook, and wrote down the date. He spelt it wrong.

'Right,' said the half-man. 'Here goes, then. You are John Athanasius, Chief Time Warden, of "Hour-glasses", Newlands Road, Bleak City, Atlantis?'

The Chief Warden nodded. 'Yes,' he said.

'John Athanasius, you are − can't read my own writing, dammit; Julian, what does that ...? Oh yes, thank you − you are charged with contraventions of the Chronological Order, in that you did knowingly and for purposes of private gain admit unauthorised persons into one of the Time Archives, contrary to Sections 3 and 67 of the said Order. How do you plead, guilty or not guilty?'

'Guilty,' said the Chief Warden.

'Oh,' said the half-man. 'How tremendously un-imaginative of you. We've been to a great deal of trouble to track you down, you know. I've got a whole corridor full of witnesses all hauled back from temporal oblivion just to say they saw you at it. Are you sure you won't change your plea?'

'I'm sure.'

The half-man shrugged – difficult to do, with only one shoulder – and reached into his bag for half a black cap. 'Is there – where *is* the dratted thing? – anything you wish to say before sentence is pronounced upon you?'

'No.'

'Ah, here we are. Are you sure?'

'Yes, sir.'

'Be like that. Now, which way round does it go? You'll have to take my word that I've got it on, of course. Just as well you aren't looking, you'd probably get a fit of the giggles, which'd be Contempt, and you're in enough trouble as it is. John Athanasius, you have been found guilty of a wholly unforgivable breach of the sacred truss – confound it, that's a T – *trust* which has been reposed in you. You try reading this with only one eye and see how you like it. I have listened with patience to your attempts at mitigation ... No, scrub round that. Pity. You have made no attempt to mitigate your crime, and I am therefore obliged to sentence you to filing in the Main Archive. *Now* have you anything to say as to why such sentence should not be imposed upon you?'

'No, sir.'

'Nothing at all? Not even *It's a fair cop, bang to rights, guv*? Nothing at all?'

'No, sir.'

The half-man sighed. 'Fine,' he said. 'The whole

evening has been a complete frost. Had we known, we could have entered judgement by default, Julian could have stayed at home, I could have gone out to dinner, Mr ... whatever his name is here could have gone to the greyhound races, or whatever it is his sort of person does in the evenings, but there it is. Sentence accordingly.'

The Chief Warden hung his head, waiting for the feel of the guard's hand on his shoulder. Instead, he heard the half-man's voice again.

'I told the driver to come back in five hours' time,' he said, 'so we're stuck here till then. How about a game of something?'

'Thank you,' said the Chief Warden, 'but I don't really feel in the mood for ...'

'I wasn't talking to you,' the half-man said. 'Julian, what about a rubber of bridge? You and you against me and Mr ... Oh, sorry, I forgot. Can't bid when you're being Infallible, might go two no trumps and get doubled, and what would that do to the Ninth Lateran Council? Oh well, this *is* going to be a jolly evening, isn't it?'

There was a long silence, during which the Chief Warden stared at the wall. By now, his wife would have given up waiting and served the cold beetroot soup with sour cream and chives. Where he was going, he reflected, not only would he never taste his wife's cooking ever again; he would also never have eaten it in the first place. The corners of his lips rose involuntarily.

'I spy,' said the half-man, 'with my little eye ... Literally, in my case, of course. Let's see. Something beginning with ... Chief Warden, is this a *complete* set of Blondel recordings?'

158

The Chief Warden nodded.

'Including the 1196 White Album?'

Without wanting to, the Chief Warden smirked. 'Yes, sir,' he said.

'The pirate edition, naturally?'

'No sir,' the Chief Warden replied – O grave, thy victory – 'the official recording, sir. With,' he added vindictively, 'Gace Brulé on drums.'

'I see,' said the half-man. 'Chief Warden, have you, er, made a will?'

The Chief Warden nodded.

'Yes,' said the half-man, 'I expect you probably have. Invalid, of course. If you never existed, you can't have made a will, which means that all your property will be forfeit to the —'

'If I never existed, sir,' replied the Chief Warden, with relish, 'then I could never have bought the very last copy of the *official* recording of the 1196 White Album. Which means,' he added happily, 'that somebody else must have bought it, sir. Don't you think?'

'I ...'

'Which is a pity, sir, wouldn't you say, since I left it to you in my will.'

'I ...'

'Specifically. And there's the Chastelain de Coucy,' said the Chief Warden, as if to himself, 'on tenor crumhorn. Blow that thing!' he added.

'Chief Warden!' The half-man's voice was suddenly as hard as diamonds. Black diamonds, industrial grade. 'Look at me when I'm talking to you.'

The Chief Warden turned smartly and smiled. No worries about looking that half-skull in the eye; not in the circumstances. For it had occurred to the Chief

Warden that, if his collection of Blondel records still existed, then Blondel too must have existed; and if he had existed, then he must, somehow or other, have got out of the Archive. In which case, sang the Chief Warden's heart within him, I'm going to get out of this mess somehow or other, quit this bloody awful job, find another copy of the 1196 White Album and retire.

'Have you any idea,' said the half-man, 'how serious an offence it is to attempt to pervert the course of *my* justice?'

'No, sir.'

'Well,' said the half-man, 'it's very serious. So don't do it, d'you hear? Leave it out completely. Understood?'

'Sir.'

'Splendid. You, whatever your name is.'

Pursuivant lifted his head from his notebook and clicked his heels smartly under the table. 'Yes, Your Highness?' he said.

'Is that the court record you've got there?' the half-man enquired.

'Yes, Your Highness.'

'Hand it to me.'

Pursuivant closed the notebook and passed it over. The half-man took it, flipped it open, and took hold of several pages between his teeth. Then he leaned his head back and pulled. The pages ripped away from the spiral binding, and the half-man stuffed them into his half-mouth, chewed vigorously with his half-set of teeth, and swallowed.

'Yuk!' he said.

'Sir!' Pursuivant shouted. His eyes were so far out of his head that he looked like a startled grasshopper.

'You can't do that!'

The half-man looked at him. Of that look there is nothing to say, except that a few hours later Pursuivant showed up at the sick bay waving a studded club and demanding to have his memory wiped.

'Next time,' the half-man said, 'don't use pencil, it tastes horrible. Shut up, Julian, you'll sprain your hands. Now then, Chief Warden. John,' he corrected. 'Or rather, Jack, my old son. Why didn't you tell me you were a Blondel man?'

'Well, sir . . .'

'Tony,' said the half-man. 'Call me Tony.'

'Well, Tony,' said the Chief Warden, 'I wouldn't have thought . . . In the circumstances, I mean —'

'Nonsense,' said the half-man. 'Just because I don't hold with the feller personally doesn't mean I can't admire his music. And I may only have one ear, but it isn't made of tin. Is it really Gace Brulé on drums?'

The Chief Warden nodded. 'There's this incredible riff,' he said, 'in the bridge section in *Quand flours et glais . . .*'

'Cadenet on vocals?'

'They do this duet,' replied the Chief Warden, 'in *San'c fuy belha . . .*'

There was silence for a while, broken only by two – one and a half – men humming. Julian looked at each other and shook his heads sadly.

'Anyway,' said the half-man, with an effort, 'this court finds insufficient evidence of the charges alleged and rules that these proceedings be adjourned *sine die* with liberty to restore.' He tried to wink but, naturally, failed. 'And let that be a lesson to you, Chief Warden.'

'Sir.'

The half-man rose to his foot. For the record, he moved in a strange – you might say mysterious – way; the half of his body which was there moved as if the other half was there too. 'All rise,' he said. 'Come on, Julian on your feet. Go and make a cup of coffee or something. You too, whatever your name is. Go and see if you can raise that blasted driver on the radiophone. Now then, Jack ...'

The Anti-Pope and his previous life shrugged and went to look for a kettle. Pursuivant, mentally exhausted, found a cupboard under some stairs and went to sleep in it. From the Chief Warden's office came the sound, in perfect Dolby stereo and highly amplified, of Blondel singing *L'Amours Dont Sui Epris*.

If anybody – apart, of course, from the man and a half in the office – joined in the second verse, nobody heard.

The waiter who brought him his iced coffee and a glass of water looked familiar, and Blondel asked him his name.

'Spiro,' the waiter said.

'Yes,' Blondel replied, 'but Spiro what?'

'Maniakis,' the waiter replied. 'Is it important?'

Blondel shrugged. 'Did your family use to farm down near Mistras, a while back?' he asked. The waiter looked at him. 'Do excuse my asking, but you remind me of someone I used to know.'

'Really?' The waiter gave him an even stranger look. 'A hundred, maybe a hundred and fifty years ago, my mother's family lived in a village near Mistras. What of it?'

Blondel suddenly remembered who the waiter reminded him of. 'Sorry,' he said, 'my mistake. Sorry to have bothered you.'

The waiter shrugged and walked away, whistling. The tune, incidentally, was a very garbled recollection of *L'Amours Dont Sui Epris*, which the waiter had learned from his great-grandmother. Blondel finished his coffee quickly and left.

A tiresome sort of day, so far, he said to himself as he wandered back towards the Town Hall; and it had been just as well that he'd noticed the door marked *Staff Only, No Admittance* in that split second before the oil rig blew up. It was good to be out of the Archives again, but disturbing that he'd heard someone singing the second verse of the song. It could just have been a coincidence, of course; but he had the feeling, although he had no scientific data to back it up with, that coincidences didn't happen in the Archives. Something to do with the climate, perhaps. Another missing person to look for, too. Just one damn thing after another.

He looked at his watch. In twenty minutes or so he planned to sing the song under the ruined Crusader castle on the promontory; then (assuming no response) he ought to be getting along to the 1750s, where he'd pencilled in a couple of Rhine schlosses to round the day off with. Then, with any luck, bed, with the prospect of looking for two characters lost in history instead of just one to look forward to. Well, it doubled his chance of finding something, if you cared to look at it that way, although it could be argued that twice times sod all is still sod all.

He decided to walk down to the promontory by way of the market, just for the hell of it. It was nine months and seven hundred years since he'd been here last – the time before that had been fifty years in the future, but that had been years ago now – and he liked to see what changes had been, or were to be, made in the places he visited. Had they filled in the enormous pothole in the road just opposite the Church?

He had stopped to buy a packet of nuts in the market and was just walking up the hill towards the steps when somebody waved at him – just waved, as if to say hello to a not particularly close acquaintance – and walked on. This was, of course, an extremely rare occurrence. He looked round and tried to find the face in the crowd by the motorcycle spares stalls, and was just about to write if off as another very distant cousin when the wave came again, causing Blondel to drop his packet of nuts.

Oh *bother*, Blondel thought.

'Hello?' Guy said.

In the darkness, something moved; something small and four-legged. Guy, who was not the sort of person who readily backed down from positions of principle, nevertheless began to wonder whether he'd done the right thing. La Beale Isoud wasn't his cup of tea, but at least she wasn't four-legged and didn't scuttle about in pitch darkness. Not so far as he knew.

'Hello?' said a voice in the darkness. 'Is there somebody there?'

'Yes,' Guy replied, feeling that his line had been stolen. 'Er . . .' he continued.

'Make yourself at home,' said the voice, and something in its tone implied that it really meant it. 'Don't mind the rat,' the voice went on. 'It doesn't bite. It's a cousin of a rat I used to know quite well, actually.'

'Oh yes?'

'Yes indeed,' the voice went on. 'The rats here are all related, you see. Generations of them. It doesn't seem to have had any adverse effect on them. If anything, it seems to have made them unusually docile and friendly.'

'Right,' Guy said. 'Good. Is there any light in here?'

'I'm afraid not, no,' said the voice. 'Are you from the cell next door?'

Guy quivered slightly. 'Excuse me,' he said, 'but did you say cell?'

'Well,' said the voice, 'yes I did, actually.'

'You mean,' Guy continued, 'that this is a, well, prison?'

There was a brief silence. 'So I've been led to believe,' said the voice. 'It's always seemed fairly prison-like to me, at any rate.'

'Oh.' Guy paused for a moment and reflected. 'You've been here a long time, then?'

'Quite a long time, yes.'

'How long?'

'Now,' the voice said, 'there's a good question. Let me see now; five, ten, twenty, twenty-five ... I make it about a thousand years, give or take a bit.'

Guy made a sort of noise. This was not his intention; he had been trying to say, 'But it's impossible for anyone to be still alive after a thousand years, let alone a thousand years in a place like this,' but it came out wrong. The owner of the voice, however, seemed to get the gist of it.

'It does seem rather a long time, doesn't it?' he said, as if he was mildly surprised himself. 'It's amazing, though, how quickly you fall into a sort of a routine, and then the time just flies by. Of course, I haven't been *here* for all of the time.'

'I was just about to say —'

'For about – oh, nine hundred and ninety-nine years

and eleven months, I was in the cell next door,' the voice said. 'Then they moved me in here. I must say, it is an improvement.'

'Improvement,' Guy repeated. Although it was pitch dark, his senses were sending him a series of reports of their initial findings, which were generally rather negative. Probably just as well, they were saying, that it *is* pitch dark in here. So much less depressing.

'Roomier,' said the voice. 'There's a bit over there, where the draught comes in, where you can almost stand upright. Talk about luxury.' Guy realised, with a feeling of intense horror, that the voice wasn't being ironic. Far from it.

'Well,' he said, 'it's been terribly nice meeting you, but, oh *gosh*, is that the time? I really ought to be getting along.'

He edged back towards the door, which wasn't there. He made a swift but thorough search for it, using his sense of touch, and arrived at the conclusion that the door had slung its hook, good and proper. He started to howl.

'Now then,' said the voice, and two hands grabbed him firmly by the shoulders. 'You'll upset yourself,' the voice said. 'It really doesn't help, you know, and you'll disturb the guard. He likes to have his afternoon nap about this time of day, and the poor fellow has a hard enough time of it as it is ...'

Guy stopped in mid-shriek. Whoever this lunatic was, he was actually concerned about the guard's well-being. You could hear it in his voice.

'I mean,' the voice went on, 'I don't suppose he gets paid very much, and it's not much of a life for a chap, sitting around in dark corridors all day making sure

167

people don't escape. I think he bears up terribly well, in the circumstances. Nice chap, too. Collects butterflies, so he told me once. Or was that his great-great-grandfather? One tends to lose track, you know.'

Guy found that he no longer wanted to shriek; a succession of low whimpers seemed much more appropriate. He could tell that the owner of the voice approved.

'Good man,' he said. 'If I may ask, and please don't think I'm prying, but, er, how did you get here?'

'Um,' Guy said. This wasn't going to be easy. 'You're not going to believe this,' he said, 'but ...'

'Don't tell me,' said the voice. 'You found my tunnel.'

'I'm sorry?'

'You came from the other cell,' replied the voice. 'Did you find the tunnel I'd been digging?'

Guy decided to take the line of least resistance. After all, there was relatively little of value that he could learn from a man who'd been in prison for the last ten centuries. 'Yes,' he said, 'that's right.'

'I think I see,' said the voice. 'You came through my tunnel, thinking it led to the ... the ... whatsitsname, outside, and then when you found it just came here you were disappointed – naturally enough – and then, well, went off your head a bit. Is that it, more or less?'

'Yes,' Guy said. 'That's it exactly. Where did I just come in by, do you think? It's hard to get your bearings in the dark.'

'Do you think so?' the voice said. 'I find it hard to imagine it not being dark, to be honest with you, but perhaps that's just me getting set in my ways. I think you'd most likely have come in through there, over where the draught comes from. Nice draught, that, don't you think? Did you have a draught in your cell, may I ask?'

'I beg your pardon?'

'Your cell,' the voice repeated, 'the one you've just come from.'

'Oh yes,' Guy said. 'Yes, it had a draught. Lovely draught. Like this one, only better.'

'Really?' There was just a tiny spark of envy in the voice. 'Well, that must be nice. But I mustn't complain. This draught is perfectly adequate for my needs, perfectly adequate.'

That seemed to conclude the conversation for a while, and Guy began to feel uncomfortable. He edged towards the draught, found the wall, and began pawing at it again. It was smooth and continuous; no sign of any door. He felt another series of howls germinating in his stomach.

'Did you have a rat in your cell?' the voice asked.

'A rat?' Guy said. 'No, I can't say I did.'

'Oh dear,' the voice said, 'I am sorry. I do find they're such a comfort, rats. I've always had rats, for as long as I can remember. Mind you,' the voice continued, 'it might be nearer the mark to say the rats have had me; it's sometimes hard to know which of us is the master and which is the pet!' There was a mild little laugh. 'Terribly independent-minded creatures, bless them. Ah well!'

The voice seemed to have subsided into a sort of reverie – doubtless contemplating the infinite variety of rats, or something of the sort – and Guy could feel the panic creeping back into the silence. He wasn't having that; on the other hand, he didn't want to start talking about rats again, or draughts, or anything else of the kind. He decided to sing something.

'Do you mind if I sing?' he said.

'Sing?' replied the voice. 'No, please, be my guest. I haven't heard singing since – oh, what was that chap's name? He was a relief warder here about, oh, six hundred and thirty years ago now, it must be, or more like six hundred and fifty. He used to sing sometimes when he brought the food …'

'Really,' Guy said. He didn't want to know about six hundred and fifty years ago; it sounded rather depressing. 'Well then,' he said, 'I'll sing something then, shall I?'

'Thank you,' said the voice, politely.

So Guy cleared his throat, and wondered what on earth he could sing. He had just decided on *They Say There's a Wimpey Just Leaving Cologne* when a sound came from outside. A distinctly familiar sound; a voice singing. It sang:

L'amours dont suit epris
Me semont de chanter;
Si fais con hons sopris
Qui ne puet endurer …'

Guy's mouth fell open. Blondel! The voice was unmistakable, and the song – well, he'd heard it rather a lot lately. It had to be Blondel.

'I say!' said the voice, quietly.

'A li sont mi penser
Et seront a touz dis;
Ja nes en quier oster …'

For a split second, Guy wasn't sure whether or not he could remember how it went on. Then he started to sing himself; loud, hoarse and flat.

>'*Remembrance dou vis*
>*Qu'il a vermoil et clair*
>*A mon cuer a ce mis*
>*Que ne l'en puis oster ...*'

'Excuse me,' said the voice. 'May I just ...'

Guy hurled the last words of the second verse out of his lungs and waited for a breathless, desperate instant; and then Blondel's voice came back, closer now and loud, clear and joyful.

>'*Plus bele ne vit nuls*
>*De le nors ne de vis;*
>*Nature ne mist plus*
>*De beaute en nul pris ...*'

The voice cleared its throat, with a sort of different urgency, and said something, but Guy wasn't listening. He was singing, very badly:

>'*Or serai ses amis*
>*Or pri Deu de la sus*
>*Qu'a lor fin soie pris,*'

and scrambling on to his hands and knees as the door flew open, letting a dim, pale light – starlight, perhaps, or a very thin moonlight – into the cell. 'Blondel!' he shouted, 'Is that you?'

'Oh,' said Blondel, outside. 'Is that you in there, Guy? Come on, then, we haven't got all day.'

Guy hurled himself at the door, which had already started to close, all of its own accord. He just managed to get through before it closed, with a very assertive click, and faded away, as suddenly as it had appeared.

In the cell, there was a very long silence. You could plainly hear the sound of a rat, snuffling about, scratching its ear plaintively and making a little, high-pitched whining noise, as if demanding to be fed.

'Oh,' said the voice. 'Oh well, never mind. Here, ratty, nice crusts! Who's a *good* ratty, then?'

It was a cold morning, that fateful day beside the banks of the Rubicon, the little river which divides the province of Gaul from Italy, and Julius Caesar wrapped his cloak tightly round his neck. He didn't want anybody to see him shivering and think he was afraid.

'Everything ready?' he said to his commander of cavalry. The soldier nodded in reply; he didn't feel like talking. The whole army was unnaturally quiet, as if they somehow knew that the history of the world was about to be changed.

To be absolutely accurate, they did know that the history of the world was about to be changed; it was only the nature of the change that was going to come as a complete shock to the whole lot of them, Julius Caesar included.

Just before noon, Caesar summoned his most intimate and trusted friends and supporters to meet him. Rain had set in; the cold, wet, malicious rain of Gaul which Caesar was only too familiar with. He pointed to a stunted oak tree that offered some vestige of shelter from the elements, and it was there that the historic council of war was held.

Caesar was, of course, bald; although, as his one concession to vanity, he took great pains to comb his remaining hair forward over the top of his head. The rain, however, threatened to wash his coiffure down over his ears in a long, soggy tress; he borrowed a leather travelling-hat from a trusted freedman and crammed it down over his wide temples. The rain fell off the brim in a steady drip.

'Friends,' Caesar said, 'we've come a long way these last ten years. First, we had to sort out Ariovistus; the man was a menace, more a wild animal than anything else, and it was our duty to deal with him once and for all. That led to a confrontation with the Bellovaci; and no sooner had we put them in their place but the Nervii rebelled; that involved us with the Veneti, and that meant taking on the Germans, and then the Britons. No sooner had we smashed one lot of them than another mob of the brutes appeared out of nowhere, just when we thought it was safe to go home. Yes, it's been a long haul.'

Caesar paused and wiped the rain out of his eyes with the back of his hand. His face was tired, they noticed; as if ten years' strain was suddenly taking its toll. They leaned forward to catch his words against the dull whistle of the wind and rain.

'But now it's over, thank the Gods; and let me tell you, I've had enough. Now there are a lot of irresponsible idiots in Rome who'll tell you that all along I've been planning to make myself Emperor, and all this fighting and conquering in Gaul has simply been a preparation for a military coup. They say that as soon as Gaul is quiet, I'm going to lead my army across the Rubicon and into Italy, on to Rome itself.'

Caesar grinned. This was the moment he'd been waiting for.

'Well, the reason I've called you all here today is to make it absolutely plain that I have no intention – no intention whatsoever – of making myself Emperor. You know as well as I do that if a single one of my men were to cross that river, it would mean a civil war; and all my life has been devoted to preventing that. I'm going

173

back now, lads; I'm crossing the river, but I'm going alone. You're all to stay here and wait for the Senate to send you a new Governor. That's it. Dismiss.'

Caesar's staff stared at each other, unable to believe what they were hearing. For as long as any of them could remember, they had all been convinced that it was only a matter of time before Caesar made his move; and now here he was, throwing it all away. The hardest part of it was that they all knew, in their heart of hearts, that it was the right decision. If Caesar's army crossed the river, the world would never be the same again. Now that the moment had come, however, they were all so thunderstruck that none of them could move. They stood, rooted to the spot, waiting for something to happen.

And happen it did. A tent-flap in the quarter-master's tent was thrown back, and two men walked out. They looked different from all the Roman soldiers milling about in the camp; one of them wore a brown sheepskin jacket, and the other a rather travel-worn scarlet doublet and hose. A number of legionaries turned and stared at them dubiously.

'God, I'm glad you showed up,' Guy said. 'I was beginning to get worried. Thanks.'

'Think nothing of it,' Blondel replied. 'At least that's one of you found. Pure luck, really.'

'Was it?'

Blondel frowned. 'I don't know,' he said. 'There I was on Aegina, having a rest before pressing on and getting back to my schedule – we're terribly behind, by the way; as soon as we can get back on to the main line we're going to have to put in a bit of overtime, I can tell

174

you – when I saw this bloke I know.'

'How do you mean?' Guy said.

'A bloke I used to know,' Blondel repeated, 'at Richard's court. He was dressed as a Greek traffic policeman, but I'd know his face anywhere. Used to be something or other in the kitchens. He just sort of waved at me – you know, the way you acknowledge someone you see in the street – and went on. Well, I followed him, naturally, and the next thing I knew I was standing under this – well, post office. So I started to sing. And then you sang back, and this ...'

'Door?'

'... Pillar-box opened, and I went in and found you. And here we are. Where are we, do you know? I just followed the arrows up the tunnel. Looks like an army camp of some sort to me.'

'Could well be,' Guy replied. 'How do we get out of it?'

Blondel looked round. 'Don't be in such a hurry,' he said, 'I don't think I've been here before, not in a long time. In fact,' he added, smiling at a legionary who was giving him a very suspicious look, 'not ever.' The legionary shrugged and went back to polishing his shield with olive oil.

'The odd thing,' Blondel continued, strolling towards the enclosure where the siege engines were parked, 'was that I'd heard someone singing the song before that.'

'Did you?' Guy asked. 'Where —?'

'In the Archives,' Blondel replied. 'Now that *was* peculiar. I must have ended up there when I went back after you into the timequake; all the escaped time from the quake – what you might call the lava – got swept up and dumped in the Archives, and I sort of got swept along with it. I wandered about for a bit until I found an oil rig —'

'Oil rig?'

'They have them in the Archives sometimes,' Blondel explained. 'It's strictly forbidden, of course. I was lucky enough to find a door just before some idiot blew the whole lot sky high. But there was definitely someone down there singing the second verse of the song – you know, *L'Amours Dont* ... Pity I couldn't stay and find out, really. May have to go back.' He stopped and looked at Guy. 'By the way,' he said, 'you haven't told me how you —'

Just then, a centurion and two troopers came up behind them and shouted at them. They turned and were about to ask politely if there was anything they could do for anyone when they were accused, in rather intemperate language, of being spies in the pay of Pompey and the Senate, and ordered not to move. Naturally, they ran for it.

'I said,' Caesar repeated, 'dismiss.'

Nobody moved. They had all turned their heads to watch something directly behind Caesar's right shoulder.

'Hey,' Caesar protested, 'so what's so bloody interesting all of a sudden that —' He looked round too, and saw a large group of angry soldiers chasing two eccentrically dressed men through the camp. They were heading directly for the oak tree.

'Don't just stand there, you morons,' Caesar snapped. 'Grab hold of them and find out what —'

He got no further. The more brightly coloured of the two intruders had come dashing up, exhibiting a quite remarkable turn of speed, and collided with the military tribune Titus Labienus, sending him reeling back. Labienus lost his footing on the damp grass, wobbled violently, and fell over. The intruder recovered his balance with an effort and was about to continue running when Caesar himself reached out a long thin arm and attached it to the intruder's ear.

'Ouch,' the intruder said. He froze.

'Now then,' Caesar said, 'just what the hell do you think you're doing, barging in here when I'm having a —'

'Let go!'

The words came from the second intruder, who was standing about ten yards away from the tree, with a mob of soldiers gaining on him fast. The second intruder didn't seem to be paying any attention to them; he was pointing at Caesar with a small black metallic object in his hand.

'Let go!' he repeated.

'Hoy!' Caesar replied angrily. 'Who do you think you're talking to?'

The brightly dressed intruder squirmed in Caesar's grip. 'For crying out loud, Guy,' he yelled, 'put that confounded thing away! You know what happened the last —'

'If you don't let go,' said the other intruder, 'it'll be the worse for you.'

Caesar gave him a blank stare; then threw back his head and burst out laughing, at the same time giving the ear in his grip a savage tweak. The second intruder swore, and then there was a loud crack, like a thunderclap. Caesar's hat jumped about a foot into the air, was caught by a gust of wind, and floated away towards the river.

'My hat!' Caesar shrieked, and clapped his hands to his bald head, too late to stop a great long lock of damp grey hair from slithering off his bald dome and flopping down over his ear. He directed a murderous look at the two intruders and set off in furious pursuit of his floating hat.

'Guy, you pillock,' Blondel panted, 'now look what you've done.'

They watched as Caesar, intent only on the recovery of his hat, dived into the waters of the river and started to swim. The current was almost too strong for him but he struck out vigorously, reached the other side and flung himself with a cry of exultant triumph on the hat, which had come to roost in the branches of a stunted thorn bush.

The army, meanwhile, was watching with fascinated attention. As soon as Caesar set foot on the far bank, a great whoop of joy rose from the ranks, as thirty thousand men shouted, all at once;

'The die is cast! Caesar has crossed the Rubicon! To Rome! Rome!'

Caesar looked up, the hat wedged once more over his slightly protruding ears. A look of supreme disgust crossed his face.

'Oh *shit*,' he said.

The army had started to cross the river. Someone had hoisted up the sacred Eagle standards. They were singing the battle song of the Fifteenth Legion.

'I told you,' Blondel said. 'Didn't I tell you?'

They were alone now in the abandoned camp. On the other side of the river Caesar was being carried on the shoulders of his bodyguard, on inexorably towards Rome and Empire.

'But I thought that was what was supposed to happen,' Guy whimpered.

Blondel shook his head. 'In a sense, yes,' he replied. 'But ... oh, never mind. Let's get out of here and go and have a drink.'

Giovanni smiled.

'What I always say to people in your situation,' he said, 'people who've fallen off the edge of the world and are sailing aimlessly about, is that one of these days you're bound to find your way back again, and in the meantime, don't you think your money should be working for you as hard as it possibly can, so that when you *do* finally get out of here ...'

The Genoese merchant gave him a blank, empty-eye-socket stare. Giovanni kept going. In his youth, when he was just another Florentine wide boy hawking scarlet hose and fragments of the True Cross door to door through Gascony, he'd come up against harder nuts than this.

'Think how long you've been down here,' he said. 'A hundred years? Two hundred? Would five hundred be nearer the mark, maybe?'

The Genoese made a little muffled noise, somewhere between a moan and a shriek. Giovanni nodded.

'Okay,' he said, 'call it four hundred and fifty years, give or take fifty on either side. Now, a modest stake of say one thousand bezants, invested at twenty-five per cent compound interest, tax-free for four hundred and fifty years ...'

The Genoese suddenly howled and tried to bite Giovanni in the neck. Being a man of action as well as a man of intellect, Giovanni sidestepped, picked up an oar and clubbed him savagely on the head. Being an insurance broker he mentioned to him the benefits of proper accident insurance and private health cover. Before he could get any forms out or unscrew the top of his fountain pen, however, the Genoese stopped twitching and lay still. Giovanni sighed; an opportunity lost, he couldn't help feeling.

'Is he ...?' Marco asked.

Giovanni nodded. 'Fool to himself,' he said. 'I suppose we could retrospectively insure his life for a couple of grand, but it hardly seems worth the bother. Come on, let's try over there.'

They walked on over the insubstantial sea, keeping their spirits up by offering passing ships the opportunity to take advantage of low-start endowment mortgages. After about an hour, they came to what looked remarkably like a bank.

'Don't look at it,' Giovanni said, 'it's probably just a mirage or something.'

Iachimo shook his head. 'Look,' he said, 'they're members of FIMBRA, it says so in the window. It must be a bank.'

'Iachimo ...'

'But Giovanni,' Iachimo said, 'they aren't *allowed* to display the FIMBRA logo unless they're ...'

Giovanni shrugged. If he was going to start hallucinating, a bank was a nice thing to hallucinate. Especially a bank which, in the circumstances, must count as definitively offshore.

'We might just wander in,' he said tentatively. 'Just on the off chance, you know ...'

It was a very nice bank, and before he knew what he was doing Giovanni had filled his pockets with leaflets.

Then he noticed something.

'Iachimo,' he said, 'Marco, there's nobody here.'

Iachimo sniffed like a dog. 'You're right,' he said.
'Completely deserted. How can they be members of
FIMBRA if there's nobody . . .?'

Giovanni rang the bell; nobody came. Mind you,
that didn't mean very much. Next he tried the door that
led to the area behind the bulletproof screen. It opened.

'Coming?' he asked.

Marco looked nervously at the security cameras. 'Do
you think we should?' he said. 'I mean, we are in the
Archives, and —'

'There's nobody here,' Giovanni replied. 'Come on.'

They walked through. At once, all the computer
screens, which had been blank, sprang into life. They
started displaying stock market results from all over the
Universe. There were one or two that Giovanni had
never heard of before.

'Here, Iachimo,' he said, 'you know about these
things. What's the $\psi\gamma\uparrow\gamma\beta\leftarrow\leftrightarrow\downarrow\phi$ 600 Share Index
when it's at home?'

Iachimo frowned and shook his head; clearly, it
worried him that he hadn't heard of it. Giovanni,
meanwhile, had sat down in front of one of the
consoles and was tapping keys. After a while, he
looked round.

'Lads,' he said, 'I think I've sorted it out.'

The others looked at him.

'It's pathetically simple, really,' Giovanni said,
with a grin. He tapped a key, and a dazzling display
of little twinkling figures appeared on the screen in
front of him. He paused for a moment and read
them. 'Getting us out of here is going to be no

trouble at all. Iachimo, what's the sort code for our bank in Geneva?'

'7865443,' Iachimo said promptly. 'Why?'

'Because,' Giovanni replied, 'I'm going to pay us into our deposit account there. By telegraphic transfer. A doddle, really. Hold tight.'

He typed in 7865443, then a couple of codes, and then their names. A moment later, they had vanished.

They stayed vanished.

'Giovanni!' Iachimo screamed. It was dark and cold and he had the sensation of falling and he couldn't feel anything – anything – with any of his limbs or senses. 'What's happening? Giovanni?'

'Sod it,' came Giovanni's voice, drifting in nothingness. 'We must be after business hours. The bastards have put us on hold.'

'What does that mean?'

'Means we've got to stay here till the bank opens for the next day's trading,' Giovanni yelled back. 'Means we'll lose a whole day's interest. When I get out of this, somebody's going to get sued.'

As if in response, there was a deafening crackle and the three brothers felt as if they were being squeezed, like toothpaste, through some sort of nozzle. Then there was a crash, and they fell, head-first, through a computer screen.

'Giovanni,' Marco said, 'you've got a bar code printed all over your forehead.'

'So have you,' Giovanni replied. He picked himself up, dusted splinters of broken cathode ray tube out of his hair, and smiled at the terrified computer operator in whose lap he had landed. She stared at him and then, without removing her eyes from his face, started to fill in an Input chit.

'Right then,' Giovanni said. 'Come on, you two. Mademoiselle,' he asked the girl, 'je vous prie, où sommes-nous, exactement?'

The girl replied that they were in Geneva, and did he want to be taken off deposit? Giovanni confirmed that he did, and the three brothers walked out of the bank into the open air.

'Quick thinking, that, on my part,' Giovanni said, 'wouldn't you say?'

'We should have offered to pay for the broken machines,' Marco replied. 'They aren't cheap, you know.'

They found a café and had a drink. They could afford it, after all; Marco's lucky silver threepenny bit, which he kept on his key ring, had just accumulated 10,000 Swiss francs interest. Accordingly, it was adjudged to be his shout. He paid.

'The next thing on the agenda,' Giovanni said, 'is to find Blondel.'

Iachimo shook his head. 'Can't do that,' he said. 'That man said he'd been destroyed, right? Blown up in a Time Archive. Means he never existed.'

Giovanni put down his glass, wiped his lips on his tie and sighed. 'Don't be a prawn, Iachimo,' he said. 'If he never existed, how come we both know who I'm talking about?'

'Who are you talking about?' Marco asked. They ignored him.

'Stands to reason,' Giovanni went on. 'If we both remember him, it follows that he must have existed. Thus he can't have been killed in the Archives. Furthermore, if we can remember him here, Topside, then he must have got out of the Archives somehow. In which case he's still here somewhere. *Capisce?*'

Iachimo wrinkled his brows, thought about it and then nodded enthusiastically. 'That's brilliant,' he said. 'How do we find him?'

Giovanni shrugged. 'There,' he said, 'you have me. That's a difficult one. I mean, we had enough trouble finding him last time.'

'You could try the phone book,' Marco said.

'I suppose,' Giovanni went on, 'we could try going back to all the gigs we set up for him which he never actually did and see if he's done any of them yet. Then we could sort of work backwards, and ...'

'There's a phone book here,' Marco said. 'Look.'

'Alternatively,' Giovanni continued, 'we could hire an enquiry agent. There's Ennio Sforza, only he's semi-retired. Or maybe we could try Annibale Tedesci; I know he really only does cross-temporal divorce work, but he might be prepared to stretch a point ...'

'Here we are,' said Marco. 'Blondel. Blondelle Cash & Carry, Blondella Hydraulic Systems, Blond Elephant Night club ...'

'Do you know how much Annibale Tedesci charges per hour?' Iachimo replied. 'We'd have to do extra gigs just to cover the fees. How about if we did a credit search? We could go back in time, issue him with a credit card, and then ...'

'Blondel,' Marco said, '32 Munchenstrasse.'

His brothers turned and stared at him.

'32 Munchenstrasse,' he repeated. 'Here, look for yourselves if you don't —'

His brothers examined the entry. They read it again.

Giovanni said something profane under his breath, and grinned.

'Now that,' he said, 'is what I call landing on your feet. Marco.'

Marco smiled, preparatory to preening himself. 'Yes?'

'Get them in, there's a good lad,' Giovanni said, indicating the empty glasses. 'And while you're at it, see if anybody's got a street map.'

La Beale Isoud tapped her foot.

'Mr Goodlet,' she said, 'enough is enough. I can take a joke as well as anyone, but this is getting silly. Either you open that door this minute, or —'

The door opened, and Blondel crawled through. 'Hello, Sis,' he said. 'Is supper ready? I'm starving. You've met Guy, haven't you?'

'Mr *Goodlet*!' said La Beale Isoud. 'Come back here at once.'

Guy, halfway back down the coal-cellar steps, froze. Like an exhausted stag turning at bay, he knew when he'd had enough. He smiled weakly.

'We have met, yes,' he said. 'Blondel . . .'

But Blondel wasn't listening; either to Guy, who was trying to explain in a loud and urgent whisper, or to La Beale Isoud, who was providing a different version of the same basic facts in a much louder voice. He waved a hand placidly and walked through into his study, leaving Guy and La Beale Isoud together. He probably thought he was being tactful.

'Mademoiselle, er de Nesle,' Guy said, 'I think we really ought to . . .'

La Beale Isoud swept past him and locked the coal-cellar door with a little silver key, which she then dropped down the front of her dress. It must have been cold, because she winced slightly. 'Now then, Mr Goodlet,' she said grimly, 'I think we most certainly ought to get a few things straight, here and now. First, if you think for one moment that I want to marry you, you couldn't be more wrong.'

'Oh,' Guy said. He felt like a boxer whose opponent has just punched himself forcefully on the nose. 'Well, I ...'

'If you were the last man in the entire world,' La Beale Isoud went on, 'and they were giving away free alarm clock radios with every wedding bouquet, I still wouldn't marry you, if it was up to me.'

'It is, surely.'

La Beale Isoud looked at him. 'What?' she asked.

'Up to you,' Guy said. 'I mean, I'm with you a hundred per cent there. Who you marry – who you don't marry, more to the point – surely that's your business and nobody else's. You stick to your guns.'

'Mr Goodlet,' said La Beale Isoud dangerously, 'the fact remains that we are married – or we will be, which is roughly the same thing, I suppose. The question is, what can we do about it?'

'We could get a divorce,' Guy said. 'If we book one now, perhaps it could be ready by the time we —'

'Divorce,' said La Beale Isoud, 'is out of the question. The scandal would be unthinkable.'

'Surely not.'

'Kindly,' said La Beale Isoud, 'do not interrupt. As far as I'm concerned, divorce is entirely out of the question. If you have any *sensible* suggestions, I should be pleased to hear them.'

Guy thought, but all he could come up with was suicide. He stared at his feet uncomfortably.

'I take it,' Isoud went on, 'that you have nothing constructive to suggest. Very well, then. I take it that we'll just have to find some – how can I put it? – some form of civilised compromise.'

Guy nodded. 'That suits me,' he said. 'I'm all for civilisation. What had you in mind?'

La Beale Isoud glowered at him. 'Frankly, Mr Goodlet,' she said, 'I feel that only one form of compromise is likely to be acceptable; namely that, after we are married, we see as little of each other as possible.'

'Fair enough,' Guy said. 'Separate beds, you mean?'

'I mean,' Isoud replied, 'separate centuries.'

Guy raised an eyebrow. 'Don't get me wrong,' he said, 'I think it's a perfectly splendid idea. But you said a minute ago that you didn't want a divorce because of how it would look. Wouldn't having a husband hundreds of years in the future look almost as bad? Or doesn't it work like that?'

'If you intend to make difficulties —'

'No, no,' Guy said quickly, 'perish the thought. Besides,' he added, 'if we're hundreds of years apart, then really the whole thing becomes pretty well academic anyway, doesn't it? I mean, you could marry someone else, I could marry someone else, nobody would ever know . . .'

'Mr *Goodlet!*'

'Oh come on, now,' Guy said, 'be reasonable. Anyway, doesn't it say somewhere in the book of rules that if your wife hasn't been heard of for seven years she's assumed to be dead? Think it's seven years, though I'd have to ask my lawyer. I mean, that way we'd have all the advantages of a divorce without the ...'

Something about La Beale Isoud's expression – perhaps it was the ferocious look in her limpid blue eyes – gave Guy to understand that he wasn't really doing himself much good. He decided to change the subject.

'Anyway,' he said, 'we can sort something out, between us, you know, later. Plenty of time for that. Um.'

That seemed to be that. La Beale Isoud, perhaps not able to trust herself to speak further, stomped out of the hall, and shortly afterwards Guy heard the sound of large copper pans being banged about.

Then Blondel came back into the hall. He had changed out of his usual outfit into another, exactly the same but cleaner, and had combed his hair. Guy had the feeling that La Beale Isoud was rather strict about such things. He shuddered; and Blondel, observing him, grinned weakly.

'Isoud told me the good news,' he said, 'I ought to congratulate you, but I'm a realist. Never mind, it may never happen.'

'Thanks,' Guy replied, 'but it already has. Or it already will have. How do you cope with all these future tenses, by the way?'

'I don't,' Blondel replied. 'When you whizz about in time like I do, you tend to get the sense of what people say rather better if you don't actually listen to the words. Just stick with the general sort of tune and you won't go far wrong. Fancy a drink?'

Guy nodded. A drink, he felt, would be almost as good an idea as something to eat. It was a very long time since he'd had anything to eat, and he didn't want to get out of practice. He mentioned this; and the words were no sooner past the gate of his teeth when there came from the far room the sound of somebody hitting a piece of quick-fry steak with a wooden mallet, very hard.

'It sounds to me,' Blondel said, 'as if Isoud's fixing something for us right now. You're welcome to stay.'

'Thank you,' Guy replied. 'But I'd hate to impose, I mean ...'

Blondel nodded. 'So would I,' he replied, 'but I'm stuck with her. Look, Guy, my dear fellow, are you *sure* you wouldn't like to marry her? Permanently, I mean. Sort of, take her a long way away? I'm sure she'd make you a wonderful wife, and then I could just get a hamburger or a couple of pancakes on my way home in the evenings, instead of having to gnaw my way through scale models of the Krak Des Chevaliers in mashed potato.'

'Mashed potato?'

'Exactly,' Blondel replied, shaking his head. 'My sister has this problem with mashed potato. She gets it confused with food. Mind you, all the women in my family believe in substantial meals. You take,' he added, with a slight grimace, 'my sister Ysabel. Give her five loaves and two fishes, and you could invite both Houses of Parliament.'

'Er ...'

'Thought not,' Blondel said. 'Don't blame you. I'm told it's worse once you've actually married them, but mercifully I'm not in a position to speak authoritatively on that point.'

'I ...'

'Pretending to have toothache doesn't help, either,'

Blondel continued, with the air of a man settling down to a cherished topic, 'because then they've got an excuse to make soup. Do you have any idea of the number of saucepans an active, able-bodied woman can use making soup? They aren't allowed to wash up, by the way, because of their fingernails. Cracks them, or something similarly absurd. On that basis, I should be walking around with half a pound of shrapnel on the ends of my arms. It's a conspiracy, that's what it is. They learn it from their mothers.'

Guy nodded. 'In the meantime,' he asked, 'have you got any biscuits, or anything like that? Sorry to be a nuisance, but ...'

'My dear fellow, I was forgetting.' Blondel looked round at the door behind which La Beale Isoud was, to judge by the sound effects, lacerating carrots, checked that it was firmly shut, and then jumped for one of the lamp-brackets. He caught it, swung himself up into one of the window mullions, picked something out of a crack in the stonework, and threw it down to Guy. It was a leather satchel containing three and a half rolls of chocolate digestives.

'It's my secret supply,' he called down in a loud whisper. 'Got to keep them hidden, or she'll pound them up for cheesecake base. She makes a cheesecake that'd stop crossbow bolts. Help yourself.'

Guy tipped some biscuits into his pockets and threw the bag back quickly. Blondel, having restored his treasure, lowered himself back down again, his jaws moving furtively.

'It's not as if she doesn't make biscuits too,' he said, through a mouthful of crumbs. 'But they're those brick-hard ones with almonds and no chocolate. I

190

mean, brilliant for lining a fireplace, but not much use for constructive eating. Now then, we were thinking about having a drink.'

But before they could get to the decanters, there was a hammering at the coal-cellar door. Blondel raised both eyebrows in astonishment.

'Expecting anybody?' he asked.

Guy shook his head.

'Well,' Blondel said, 'I'm not, and unless it's double glazing then someone would appear to have followed us. And we don't get many offers of double glazing in the eleventh century. Be different if this was Chartres or Saint Denis. I think I'd better see who it is.'

With a swift movement of his hand, he drew a sword down from the wall and hid it behind his back. With the other hand he undid the bolts on the door and pulled it open. Through the door came Giovanni, Iachimo and Marco.

'I wasn't far wrong,' he said, 'at that. What on earth do you gentlemen want?' He produced the sword and smiled. 'You'd better come in,' he said. 'And take your hats off quick.'

The Galeazzo brothers uncovered their heads immediately. Blondel grinned and put up his sword.

'Drink, anybody?' he said. 'I hope you all like mashed potato. Now, how did you get here, and what do you want?' He poured out five glasses of mead with a flourish and handed them round.

'We were telexed,' Marco said, and would undoubtedly have explained further had not Giovanni trodden on his foot. He had to get up and walk across the hall to do it; but Marco was trained to obey certain signals, and if one didn't use them it only confused him.

'We were just passing,' Giovanni said, 'on our way back from the Archives; stopped off for a drink, happened to notice your name in the phone book, thought we'd drop in on the off chance you were in.' He looked about him. 'Nice place you have here,' he said. 'I wonder if you've ever considered whether you've got it adequately insured. We can offer you ...'

Blondel shook his head. 'No point,' he said. 'In five days' time it gets burnt down. Not a stone left standing.'

'Ah.'

'Mind you,' Blondel went on, 'every four days I move it back in time. That means I get to pay reduced rates, too. Handy.'

Giovanni looked at his brothers and shrugged. 'Anyway,' he said, 'this isn't entirely a social call.'

Blondel grinned. 'You amaze me,' he said.

'In fact,' Giovanni went on, 'we have some very serious business to discuss. You realise that you are in breach of your contract?'

'Oh yes?'

Giovanni nodded gravely. 'Clauses 1, 2, 3, 4, 5, 6, 7, 8, 9, 10, 11, 12, 13, 14, 15, 16, 17, 18 and 20.'

'Really?' Blondel said. 'What's Clause 19 about, then?'

'There isn't one,' Giovanni replied. 'Originally it was your right to receive a duly audited account every financial year, but it got deleted.'

'Did it?'

'Yes.'

'I see.' Blondel poured himself another glass of mead, picked some beeswax out of it with his finger-nail, and smiled. 'But I'm in breach of the rest of it, am I?'

'I'm afraid so,' Giovanni said. 'However —'

'That's very serious, isn't it?'

'It could be,' Giovanni replied, 'potentially. That's why —'

'If I was you,' Blondel purred, 'I'd sue.'

Giovanni blinked. 'You would?'

Blondel nodded vigorously. 'Too right,' he replied. 'Can't have people going about the place playing fast and loose with binding agreements, can we? No, bash on, that's what I'd do, and stand up for your rights.'

'Um . . .'

'In fact,' Blondel said, 'there's no time like the present, is there? Now it so happens,' he said, standing up and taking down a sword and a shield from the wall, 'that this castle is within the jurisdiction' – he swung the sword in his hand to check the balance; it passed – 'of the Supreme Court of the Barony of Nesle, of which I' – he tested the point, swore, and licked his finger – 'am hereditary Chief Justiciar. Normally, there's quite a backlog of cases, but just at present I think we could fit you in. Trial by combat, naturally.'

Giovanni swallowed hard. 'Combat,' he repeated.

'Absolutely,' Blondel replied. 'We tried the other way, but we kept on coming back to combat. Quicker, cheaper, and above all, fairer; not to mention a damn sight less traumatic for the participants. Would you like me to lend you a shield? You seem to have come out without one.'

'Actually,' Giovanni said, 'perhaps we ought to try a little without prejudice negotiation. I find litigation positively counter-productive sometimes, don't you?'

'Ah yes,' Blondel replied, making his choice from a rack of double-bladed battle-axes, 'but that's because

193

you've never had the advantage of the Nesle judicial system. No, I think a couple of bouts ought to' – he weighed two maces, picked the heavier one and put the other back – 'get this business knocked on the head – if you'll pardon the expression – in two shakes of a lamb's tail. Here, catch!' He tossed a helmet to Giovanni, who dropped it with a clang. 'Up to you,' Blondel said, putting on his own helmet and feeling the edge of his axe. 'Helmets are optional, and I can understand your feeling nervous, what with Mr Goodlet being in the same room. Shall we make it best of three, do you think? Or would you prefer sudden death?'

Giovanni made a small, whimpering noise and looked round at his brothers for support. They weren't there. They were right behind him, hiding.

'Alternatively,' Blondel said, removing his helmet and putting down his axe on a handy coffee table, 'we could forget all about the contract. I mean, we all trust each other, don't we? Nod if you agree.'

The Galeazzo brothers nodded in perfect unison, like a miniature Cerberus in the back window of a Vauxhall Cavalier.

'Glad you think so, too,' said Blondel. 'You wouldn't happen to have it with you, by any chance?'

Marco put his feet carefully out of Giovanni's way and said 'Yes.' He went on to explain that it was in Giovanni's briefcase, inside an envelope marked *Tax Returns 1232/3*, and would have enlarged on the theme had not his brothers put a helmet on his head, the wrong way round, so that the neckguard obstructed his mouth. By then, however, the contract was on the fire.

'Now then,' Blondel said, 'I think it's time for some food.'

Giovanni was looking at the contract curling up on the fire. It was possible that he might have felt similar sensations of loss and sadness for the death of his grandmother; but the theory would be hard to prove, given that he'd sold her to Barbary slavers hundreds of years earlier, and since then they'd lost touch. He moistened his lips with the tip of his tongue.

'Right,' he said. 'Well, I think we've now established a forum for negotiations leading to a new contract ...'

Blondel turned round slowly and looked at him. 'You think so,' he said.

'Absolutely,' Giovanni replied. 'I mean,' he added, and his will to profit battled briefly with his instincts of self-preservation; the will to profit won. 'Perhaps a little fine-tuning of some of the clauses might be called for, what with the passage of time and changes in circumstances; but what the hell, Blondel, you're still an artist, and artists need agents. Now then ...'

'Just for that,' Blondel said, 'you get a double helping of mashed potato.'

Giovanni looked wounded. 'You disappoint me,' he said. 'I think we can do business together. After all,' he said, 'you'd be interested in finding the Chastel des Larmes Chaudes, now wouldn't you?'

Blondel gave him a long look. 'You're bluffing,' he said.

'Maybe.'

'You don't know where the Chastel des Larmes Chaudes is, any more than I do.'

Giovanni smiled. 'True,' he said. 'But I know where they bank.'

There was a long silence, broken only by the sound of Guy eating a few stale peanuts he'd found in a deserted finger-bowl. Finally Blondel stood up and walked about the room for a while.

'Where they *bank* . . .' he said.

'Absolutely,' Giovanni said. 'After all, it's a fundamental rule of nature. Everybody banks somewhere.'

'Oh yes?' Blondel replied. 'What about . . .' He tailed off.

'What about?' Giovanni repeated.

Blondel suddenly grinned. 'I was trying to think of an example,' he said, 'and I couldn't. All right, then, tell me how you know where the Chastel des Larmes Chaudes banks.'

Giovanni shook his head. 'I wasn't born yesterday,' he said. 'We've got to have a contract first.'

Blondel sighed. 'Have it your own way, then. Even when I've found out where their bank is, how does that help me find them?'

'That's up to you,' Giovanni replied. 'You're a very resourceful man. Now then, we were discussing terms.'

'Were we?'

'Yes.'

'Oh,' Blondel shrugged. 'Go on, then.'

'Just one gig,' Giovanni said. 'One very big concert. We'll network it, naturally; every country, every century, every dimension.'

Blondel frowned. 'How?' he said.

'Simple.' Giovanni spread his hands in a gesture of extreme simplicity. 'We'll do it in every country, in every century, simultaneously.'

'Hang on,' Blondel said. 'Nobody's ever done that before.'

Giovanni's smile widened until it came close to being a geographical feature. 'They soon will have,' he replied. 'Just one gig, Blondel. How about it?'

As he spoke the kitchen door opened, and Isoud trotted angrily out, plonked down a huge dish of mashed potato on the table, and trotted back again. The door slammed behind her.

'All right,' Blondel said. He looked at the mashed potato and shuddered. 'Just this once.'

FAX
From: Galeazzo, Galeazzo and Galeazzo, Beaumont Street, Londinium
To: The Chastel des Larmes Chaudes
Your reference: AC
Message follows

'If it's one of those junk faxes,' Mountjoy's secretary said, 'I'll get him to write to the company. I've got enough to do without running up and down stairs delivering mailshots.'

Congratulations! the message continued. *You have been selected as this month's lucky winner in the Galeazzo Brothers Financial Services Draw. This month's fabulous prize is two tickets for the greatest ever Blondel concert.*

'Thought so,' said Mountjoy's secretary, and she went to pull the paper out of the machine. An arm stopped her.

'Leave it,' said a voice harshly behind her. 'I want to see what it says.'

'Yes, *sir*,' squeaked the secretary. She retreated.

All you have to do to receive your fabulous prize, went on the message, slowly ballooning out of the printer, *is to invest ST50,000 or more in a Galeazzo Brothers*

197

Managed Fund of your choice before the end of the month; but hurry! If you don't claim your fabulous prize within the specified time, then Galeazzo Brothers Financial Services reserve the right to offer your fabulous prize to another lucky winner. All enquiries about Galeazzo Brothers Managed Funds should be addressed to ...

And then the paper got wedged and the toner ran out and the rollers jammed and the printer got stuck, and a few moments later the whole thing seized up and started beeping hysterically. An arm reached out and tweaked the paper free. Someone opened a door for the distinguished visitor, and he left. Gradually, life in Reception returned to normal.

'Who was that?' Mountjoy's secretary asked. Everybody looked at her.

'Funny,' said the office junior. 'Dead comical.'

'Straight up,' she replied. 'Who was it? I've never seen him before.'

'That,' said the postboy, 'was Mr A.'

'Who's —'

'So next time,' the postboy went on, 'if I was you, I'd mind your manners, right? It doesn't do to get on the wrong side of Mr A.' The postboy frowned. 'So to speak,' he added.

'I still don't know ...'

But everyone was wandering off; some to make coffee, others to file memoranda, others to stand around waiting for the man to come and fix the photocopier. Mountjoy's secretary was just scratching her head, wondering if she'd missed something somewhere, when the phone rang. She hurried back to her place, sat down and put on the headphones.

'Chastel des Larmes Chaudes, can I help you?' she warbled.

'I want to speak to the proprietor,' said the voice at the other end. A nice voice, Mountjoy's secretary thought; not the sort to bite your head off.

'Thank you,' she replied. 'Who shall I say is calling, please?'

'My name's de Nesle,' the voice said. 'Jean de Nesle. I think he'll take my call.'

The atmosphere at a Blondel concert is not easy to describe. When the concert in question has been billed as the Very Last Ever Farewell Charity Concert, the atmosphere is heightened to such an extent that barometers are brought into the auditorium entirely at their owners' risk.

For the occasion the Galeazzo Brothers had built – over the course of centuries, naturally, and entirely funded by retrospective borrowing (which meant that the bank ended up paying *them* interest) – the biggest, grandest, most garish neo-Gothic auditorium ever. Every inch of the surface area of the huge massed banks of speakers was carved with intricate scroll-and-acanthus work, and the leads entered them through the mouths of grinning gargoyles. The stage itself was supported on slender pinnacles of stone at a dizzying height above the ground, and was roofed over with a breathtaking canopy of stained glass, providing an unrivalled light show without the expense of electric power.

Up in his dressing room, Blondel wasn't feeling the

slightest bit nervous. As far as he was concerned, he was going to sing. He quite liked singing, although he found it got a bit tiresome if you did it day in, day out, and since he'd written all the songs himself he wasn't worried about forgetting the words. Even if he did, he could make up some more. They'd like that, probably.

'I do wish you'd stop walking up and down like that,' he said to Giovanni, who had worn a little freeway in the pile of the carpet. 'You know I like to get forty winks before I go on, and you're keeping me awake.'

Giovanni spat out a mouthful of fingernail and scowled at him. 'The biggest gig in the history of the world,' he snarled. 'If they suddenly ask for their money back, it'll wipe out the financial structures of the entire civilised world. For God's sake, most of the money we've been paid for seats hasn't even been made yet. I've got a right to be nervous.'

Blondel shrugged. 'Fair enough,' he said, 'if it makes you feel any better, by all means be nervous. But it'd be awfully sweet of you if you'd just go and do it somewhere else.'

Giovanni shook his head furiously, until it became a blur of movement. 'Oh no,' he said. 'I'm not letting you out of my sight till this is all safely over. Not after Wurtemburg.'

'Come on, Giovanni,' Blondel sighed. 'Not Wurtemburg *again*.'

Giovanni ignored him. 'A sell-out,' he said. 'Not a seat to be had for any money. Crown Prince of Denmark sitting in the front row, eating popcorn. And you take it into your head to slope off and sing under some castle instead, just because —'

'It was seeing the Crown Prince put it into my head,

201

actually,' Blondel commented. 'I thought, Elsinore, haven't been there for ages, worth a try. A complete washout, actually. I nearly got spitted by a nervous guard with a halberd, but that was all.'

Giovanni growled at him. 'That was not bloody well all,' he snapped. 'I had to pay out ninety million groschen in returned admittance. The Crown Prince nearly did his nut. Tried to stab me through the safety curtain. And that's why I'm not letting you set foot outside this room until ...'

Blondel shrugged. 'All right,' he said amicably, 'entirely up to you. I just thought you might be more comfortable sitting down. Have an aspirin or something.'

'I don't want an aspirin,' Giovanni replied. 'For two pins I'd take a short cut through a couple of hours and only come back when it's all over. Only then I wouldn't be able to keep an eye on you ...'

The door opened and Guy came in with a tray. It contained a glass of water, a dry biscuit and a handful of seedless currants.

'There's a man outside,' he said, 'claims he's from the *Anglo-Saxon Chronicle*, wants an interview. I told him to get lost.'

Blondel drank half the water and nibbled the edge of the biscuit. 'He was probably telling the truth, actually,' he said. 'Still, I don't much care for reporters. Silly of me, I know, and they're only doing their job, but —'

'Job nothing,' Giovanni interrupted. 'We've done an exclusive deal with the *FT*.'

'Never mind,' Blondel said. 'Now, if it'll take your mind off worrying, we can run through the programme.

Will that make you feel any better?'

Giovanni nodded. He'd grown his fingernails for two years just to be ready for tonight, and he'd finished them already.

'Well,' Blondel said, 'we'll start off with *Purgator Criminum*, something with a bit of go to it; then we'll have *Ma Joie*, follow that up with a couple of numbers from the CB —'

'Which ones?'

'I thought *Estuans Intrinsecus*, followed by *Imperator Rex Grecorum*. Or do you think that's wise, after what happened at Antioch?'

'Don't worry about that,' Giovanni reassured him, 'I've brought in the whole of the Knights Templar to cover security. First sign of any trouble, they'll be out, dead *and* excommunicated.'

Blondel shrugged again. 'Nothing to do with me,' he said. 'Then I thought we'd do the rest of the White Album stuff, finish off with *Mihi Est Propositum*, and have the break there. That sound OK?'

Giovanni nodded. 'That's good,' he said. 'That way we'll sell a hell of a lot of peanuts in the interval. So what about the second half?'

'Pretty straightforward,' Blondel said. 'We'll do all the new material there.'

'New material?' Guy interrupted. 'You mean you've written more songs since you ...'

Blondel grinned. 'I like to keep my hand in,' he said, 'just for fun. So I reckon we might as well do *Greensleeves, Molly Malone, Shenandoah, Au Près De Ma Blonde, Liliburlero* and *The Bonnie Banks of —*'

'Hang on,' Guy said.

Blondel wrinkled his nose. 'Maybe you're right,' he

said, 'not *Loch Lomond.* Don't know what I was thinking of. How about *Swing Low Sweet Chariot?*'

'Ever since Blondel ... retired,' Giovanni explained, 'he's written under a nom de plume.'

'What's that?'

'Anonymous.'

Guy closed his eyes and then opened them again. 'What, all of them?' he asked.

Blondel made a tiny movement with his shoulders. It might have been wincing. 'Pretty well,' he said.

'Did you write *Kiss Me Goodnight, Sergeant Major?*'

Blondel nodded. He did not speak.

'And *Frankie and Johnny?*'

Blondel's head dipped, just perceptibly.

'Really?'

Blondel nodded again and smiled; or at least he lifted the curtain of his lips on a set of clenched teeth.

'Gosh,' Guy said. He seemed to experience an inner struggle, as perhaps between hero-worship and extreme embarrassment. 'Er, can I have your auto —'

Blondel gave him a cold look. 'I also,' he said, 'wrote —'

'It's not for me,' Guy went on, 'it's for my —'

'*Western Wind, When Wilt Thou Blow, Silent Night* and *The Vicar of Bray,*' Blondel went on. He signed the envelope-back that Guy had thrust at him without comment. 'Anyway,' he added, after a while, 'that ought to do for tonight. And of course we can finish up with *L'Amours Dont Sui Epris.* End up with something they can hum on the way home, you know.'

'You didn't write —'

'No,' Blondel snapped, 'certainly not. Look, unless anyone's got anything important they want to talk about, I really am going to try and get a nap now. All right?'

'Anything you say,' Guy said. He folded the envelope carefully and put it away. Even then, he felt he had to add something. You don't meet a seminal genius every day, after all.

'Mr Blondel,' he said, 'I take my hat off to you.'

'So long it's your own hat,' Blondel replied sleepily, 'that's fine by me. Shut the door behind you when you go.'

Guy did so. By this time, Giovanni had disappeared to have another tearing row with the electricians. The man from the *Anglo-Saxon Chronicle* had retired to the bar, and was probably trying to coax a story out of the PR people in an attempt to scoop the *Tres Riches Heures Du Duc De Berri*. There was nothing, Guy decided, that he could usefully do; which meant he had time to go and find something to eat. Now that was a good idea.

A section of the audience was having trouble finding its seat.

'This,' it said, 'is Row 8765, right?'

'Yes,' said the usher, 'but —'

'And this is a ticket, right?'

'Looks like one,' the usher admitted, 'but —'

'Read me,' said the section of the audience, 'what it says on the ticket.'

'Row 8765 Seat 3654,' said the usher, 'but —'

'Thank you,' said the section of the audience. 'Now, if you'll kindly throw out the man who's sitting in my seat, I can take the weight off my foot and sit down, and you can go and do something else.'

But he's got a ticket too, the usher would have said, if he hadn't met the full force of the section of the audience's eye. As it was, he said, 'Yes, sir,' and shortly afterwards, 'You, out of it.' This remark was addressed, as it happened, to the music critic of the *Oceanian*, whose great-great-great-great-great-grandfather had booked the seat five hundred years in advance and left it in his will, together with strict instructions to his descendants to devote themselves solely to preparing themselves for this event.

'Thank you,' said the section of the audience, as the music critic of the *Oceanian* was carried away on an improvised stretcher. 'You can go now.'

'Yes, sir.'

The section of the audience turned to the two men sitting beside him. They looked identical; not surprisingly.

'Pity,' he continued, 'we could only get two tickets. I don't like having to pull rank like that, let alone use a forged ticket. Bad form. Still, I didn't want you two to miss the fun.'

His two companions nodded. Simultaneously. With one voice they said, 'Thanks.'

The section of the audience waved a deprecating hand. 'That's all right,' he said. 'Now then, let's have a look at the programme. Oh *good*, he's doing *Mihi Est Propositum*. I remember at the Orleans gig of '88 ...'

Guy wasn't having the best of luck. The bar was packed, the hot dog stall had been stripped down to bare wood within thirty seconds of opening, and he found when he reached the front of the queue that the candy-floss, at ST125 a go, was beyond his means. He was beginning to feel decidedly peckish.

He walked along the front of the stage, trying not to trip over the various serpentine bunches of wires, heading for the electricians' staff canteen. With luck there might be a cheese roll or so over there. Electricians of this particular type were outside his immediate knowledge, but the rules of their guild never change; if these electricians were anything like the ones they'd had in the 1940s, they never moved a step without an adequate supply of cheese rolls. Stale, usually, and with bits of translucent yellow rind on the exposed edges of the cheese; but edible, within the broad meaning of the term.

He stopped. In the middle of one of the middle rows there was a man who was only half there.

Guy's mother had taught him three guiding rules of civilised behaviour, and his ability to forget them was a pretty effective gauge of his efficient functioning as a human being in the real world. They were:

(1) Don't push in queues.
(2) Don't talk with your mouth full.
(3) Don't stare.

As to the first; if he'd ever paid any heed to it, he'd still be standing in line in the sub-post office at the end of Garner Street waiting to buy ten first-class stamps for the cards for Christmas 1931. As to the second; as matters stood at present, chance would be a fine thing. And as to the third; well, the possibility of men who were only half there had obviously not been within his mother's contemplation when she formulated the rule. He stared.

The man – he could see him very clearly indeed, although he was quite some way off – didn't seem at all put out about being only fifty per cent present. He was laughing at a joke or something similar, and his hand was extracting peanuts from a packet balanced precariously on his one knee. Peanuts!

Guy wrenched his mind away from thoughts of peanuts. There were plenty of odd-looking people in the audience – the party sitting in the front row were not the sort of thing Guy had ever come across outside the Saturday morning Buck Rogers serial – but none as odd as ... The man was split neatly and precisely down the middle. The dividing line ran down across his forehead, followed his nose down through his lips and chin, bisected his neck and continued down his shirt front. Guy felt a strong urge not to find out what the man looked like viewed in right profile.

'I'd better tell Blondel,' he said to himself.

He turned and walked up the stage towards the small door in the back, which led to the dressing rooms; and would undoubtedly have reached his destination, woken Blondel, told him what he'd seen and so changed the course of past and future history, if only he hadn't caught sight of an unfamiliar figure holding a heaped plate of individual pork pies flitting like a shadow through the wings. He changed course abruptly and followed.

It goes without saying that the pork pie carrier was Pursuivant, and that he wasn't wearing a hat.

Guy made a muffled grunting noise and tried to move his feet. Pointless.

Out of either irony or compassion, they had stopped his mouth with a ham and watercress club sandwich of phenomenal proportions; too thick to bite through without the use of one's hands, at any rate. His tongue could sense the presence of tomato, cucumber and (he felt sure) green peppers and English mustard. He gave up grunting and tried growling instead.

No chance of being heard, of course; not with that noise going on out there. To be sure, it wasn't an unpleasant noise – it was Blondel singing the big numbers from the White Album, and on a number of occasions Guy would have stopped struggling and sat open-mouthed with admiration if it hadn't been for the club sandwich – but what with the amplification and the acoustics and Blondel's natural power of voice projection, the likelihood of anybody hearing his frantic oinking noises, or wishing to leave the music and come and investigate if they did, were pretty well minimal. He was stuck.

Being a realist, therefore, he stopped making a noise and tried thinking instead. The only conclusion which ensued, however, was the feeling that contemplation was probably overrated as against, for example, escaping from tight knots or eating. The thinking made his head hurt, especially on the lower left back where whoever it was had hit him, and he packed it in. The only thing left to do was to sit still and stare at the heaped plate of sausage rolls which some sadist had left on the straight-backed chair opposite.

In the auditorium, Blondel was launching into yet another popular favourite. Guy stretched out his hands, which were tied firmly behind his back, and groped to see if his fingers could encounter anything sharp and useful. No such luck; only what felt, to Guy at least, like a plateful of cheese sandwiches.

Then the door opened and a man came tiptoeing in.

Guy froze (not that that made a vast amount of difference in the circumstances, but he was always one to show willing) and watched.

The man's eyes clearly hadn't got used to the nearly complete darkness in the room (whatever sort of room it was) and quite soon he barked his shin on something, swore quietly and stopped to rub himself. Then he lit a cigarette lighter, and found himself staring straight at Guy.

'Mnnnnnnnn,' Guy said, tersely.

'Who are you?' the man replied, thereby demonstrating a complete absence of all the qualities that Guy had hoped to find in him.

'Mnnn,' he explained. 'Mnnnn mnnnn mnn mnn mn.'

'What?'

By the light of his cigarette lighter, the man appeared to be of medium height, thirtyish, with scruffy long hair, dressed in a sports jacket, an open-necked shirt, light blue baggy trousers and white canvas shoes. He wore spectacles and had the kind of face you'd expect to register bewildered surprise no matter what you said to it. Guy shook his head, causing the club sandwich to oscillate wildly.

'Has someone tied you up?' the man said.

'Mnn,' Guy replied with studied irony. 'Mnnn mnn mnnnn.'

'Here,' the man said, 'this is my card, I'm with BBC television. My name's Danny Bennett.'

'Mnn.'

The man thought for a moment, and then said, 'Would it help if I took that sandwich out of your ...? Right, fine, hold on.'

'Thank you,' Guy replied. 'Now get these ropes off me, for crying out loud.'

'Ropes?'

'The ropes with which my hands are tied behind my back,' Guy said. He remembered something his mother had told him, many years ago. 'Please,' he added.

'Sure, sure,' the man said. He picked up a bread-knife – someone has been using that to make *sandwiches*, Guy reflected – and started to saw at the ropes.

'I'm covering this concert,' the man said, 'for the North Bank Show. Perhaps you could explain something for me. When is this?'

'Ouch,' Guy replied, 'that was my —'

'Sorry,' the man said. 'Only my producer said I was to get in the car and not ask daft questions, and when I got here my calendar watch was reading 35th March 2727, I reckoned – sorry – that it must have gone funny so I reset it, and now it says 43rd August 1364. And not only that, but —'

'What's a calendar watch?' Guy asked.

'Um ...'

'Don't worry about it,' Guy added quickly. 'Look, if you could just hurry up with these ropes ...'

The man leaned forward and whispered. 'It's OK,' he said, 'you can tell me, I'm a reporter. Is something going on around here?'

'Yes,' Guy replied.

The man stared – at least, he stared even more. 'You mean —'

'It's a ... a plot of some kind,' Guy said. 'And I've got to go and tell someone something terribly important, so if you'd just —'

'Can I come?'

Guy turned his head and stared. 'You *want* to come?' he said.

'Sounds to me like there's a story in it,' the man replied. 'You know, like a scoop or something.'

Guy narrowed his eyes for a moment. 'Are you from the *Anglo-Saxon Chronicle*?' he asked.

'You what? I'm from the BBC.'

'The BBC?' Guy repeated. 'You mean the British Broadcasting Corporation?'

'Yes, of course I mean the —'

'What date was it when you left home this morning?'

The man gave him a look of almost liquid bewilderment. '5th April 1994,' he replied. 'Look, what *is* —'

'Thank you,' Guy said. 'Have you nearly finished with that rope?'

'There,' the man answered, 'try that.'

Guy flexed his arms and felt his hands come free. He dived forward, snatched up the club sandwich from where it had fallen, and ate it, very quickly.

'That's *better*', he said. 'You have no idea how much better I feel now.' He grabbed the breadknife and started sawing through the ropes that constrained his ankles.

'Don't mention it,' the man said. He had reached into his pocket and taken out a notebook. 'Now, then,' he said, 'what's happening?'

Guy cut the last strand of rope, put down the knife, and levered himself gingerly to his feet. 'Don't worry about it,' he said, 'it's nothing, really. Just a little —' he searched for the right word – 'temporary problem. Soon get it sorted out. Have a sausage roll, they're really good. Really good.'

'No thanks. Look —'

'Suit yourself,' Guy replied, and he tipped the rest of the plateful into his pocket, shoved a jam tart into his mouth, and started to run. The man tried to follow him, but fell over a packing-case, banged his head and passed out.

This was a pity, because if he hadn't he would have been the only reporter to have witnessed one of the most crucial events in history – in all history, past, present and future. As it was, he came round to find himself fast asleep on a bench in Central Park, with a sore head and a calf-bound copy of *Silas Marner* in his left hand, where his reporter's notebook had been when he fell over.

Some people are just plain unlucky.

Guy ran out of the room into what turned out to be a corridor, stopped and looked both ways. Nothing. Nor any indication of which way he should go. He could hear the music, which seemed to be coming from directly above his head. A great deal of help that was.

Being one of those people who automatically turns left unless firmly directed to do otherwise, Guy ran down the left branch of the corridor, and so arrived at a glass fire door, which was locked.

Oh *good*, he thought, I've always wanted to do this.

He picked up a nearby fire extinguisher, ate a sausage roll, and attacked. The glass was much tougher than it looked, but not nearly tough enough, and when Guy had quite finished, he reached through, found the bolt on the other side, drew it back and opened the door. Easy.

Standing on the other side of the door, hands on hips and looking decidedly unfriendly, was La Beale Isoud.

'There you are,' she said. 'I've been looking for you everywhere.'

Guy noticed that he was still holding the fire extinguisher, and that he had slightly grazed his hand on the glass. He put the extinguisher down slowly and found a weak smile from somewhere.

'You have?' he said.

'Yes,' replied La Beale Isoud. 'You've got to warn Blondel.'

'Why can't you do it?'

'What?'

'You've got the message,' Guy replied. 'You probably know what's going on. You tell him.'

'Don't be *stupid*,' La Beale Isoud replied. 'You're supposed to be a man, aren't you?'

'What's that got to do with —'

'It's probably dangerous,' said La Beale Isoud, fiercely. 'Are you saying you'd just stand there and leave a defenceless woman to —'

'All right, all right,' Guy said. 'You tell me how to find Blondel and I'll give him the message.'

'He's up there,' said La Beale Isoud, pointing to where the sound of someone singing *Floret Silva Nobilis*, rather well, was coming from, 'on the stage.'

'Yes,' Guy replied, 'thank you, I had actually worked that one out for myself. How exactly am I supposed to —'

'Go back down the corridor,' La Beale Isoud replied coldly, 'the way you came. It leads straight out into the wings. I suggest you wait for him to come off stage at the end of the first half.'

'What a truly brilliant plan,' Guy said. 'All right, what's the message?'

'Come on,' said Isoud. 'Follow me, and I'll tell you as we walk. But for heaven's sake don't *dawdle*.'

She turned and trotted briskly away. After a moment's instinctive thought, Guy ran after her and caught her up.

'I was sitting at home,' said La Beale Isoud, 'looking at the hyperfax —'

'What's a —'

'When the message came through which I couldn't make out. It said, *Beware the one-armed man.* Now even you'll agree that that's a very unusual message to get out of the blue like that.'

Guy ignored the even-you bit. 'Odd,' he agreed politely. 'Perhaps it was an advertisement for something.'

'Please, Mr Goodlet,' Isoud said, 'don't interrupt. Your untimely flippancy is quite probably your most disagreeable characteristic. I was wondering what on earth this message could possibly mean when — Mr Goodlet, is that gentleman a friend of yours?'

Guy looked up, blinked twice and reached for where his revolver ought to be. Of course, it wasn't there any more.

'Looking for this?' Pursuivant said. He waggled the revolver tauntingly. Probably out of sheer spite, it went off.

'Eeek!' said La Beale Isoud, and for the first time Guy noticed that she was wearing — had been wearing — one of those tall and picturesque pointed female headdresses that one sees in illuminated manuscripts. He suppressed a snigger, jumped on Pursuivant, and banged his head hard on the ground.

'Here we go again,' Pursuivant sighed, and died.

215

Guy looked down. 'Damn,' he said, 'I've killed him. Oh well, can't be helped.' He prised his revolver out of Pursuivant's fingers and slipped it back in its holster. 'Sorry,' he said, 'you were saying?'

But La Beale Isoud didn't reply. She was staring at him; no, not so much staring as *looking*.

'Mr *Goodlet*!' she said.

Guy frowned in puzzlement for a moment, and then a light bulb went on inside his head. He got up, retrieved Isoud's perforated headdress and handed it to her.

'All in a day's work,' he said, smiling.

'That was very —' Isoud said.

'Brave?'

'Yes,' replied La Beale Isoud, with just a touch of irritation. 'That was very brave of you, Mr Goodlet. You saw that I was in danger and you unhesitatingly ...'

'Yes,' Guy replied, 'I know. It's not every chap who'd do that, you know. Anyway, there you were, pondering this message.'

'Oh yes. I was just wondering what on earth it could mean when another message came over the hyperfax. And do you know what it said?'

'No.'

'It said, *Beware the one-legged man*, Mr Goodlet. Well of course, that started me thinking, as you can imagine.'

'Did it?'

'And I was just beginning to get an inkling of an idea when a third message came through. *Beware the one-eyed man.* So of course I came here as fast as I could.'

'You did?'

216

'Naturally.'

'Have a sausage roll?'

'No, thank you, I had tea before I came out. The question is, Mr Goodlet, will we be in time?'

'Who can say?' Guy replied. 'In time for what?'

He got the feeling that under normal circumstances, La Beale Isoud would have said something less than complimentary. She didn't, however. How nice.

In front of them was a door marked *Stage Door; No Entry*. On the other side of it, Blondel's voice stopped singing, there was a moment of complete silence, and then a deafening outburst of applause.

'It's the interval,' Isoud cried. 'Come on, quickly!'

She pushed the door and, before Guy could stop her, walked through.

'Isoud!' Guy shouted, but it was too late. Too late to point out what was written on the door.

He hesitated, just for a moment. It wasn't, he told himself, just the fact that he would be delighted to be rid of her; there was also the question of this cryptic message and the mysterious man who, despite his apparently overwhelming disabilities, was perceived to be so dangerous. On the other hand ...

'Sod it,' he said, and followed.

It wasn't a big apple; but to a man with a bad head, brought on by drinking slightly too much mulled ale in the *Three Pilgrims* the night before, it was plenty big enough.

'Ouch!' said Sir Isaac Newton. He stood up, winced, and looked round for the gardener.

'George!' he yelled. 'Come here this instant.'

The gardener, an elderly man with a face that

seemed to indicate feeble-minded dishonesty, waddled across from the asparagus bed. He was hiding something behind his back, as usual.

'Look, George,' said Sir Isaac, 'didn't I tell you to get those damned apples picked last week, before they fell off the tree and spoiled?'

George looked blank. Everyone, after all, is good at something.

'Why haven't you picked the apples, George?'

'Dunno, Master Isaac.'

'Well,' said Sir Isaac, 'bloody well pick them now, all right? Before they do somebody a serious injury.'

'Yes, Master Isaac.'

'And if anybody wants me, I'll be in my study.'

'Yes, Master Isaac.'

As soon as Sir Isaac was safely out of sight, George took the bundle out from behind his back, unwrapped it carefully, and looked at it with pleasure.

It was a pigeon. Very dead. Dead for some time. Still, a poor man has to eat, and on the wages Master Newton paid, a pigeon was a pigeon and to hell with minor decomposition. George grinned.

Then the small gate in the wall opened and a young lady came bursting through. She was wearing funny, old-fashioned clothes, like someone out of one of those old stained-glass windows George had helped smash up during the Civil Wars, and she wore a sort of white witch's hat with a hole in it. George frowned, puzzled.

The lady came to a sudden halt and stared at him.

'Excuse me,' she said. George nodded vigorously. It was just possible that she hadn't noticed the pigeon.

'Excuse me,' the lady repeated. 'Where —'

'In the study, miss,' George replied. 'That way.' He pointed with his left hand.

'I beg your pardon?'

'In the study, miss,' George said. 'Just this minute gone in, miss.'

The door flew open again, and this time it was a man.

'Come on,' the man said to the lady, 'we'd better get back.'

The lady turned. 'Mr Goodlet,' she said, 'what's going on?'

'The door,' said the man. 'It had *No Entry* on it. Didn't you see?'

The lady looked puzzled. 'What do you mean? Oh,' she added. 'It was one of those doors, was it?'

George coughed deferentially. 'He's in the study, sir,' he said.

'Exactly,' said the man to the lady, ignoring George. 'So here we are. We'd better find a town hall or something quick. With luck, we might just be able to find our way back to precisely the right moment. Have you got one of those maps?'

'What maps?'

'Ah,' the man said, 'that means you probably haven't. Never mind.' He turned and faced George. 'Excuse me,' he said.

'He's in the —'

'Which way to the town hall?' the man asked.

George frowned. 'What town hall, sir?' he asked.

'All right then,' said the man, 'what about a police station. Army barracks. Magistrate's court. Something like that.'

George couldn't help shuddering. In court, at his

age, and all for one lousy pigeon. He started to whimper.

The noise had obviously reached the study, because Sir Isaac came out. He was holding a cold towel to his head, and he wasn't looking happy.

'Will you please,' he said, 'keep the noise down?'

'Sorry,' the man said. 'I wonder if you could help us. We're looking for a public building.'

Sir Isaac gave them a look, as if trying to work out what on earth they were on about. A thought occurred to him, painfully. 'If you're desperate,' he said, 'you can use the one at the bottom of the kitchen garden.'

'No, thank you,' the man replied, 'a public *building*. Like a corn exchange or a guildhall or something like that. Something with *No Entry* on the door.'

'I ...' Sir Isaac said. 'Look, I don't want to seem inhospitable, but if this is some sort of a joke ...'

'Really,' the man replied, 'this is an emergency, so if you could just ...'

Sir Isaac closed his eyes. He had known it help sometimes. 'George,' he said, 'escort these people to the Municipal Hall.'

'Yes, Sir Isaac.'

The man was staring; looking at Sir Isaac's clothes and his periwig, apparently making some connection in his mind.

'Sir Isaac?' he said.

'Yes,' said Sir Isaac, 'that's right. Now if you'll just —'

'Sir Isaac *Newton*?'

'That's right. Do I know you?'

The man was looking at him with something resembling awe. '*The* Sir Isaac Newton? The Sir Isaac

Newton who discovered gravity?'

'I beg your ...' Sir Isaac stopped suddenly. In his ale-clogged mind, something suddenly clicked into place. '*Gravity!*' he exclaimed. 'Yes, of course, that's it! Gravity!'

The man was looking sheepish. 'Whoops,' he said, 'there I go again, putting my foot in it.'

Sir Isaac's face was alight with joy. 'My dear sir,' he said, 'how can I ever ...?'

But the man and the woman had gone.

In the beginning, God created the heaven and the earth.

And the earth was without form and void, and darkness was upon the face of the deep. And God saw that it had potential, if it was handled properly.

Originally, he had in mind a three-tiered development programme, with a residential area of high-quality executive starter-homes, a business and light industrial park and a spacious, purpose-built shopping precinct, all centred round a general amenity area and linked with a grid-pattern road layout. It was good; and maybe it wouldn't have won any design awards, but it would have done the job and returned something like 400 per cent on the initial outlay.

The problem was the Eden (Phase II) Area Plan, and it was the same old story all over again. You hire an architect, he draws the plans, the quantity surveyor does the costings, the contractor does the schedules, everything's ready to roll and some shiny-trousered bureaucrat refuses to grant planning permission. And there you are, with a thousand billion acre site, eighty billion supernatural brickies, forty million miles of

221

scaffolding, nine hundred thousand JCBs (all balanced on the head of a pin) and terminal planning blight.

God, however, has patience. With a shrug of his shoulders, he walked away from the whole mess and occupied himself with a forty billion acre office development on Alpha Centauri. By the time he'd finished that, plus a little infilling in Orion's Belt and a couple of nice barn conversions in the Pleiades, there had been a number of changes in the political makeup of Eden County Hall. At long last, there were people in charge there whom he could do business with.

Of course, there had to be a public enquiry; there always is. But the problem was that, since the earth was still without form and void, there were no human beings, therefore no public, therefore there could be no enquiry and the previous decision would have to stand. Deadlock.

It was then that the venture capital consortium funding the project, Beaumont Street Retrospective Developments Inc., took a hand. The three members of the consortium were admittedly domiciled millions of years in the future, but they were all bona fide human beings, and they would be delighted to hold an enquiry. No problem.

The result of their deliberation was that the whole purpose of planning controls is to preserve the environment; but no development can actually damage the environment in the long term, because eventually, in the fullness of time, the physical laws of entropy will have effect, the world will come to an end, the Void will creep back, matter will implode into nothingness, and everything will be exactly the same as it originally was. The proposed development was, therefore, strictly temporary, and planning consent was not required for temporary structures.

In the end, they did a deal: God was granted a ten billion year lease, the paperwork was tidied up, bulldozers rolled, and the rest is theology. Almost.

It was, of course, the lawyers who cocked it up. When they sublet the development to the human race, there was some sort of snarl-up in the small print, and when the Antichrist turned up in AD 1000 to serve notice to quit, the human race grinned smugly, pointed to the appropriate page and refused to budge.

The various flies on the wall of God's office that afternoon of 31st December AD 1000 all agree that the ensuing meeting was stormy. There was a free and frank exchange of views, which resulted in the Antichrist being turned into a skeleton and split down the middle (or as we would say nowadays, promoted sideways); the upshot was that the Antichrist was sent off to find a loophole in the lease, which he did.

One of the conditions of the lease was that Mankind was obliged to worship the Landlord regularly and according to the forms prescribed by Mother Church. The Antichrist therefore immediately founded a rival church, presided over by Anti-Popes, with the aim of subverting religion, destroying faith, and nipping in to get the locks changed and the suitcases out on the street before 1690. It worked well to begin with, and eviction proceedings were actually under way when a minor human potentate called Richard Coeur de Lion started in motion a chain of events which would inevitably lead to universal peace, a return to the True Faith, and the building of the New Jerusalem. And there was absolutely nothing that anybody could do about it.

Until, that is, the Antichrist overheard a minor Chastel des Larmes Chaudes functionary by the name of Pursuivant remarking that it would have been better all round if Richard had never been born. Something fell into place in the Antichrist's mind, and the result was the concept of time revision, editing and the archives. All they had to do was edit Richard out of history, and they could have Mankind out of there in a hundred years flat, with a massive bill for dilapidations thrown in.

It would have worked, if it hadn't been for one Blondel, a courtier, who inconveniently refused to accept that Richard had never existed, and started looking for him everywhere. As long as Blondel knew Richard had existed, Richard would have to continue to exist. The man was, to put it mildly, a menace.

Somehow, all the efforts of the Chastel staff to find Blondel failed – remarkable enough in itself, since he spent a material amount of his time appearing at well-publicised concerts – until the day when the Antichrist received two tickets for the biggest Blondel gig of all; according to the pre-concert hype, the very last Blondel gig of all.

Well yes, the Antichrist said to himself, the very last. The very last ever.

'Do come in,' Blondel said. 'Would you like a drink? Do please sit down.'

The Antichrist found no difficulty in walking, despite the lack of one leg; he walked perfectly naturally, as if he refused to believe that the other leg wasn't there. He could even stroll, trot and run if he saw fit. Just now, he was swaggering.

'Thanks,' he said. 'I'll have a dry martini.'

Blondel nodded and fiddled with the bottles on the drinks tray. 'What about you, Your Excellencies?'

The two Popes Julian – or, to be exact, Pope and Anti-Pope – shook their heads. 'Not while they're on duty,' the Antichrist explained.

'I thought that was only policemen.'

'And Popes,' he replied, 'but only when they're being simultaneous.'

'Ah yes,' Blondel said, handing the Antichrist his drink. 'I meant to ask you about that. They don't mind being discussed like this, do they?'

'Not at all,' the Antichrist said. 'Since they can't speak, I do the talking for them. Not that they matter a damn, anyway, since I'm here. I only brought them in case they wanted to see the show.'

'Thank you,' Blondel said, accepting the compliment. 'I gather that you're a fan, too.'

'Absolutely,' the Antichrist replied. 'I've got a complete set. In fact, quite soon I shall have the only complete set in existence. It'll be a nuisance having to go down to the Archives every time I want to hear it, but never mind.'

Blondel raised an eyebrow. 'The Archives?' he said. 'How do you mean?'

'Now then,' the Antichrist said, 'don't be obtuse. You're coming with me, Blondel, whether you like it or not. You've had your bit of fun, but it's all over. You do understand that, don't you?'

'Have an olive,' Blondel replied. 'They're quite good, actually.'

'Thank you.'

'Enjoying the show?'

'Yes. Very much.'

Blondel sat down and put his hands behind his head. 'Pity you won't hear the second half, then.'

The Antichrist shrugged. 'That's how it is,' he said. 'Why did you do it, Blondel? Have you just got tired of running? Or have you finally seen how much damage you've been doing all these years?'

'You mean,' Blondel replied, 'why did I invite you to my concert?'

'That's right.'

Blondel leaned forward and rested his chin on his hands. 'Simple,' he said. 'I'd have invited you to all my concerts, but I've only just found out your address. Or at least your telephone and fax numbers. I've wanted to get in touch with you for a *very* long time.'

The Antichrist grinned. 'I'll bet,' he said. 'But why didn't you just go along with Pursuivant and Clarenceaux? I sent them to fetch you, hundreds of times.'

'And it was very kind of you,' Blondel said. 'To be absolutely frank – another olive? – I don't feel entirely comfortable with Clarenceaux and Pursuivant and that lot. If I'd gone with them when you so kindly sent them to fetch me, I'd have felt – how shall I put it?'

'Captured?'

'Yes, that'll do. Captured. How is Richard, by the way?'

The Antichrist smiled. 'I don't know,' he said. 'I gather he's still down there, somewhere. Can't be very comfortable for him, what with the rats and the complete isolation and the darkness and the damp and everything, but until you've been sorted out, we can't send him on to his Archive. Pity, really; it's a nice Archive. He'll like it. And so will you.'

'No doubt.' Blondel sat on the arm of the sofa and looked at his watch. 'Look, I hate to rush you, but I've got to be back on stage in five minutes, and I want to have a word with the idiot in charge of the lights. Don't you think it's time we did a deal?'

The Antichrist laughed. It wasn't a pleasant sound.

'Listen, mortal,' he said. 'You're in no position to make a deal. You're coming with me, and that's that.'

'Actually,' Blondel said, 'you're wrong there. I took the liberty of putting something in your drink. Apart from vermouth and gin, that is. In a very short time you'll be sleeping like a baby.'

The Antichrist tried to get up, but his knee refused to operate. His mouth opened but nothing came out of it except an olive stone.

'Oh good,' Blondel went on, 'it's starting to work. I will be brief, for a change. What I propose is a simple exchange of hostages. You for Richard.'

'But I'm not a ...' The words came very slowly out of his mouth, which was scarcely surprising, since his jaw was setting like concrete.

'Very soon,' Blondel said gently, 'you will be in the dungeons of the Chastel de Nesle. I'll try and make things as comfortable for you as I can. Clean straw once a year, all that sort of thing. Honestly, I'm surprised at you; and you, Julian and Julian. Didn't you realise this was likely to be a trap?'

The two Popes tried to get to their feet; unfortunately, the effort of manifesting themselves simultaneously without cocking up the balance of history was too great, and they flopped back against the cushions. Blondel pressed a buzzer and the door opened.

'Be a good chap, Giovanni, and fetch that laundry

basket,' he said. Giovanni nodded and left.

'You won't get away with this,' the Antichrist managed to say; but by the time he'd finished the last word he was fast asleep. Blondel removed the glass from his hand, smiled gently and put a pillow behind his head. They might be mortal enemies, but there was no point in letting the fellow get a crick in his neck for no reason.

'Here we are,' Giovanni said. 'You two, give me a hand.'

The Galeazzo brothers gently transferred the Antichrist and the two Julians into the basket, secured the lid and sat on it. Blondel nodded his approval.

'Right then,' he said. 'Let's be getting on with it. You take the basket back to the Chastel and we'll meet there after the show.'

'Will do,' Giovanni replied. 'And I can be getting on with the ransom note.'

Blondel shrugged. 'If you like,' he said. 'I don't think that's entirely necessary, though, do you?'

'Maybe not,' Giovanni said with a grin, 'but it'll be fun.'

'We're lost, aren't we?' Isoud said.

Guy sat down on the step and nodded. They'd been down here for a very long time, and there were no more sausage rolls left. This was a silly game.

'It's not your fault,' said La Beale Isoud reassuringly, and while Guy was still recovering from that one, she added, 'I think you're coping very well, in the circumstances.'

'You do?' Guy asked, bewildered.

'Oh yes.'

'Oh.'

They sat together for a while in silence. If it wasn't so dark, Guy would have been able to see that Isoud was looking at him with something approaching affection. It was probably just as well that it was so dark.

'Mr Goodlet.'

'Call me Guy,' Guy said wearily. 'If it's all the same to you, I mean.'

'Thank you, Guy,' Isoud replied. 'And you can call me Isoud, if you like.'

'Thank you, Isoud, that's a great weight off my mind.'

Isoud either didn't hear that or else she ignored it. 'Guy,' she went on, 'I've been thinking.'

'Oh yes?'

'Would it help,' said Isoud, 'if we had a map?'

Women, thought Guy darkly. 'Probably,' he said. 'But we don't.'

'No,' Isoud agreed. 'But perhaps we could get hold of one.'

'Oh yes? How do we manage that?'

Isoud was fumbling in her handbag. It was the first time that Guy had noticed she'd got one with her; but women's handbags aren't things one tends to notice, not consciously at any rate. One assumes that they have them without looking, just as one assumes that they have feet.

'We could try the hyperfax,' she said.

'You mean,' Guy said, as sweetly as he could manage, 'that you've had that ... that thing with you all this time and you haven't seen fit to —'

'Sorry,' Isoud said, girlishly. 'Have I been very silly?'

On balance, Guy said to himself, I think I preferred her when she was being unpleasant. 'No,' he said, 'not at all. You *have* got the wretched thing?'

'Here,' Isoud replied. She took a tiny metal cube from her bag and handed it to him.

'This is it, is it?'

'It folds away,' La Beale Isoud replied. 'I'd forgotten all about it until —'

'That's fine,' Guy said. 'Now, just show me how it works, and we can be getting on.'

Isoud reached across and pressed a tiny little knob

230

on one side of the cube. At once it opened up into a miniature replica of itself. 'Now all we have to do is plug it in,' Isoud said.

'Plug it in?'

'Yes.'

'Plug it into what?'

'Oh.'

Guy made a tiny, thin noise like linen tearing. 'Oh, for crying out —'

'Sorry,' Isoud said, and snuffled indistinctly.

Very much against his better nature, Guy reached out a tentative hand and patted Isoud on the shoulder. Under normal circumstances it was the very last thing he would have done, but if the bloody woman started crying on him he doubted whether he'd be able to cope. There are limits.

'There there,' he said stiffly, like a bank manager addressing a small, overdrawn child, 'it doesn't matter. And it was a very clever idea, really. Just a shame there isn't —'

To his horror, Guy felt a small, warm hand slip into his. His mouth went dry and he felt like a fish who has realised, too late, that if earthworms suddenly appear out of thin water and hover invitingly above one's head, there is probably a catch in it somewhere. Numbly, he gave the hand a little squeeze. One must, after all, be civil.

'Anyway,' he said in a strained voice, 'we mustn't sit about here all day, must we? Let's be getting along.'

'Yes, Guy,' said Isoud, meekly. 'Shall I put the hyperfax away again?'

'Yes,' Guy replied. 'Or rather, no. I've just had an idea.'

Which was actually true.

★

The President of Oceania was sweating.

What he wanted to do most of all was get out his handkerchief and wipe his forehead; but if he did that, the Chairman of the Eurasian People's Republic would see him do it on her Visiphone monitor, and might take it as a sign of weakness. And that would never do.

'Is that your last word, Madam Chairman?' he said.

'It is.'

Despite the flickering screen he could see that her face was set in an expression of monolithic determination. Bloody woman.

'In that case,' he said 'I fear that the United States of Oceania has no alternative but to consider itself at war with the Eurasian People's Republic. Madam Chairman, we have switched out a light that shall not be relit within our ...'

Hold on, thought the President, somebody *has* switched out the light. 'Are you still there, Madam Chairman?' he asked. But the screen had gone blank.

'Hey,' said the President angrily, 'what the hell is going on around here?'

From a corner of the darkened room a voice said, 'Sorry.'

The President wheeled round in his swivel chair. 'Who is that?' he demanded.

'It's all right,' said the voice, 'won't keep you a minute. Just borrowing your plug.'

The President groped for the security buzzer under his desk, and then realised that that wouldn't work either. All the electrics in the room were fed off just the one plug. Damn fool of an electrician had said it would be cheaper that way.

'Who are you?' said the President. 'And what do you want?'

'We're just using your plug,' said the voice. 'Sorry if we're disturbing you. Is that something coming through, Isoud?'

'Put that plug back on *immediately*.'

'Certainly, certainly,' replied the voice. 'Won't be two ticks.'

The President leapt to his feet, tripped over the leg of his desk, and fell over. 'Ouch,' he said.

'Careful.'

'How did you get in here?'

'Through that door over there,' replied the voice. 'It's probably got *No Entry* written on it, all the others do. I assure you it's nothing personal,' the voice added. 'It's just that yours was the first door we came to that didn't lead to somewhere in the Middle Ages.'

'I ...'

'Yup, it's the map all right,' said the voice, 'just the ticket. All right, then, Isoud, you can switch the thing off and let the gentleman have his electricity back. Sorry for any inconvenience,' the voice added.

A few seconds later, the lights went on, just in time for the President to catch a glimpse of the door marked *Maintenance Staff Only* closing. The Visiphone screen crackled and lit up. He dived for his chair and tried to look nonchalant.

'All right,' said the voice of the Chairman, 'you win.'

'You what?'

'You win,' replied the Chairman bitterly. 'You have – how you say? – called our bluff. We withdraw our missiles from Sector Three.'

'Oh,' said the President. 'Thank you.'

'Mr President.'

The screen went blank. Gasping slightly, the President found his handkerchief and wielded it vigorously. Obviously, the screen had been switched off *before* he'd made his declaration of war. Lucky.

He switched on the intercom. 'Frank,' he said, 'get me the briefing room. And,' he added, 'get me that god-damn electrician.'

'This way.'

Guy folded the map, put it away and pointed. Absolutely no doubt in his mind this time. The map had said *Stage Door of Blondel's Concert* on it in big bold letters. He turned the handle and pushed.

And fell forward.

A split second later, Isoud followed him, landing on the small of his back. He complained.

'Sorry,' Isoud said. 'Are you all . . .?'

Guy raised his head and groaned. It wasn't just because Isoud had nearly broken his spine; it was more because he had a very strong feeling that he knew exactly where he was.

'Guy, are you all right?' Isoud repeated. Then, sensibly, she moved off his back and let him breathe.

Guy rolled over on to his side and groped for the map. Not that there was any light to read it by, of course. Something small and furry brushed past his hand.

'Hello,' said a sleepy voice in the depths of the gloom, 'who's there?'

'Oh, hellfire,' Guy moaned. He was right.

'Hello?' said the voice again. 'Why, my dear fellow, you've come back again.'

Guy moved his hand – slowly, so as not to startle the rat – and buried his face in it. A trap. The faxed map hadn't been sent from the Chastel de Nesle at all. It had come from ... Well, it didn't take a genius to work it out. From here.

'Guy?' Isoud said.

'Yes, all right,' Guy replied testily. 'Excuse me,' he said, projecting his voice into the darkness, 'but I wonder if you can tell me, is this the Chastel des Larmes Chaudes?'

'Certainly, my dear fellow,' replied the voice. 'Didn't they tell you at Reception when they brought you in?'

'I ...' Guy shook his head; for his own satisfaction more than anything else. He wanted to see if anything rattled about in it.

'Isoud,' he said, 'I'm afraid we've come the wrong way.'

Pursuivant woke up, opened his eyes, and wiggled his toes. They still weren't right. Typical. If he'd mentioned the duff bearing in the offside right joint once, he'd mentioned it a hundred times, but nobody listened. Next time he was brought in to the Service Bay, he'd damn well insist.

'I don't know why I bother.'

It was the voice of the Head Technician, and now he came to think of it, Pursuivant could see his face glowering down at him. He shrugged his shoulders, only to find they weren't there. Probably off having the rubbers changed.

'I mean,' the Head Technician was saying, 'why don't I just scoop the whole lot out and fill in the hole with wet newspaper or something? Then, next time you get them all bashed out, it won't take me an hour and a half with the small scalpel to put them back together again.'

'Bad, was it?' Pursuivant asked.

The Head Technician pulled a face. 'For two pins,' he said, 'I'd have binned the lot and put in a brand new unit. Only then I'd have the bloody Quartermaster down on me like a ton of bricks. First thing in the morning, I'm going to ask my brother-in-law if there's any jobs going down the canning factory.'

He waved to the orderlies, who switched on the conveyor, transporting Pursuivant to the Armery section.

'What the hell did you do to it this time?' the Armerer demanded. 'Roll about on it? Try and use it to lever open a safe? These are precision instruments, you know.'

'Sorry,' Pursuivant said. 'Can I have a new one?'

'No,' replied the Armerer. 'Instead, you can have arthritis. I've fitted it,' he added with a malicious grin, 'personally.'

'Hey, doc, that isn't —'

'Nobody said it had to be,' replied the Armerer, swinging his ratchet spanner like a football rattle. 'Next.'

Three quarters of an hour later, Pursuivant was standing outside Mountjoy's office, waiting to be told he could come in.

'Let's just go through this one step at a time,' Mountjoy said. 'You and your colleagues captured the renegade Goodlet backstage and tied him up. Then you left him.'

'Yes, sir.'

'Then,' Mountjoy went on, glimmering unpleasantly, 'a quarter of an hour later you meet him sauntering down a corridor with a girl.'

'Yes, sir.'

'Whereupon he kills you.'

'Sir.'

'Pursuivant,' Mountjoy said, glowing like a constipated firefly, 'you excel yourself. Thanks to you, they've disappeared. Completely. Without trace.'

'They, sir?'

'The Pope, you idiot. And the Anti-Pope, And ...' Mountjoy mimed a one-armed, partially-sighted man. 'Vanished into thin air. What were you playing at?'

'I was being killed, sir.'

'When I've finished with you,' Mountjoy roared, 'you'll wish you were dead ...' He tailed off, and a few desultory sparks crackled from his nose, singeing the hairs. Pursuivant stayed rigidly at attention. He knew from long experience that having your arms drawn tightly in towards your body made you a smaller target.

'Anyway,' said Mountjoy, 'the question now is, what are you going to do about it?'

'Me, sir?' Pursuivant said, realising as he did so that he'd gone and cocked it up again. 'I mean, sir —'

'Yes, soldier, you.' Mountjoy stood silently for a moment, looking for all the world like a pensive table lamp. He turned as the door opened and White Herald came in. He was limping, probably because they'd run out of offside tibias in 63E again. He held a sheet of paper.

'Fax just come through, sir,' he said. 'Marked *F.A.O. Acting General Manager*. Brought it straight here.'

Mountjoy frowned and grabbed at the paper. A

moment later he made an unpleasant noise in the back of his throat, grating and ominous, like the sound of hubcap on kerb.

'Now look what you've done,' he said. 'This is from de Nesle.'

'Sir.'

'Stop saying sir like that. He claims to have overpowered them and locked them up in his dungeons.' Mountjoy sighed. 'Well now, this is a bit of a problem, isn't it? Well?'

'Yes, sir.'

'Yes, sir. And there's not really much point in sending you to get them out again, is there?'

'No, sir.'

'No, sir. Because you don't know where to look. And even if you did, you're too incompetent to do even the simplest ... What is it?'

Pursuivant knew better than to look round. In the arcane and convoluted code of regulations by which the Chastel guard was governed, looking round in the presence of a superior officer was punishable in a number of cleverly devised ways, most of which included swapping components around between the individual offenders. When the newcomer spoke, however, he recognised the voice of the chief warder of the dungeons.

'Sorry to interrupt, chief,' said the warder, 'but I thought you ought to know. I was just doing my rounds when I noticed, there's two new prisoners in Cell Fifty-Nine.'

Mountjoy dimmed incredulously. 'Two *new* prisoners?'

'Yes, chief.'

'You mean somebody's broken *into* the prison?'

'Looks like it, chief.'

The Chaplain furrowed his brows, producing interesting kaleidoscopic effects on the ceiling. 'Cell Fifty-Nine? You're sure?'

'Sure, chief.'

'Well, now,' Mountjoy said, 'I think we'd better have a look at this.'

Musicology records that the concert was a success.

'His lambent woodnotes,' wrote the critic of the *New Theosociologist,* 'blended pellucid *leitmotiven* with an extravaganza of polychromatic detail, often resulting in a vibrant antagonism between line and length which found its ultimate apotheosis in the semi-cathartic culmination of *Nellie Dean.* De Nesle continues to build on the firm foundations of his earlier flirtation with the neo-structural; and if he manages to resist the meretricious temptations of the merely beautiful, may yet prove that his pan contains further and more transcendent flashes.'

As far as Blondel was concerned, though, it had been a good sing-song, it was nice when the audience all joined in the final verse of *L'Amours Dont Sui Epris,* and what he really needd now was a shower and a cup of warm milk.

He was annoyed, therefore, to find his dressing room deserted and in rather a mess. In fact, ransacked would be a better word. It looked like a haystack in which someone has eventually managed to find a needle.

'Mmmmmmmm,' said a voice from inside the wardrobe.

Blondel raised an eyebrow. One of the wardrobes in

this room led directly to the past, the future and a tasteful selection of presents. The problem was, there was no way at any given time of knowing which.

'Hello?' he enquired

'Mmmmmm.'

'Giovanni? Is that you?'

'Mmm.'

'What on earth are you doing in there?'

It's remarkable how quickly you can pick up a new language. Quite soon, Blondel was fluent enough in gagged noises to understand that Giovanni was trying to tell him that he'd explain much better if only somebody took this sock out of his mouth.

'Coming,' Blondel said.

He tracked the noise to the smaller of the two wardrobes and opened it. A quick glance revealed three bound and muffled investment consultants.

'My dear fellow,' Blondel said, gently removing the sock from Giovanni's mouth, 'whatever's been going on?'

Giovanni gurgled, made a noise like a rasp on formica, and said, 'Revenue.'

'I beg your pardon?'

'I think,' Giovanni muttered, 'they were from the Revenue. Looking for receipts or something.'

'Who?'

'The men,' Giovanni replied. 'The men who searched the place. We tried to stop them but . . .'

Blondel looked round. Come to think of it, the place did have a distinctly frisked look. 'What makes you think they were tax men?' he asked.

'Just look at the place, for God's sake.'

Blondel scratched his head. 'Good point,' he said;

then he thought of something. 'My dear chap,' he said, 'what must you think of me? Do let me help you out of those ropes. They look awfully uncomfortable.'

Once freed from his bonds, Giovanni immediately ran across the room, upended a tubular metal chair and fished around for something inside one of the legs. After a short, frantic burst of activity he produced a tight roll of papers and waved it round his head in relief.

'It's all right,' he said, 'they didn't find it.'

'Oh yes?' Blondel said. 'What's that?'

'Er . . .'

'Do you know,' Blondel went on, 'I don't think they were from the Revenue at all.'

'No?' Giovanni paused, balanced on one leg, in the act of stuffing the papers inside his sock. 'Customs and Excise, you reckon?'

'Maybe,' Blondel replied. 'Or perhaps they were some of the Antichrist's people.'

'You think so?'

Blondel picked up something from the floor and displayed it on the palm of his hand. 'Look at this,' he said. 'It's a button off a tunic. See there, that's the arms of the Chastel des Larmes Chaudes. I think they're on to us already.'

'Phew!' Giovanni said. 'Thank God for that. I thought we were in trouble there for a minute.' He sat down and pulled his shoe back on.

'How long since they left?' Blondel asked. He threw the button up in the air and caught it. 'Not long, I don't imagine.'

'Dunno,' Giovanni replied. 'Five minutes, maybe, perhaps ten.'

'And it wasn't Pursuivant and Clarenceaux or any of that lot.'

Giovanni shook his head. 'I'd have recognized them,' he said. 'Like I said, this lot were *frightening*.' He reached out for his briefcase and started riffling through papers.

'Ten minutes,' Blondel repeated, 'and not Pursuivant and Clarenceaux. So it must be the other squad.' He turned to the Galeazzo brothers. 'If I were you,' he said, 'I'd head for the wardrobe. The other wardrobe. Now.'

'But you said ...'

'Now. If it'll help create an illusion of urgency, pretend there's a party of Department of Trade investigators coming up the stairs.'

Very shortly afterwards, the wardrobe door slammed, hard. Blondel started to count to ten. Give them a head start, he reckoned, and then follow. Because if he was right, the gentlemen who would very shortly be coming back were not the sort of people he wanted to meet.

Every military and paramilitary outfit has an elite force of some kind, a hand-picked bunch of utterly ruthless and determined professionals who think nothing of dyeing perfectly good balaclava helmets jet black and cutting holes in them. The Chastel des Larmes Chaudes is no exception. It has the Time and Motion department.

Some special units are trained to operate in specific conditions, such as mountains or the arctic. The TAM is designed to operate in time.

They know how to live off the land, snaring lost

opportunities and roasting them on spits; how to blend imperceptibly into the temporal landscape, disguised as fleeting moments; how to ambush unsuspecting hostile forces by attacking them before they've even been born. Intensive training has taught them to withstand the devastating metabolic effects of rapid time travel, which can only too easily lead to a meal being digested before it is eaten. And they can follow a trail through history better than the combined postgraduate resources of all the universities in the world.

The TAM is recruited exclusively from temporal misfits – men who have somehow or other fallen out of their own time, anachronisms; as can readily be deduced from the narrow lapels and flared trousers of their battledress uniforms. As might be expected, therefore, they are pitiless, determined and incorrigibly unpunctual.

It stands to reason, then, that when the Chastel des Larmes Chaudes sees fit to turn the TAM loose, it's probably had enough of messing about.

Once Zeitsturmbahnfuhrer Uhrwerk had satisfied himself that Blondel wasn't hiding under the floor-boards or inside the sofa cushions, he started to search for the time door. He was equipped with the latest in Chronological Anomaly Detectors and it didn't take him long to find the right wardrobe door. The fact that it was open and palpably led nowhere helped, of course.

'Right, men, follow me,' he snapped. 'Synchronise your watches.'

The platoon laughed dutifully. Zeitsturmbahnfuhrer Uhrwerk was essentially a one-joke man.

It was dark in the tunnel, but TAM soldiers are equipped with both foresight and hindsight, and can if

243

necessary navigate by sound alone, listening out for their own future muffled curses as they stub their toes on concealed obstacles. It was not long before they picked up the trail. The litter of bent and distorted historical potentials, imperceptible to the naked eye, were easily detected by the CADs. The squad broke into a run.

For the first time in a very long time, Blondel wasn't sure where to go next. His basic instincts told him to head for the Chastel de Nesle, bolt the doors behind him and get Isoud to heat up a huge cauldron of boiling mashed potato for pouring on the heads of would-be besiegers. The thing to remember about basic instincts, however, is that they don't always work. If beavers and rabbits used their brains instead of following their natural instincts, fur coats would be rather more expensive.

The alternative, of course, was to try and lose them somewhere in time; but that was rather like trying to drown a fish. The third alternative, standing his guard and fighting it out with cold steel, made his basic instincts look quite intelligent by comparison.

Standing at a fork in the tunnel, Blondel hesitated and tried to reach a decision. The right hand fork led, via the Icelandic Foreign Office and the Cultural Revolution pension scheme, to the Chastel de Nesle. The left hand fork led to DVLC. He had no idea what lay beyond. To the best of his knowledge, nobody did.

Behind him, he heard the sound of heavy boots and the distant muffled swearing noises of men learning by mistakes they never got around to making. He turned left. Robert Frost would have been proud of him.

To get to DVLC you have to pass through some undeniably hairy situations, as anyone who has ever tried to get hold of a replacement logbook for a 1978 Cavalier will confirm. First you have to go past the Arts and Heritage secretariat of the Long Parliament (watch out for splinters of broken stained glass underfoot), then turn left at the Irish Postmaster General's office, circa 1916 (a terrible beauty is born, so be ready to duck) and left again through the Spanish Feudal System. It's at this point that it's all too easy to get lost. The through route across the Customs and Excise of the later Byzantine empire is, well, byzantine in its complexity, and if you aren't careful you can easily find yourself in the Ottoman Ministry of Works; which is remarkably like being dead, only not as restful. You'll know you're on the right road if you come to a long corridor which you try running down only to find that you're either staying exactly where you are or moving slightly backwards. That means you're in driving licence application territory.

The main thing to remember, once you're there, is *not to go through any of the doors.*

Blondel stopped, selected a door at random, opened it and fell through. These guys, he told himself, know the score. They'll never follow me in through here.

The true nature of Time has puzzled the best brains in the human race throughout history; but only because nobody has ever grasped the fact that the stuff comes in two quite different isotopes.

There is Time; and there is Overtime.

Time is the shortest distance between two events. Overtime is the scenic route. In Overtime, things

245

happen in the same order as they do in Time, but temporal units have different values of magnitude. To put it another way, an egg boiled for three minutes in Overtime would penetrate steel plate.

The trick is to be able to tell which system is in force on any given occasion. There are no hard and fast rules, but here are a couple of examples of situations where you can expect to find Overtime:

(a) Public transport; for instance, someone who arrives at an airport two hours early will have to wait another two hours because his plane is late getting in, whereas someone who turns up three minutes before takeoff will invariably find that the plane left three minutes early.

(b) Government departments; consider how entirely different temporal concepts apply when you want them to do something, and when they want you to do something. It's a little-known but revealing fact that the supertemporal forces inside the IRS Headquarters in Washington are so strong all the clocks in the building had to be specially designed by Salvador Dali.

The effects of mixing Time and Overtime were harnessed by a pioneer firm of time-travel agents, who used them to make it possible for their clients to take relaxing and indefinite holidays in the past or the future. In order to travel, holidaymakers booked an ordinary holiday with an ordinary package tour company. Three weeks before the holiday, they sent their passports off for renewal. Two days before the departure date, they cancelled the holiday.

The result of sending the passports off was the creation of a massive Overtime field which would ensure that the passports would take at least four months to

246

process. Cancelling the holiday broke the field, bringing the most tremendous pressure to bear on the Time/Overtime interface and tearing holes in it large enough for human beings to pass through. The time-holiday was spent in Overtime, which meant that you could spend six weeks in Renaissance Florence and still be home in time to go to work the morning after you'd left.

In other words, the earth's temporal system, which was installed on the afternoon of the fifth day by a team of contractors found by God in the Golden Pages under the trading name of Cheap 'n' Cheerful Chronological Engineers, is a classic example of a Friday afternoon job, and fundamentally unstable. If Man had stayed put in the Garden of Eden, where the chronostat is jammed stuck at half past six on a summer afternoon, it wouldn't have mattered. Once Adam cut loose, however, it was inevitable that any sudden violent dislocation – a successful Crusade, for example – could knock the entire thing into the middle of next week. Or possibly worse.

Accordingly, on the eighth day, God telephoned his lawyers and began asking all sorts of questions about product liability.

Blondel stared, and grabbed at the doorframe to stop himself falling. The problem was that the doorframe wasn't there any more.

Which was reasonable enough; you don't need a doorframe on a cave, and a cave was quite definitely what Blondel had just come out of. A cave opening directly on to the sheer side of a cliff. Oh well.

Four seconds later he was relieved to find himself in

water. It could just as easily have been rock, or sun-baked earth, or a thick brown bush, but it wasn't. Having thrashed his way to the surface again and spat out a newt, Blondel trod water for a moment and tried to work out what was going on.

He was still, he gathered, in a cave; a cave inside a cave; a cavern. High above him he could see the roof, with a tasteful display of stalactites. The entrance he had fallen out of was one of several. There were crudely-made ladders tied to the walls, which led down to the narrow strip of beach, or whatever you liked to call it, that ran round the edge of the pool he was currently bobbing about in.

It was perishing cold, too.

With slow strokes he swam to the edge and pulled himself out. As he did so, he noticed a pair of feet directly in front of him. He stayed where he was.

It was hard for feet to look menacing, but these ones seemed to have the knack. It wasn't so much the size of them or the inordinately bizarre cut of the toenails. It wasn't even the context. The feeling of being in deep trouble was a purely intuitive one, but Blondel had always had an excellent working relationship with intuition. He looked up.

The owner of the feet stood about five foot four and was distinctly hairy. What little of his face was visible through the undergrowth had a simian look, mostly to do with the jaw, which looked as if it had been carelessly left out in the sun and had melted. As if that wasn't offputting enough, there was a heavy-looking rock in the stranger's hands, and he probably wasn't lifting it over his head like that simply to exercise his pectoral muscles. For one thing, they didn't look like they needed it. Blondel ducked, and a moment later the rock hit the patch of beach he'd just been using.

'Steady on,' Blondel said, resurfacing a few feet out into the pond. The stranger grunted irritably and picked the rock up. It looked unpleasantly as if what he lacked in intellectual stature he made up for in dogged persistence.

Out of the corner of his eye, Blondel saw another, similar figure approaching. This one was carrying a stone axe, and gave every indication of having been woken up from a badly needed sleep. There were others following. Bad news.

'Excuse me,' Blondel said, in the most nonchalant voice he could find, 'but could any of you gentlemen direct me to the nearest —'

There was a loud and disconcerting splash in the water about a foot from where he was standing, and a wave hit him in the face. The rock, probably. That one or one just like it. Blondel dived down again and resurfaced some way further out.

It was difficult to know what to do for the best. If these were, as Blondel suspected, cavemen, there was a fair chance that if he stayed there long enough they would probably catch some disease or other from him to which they had not yet had a chance to build up an immunity, and die. On the other hand, that might well take some time, and the water was quite distressingly cold. So Blondel decided to try his other option. He sang *L'Amours Dont Sui Epris*.

With hindsight, Blondel realised, he'd been expecting a bit much there. The romance tradition of chansons and trouveres, though considerably more accessible than many other musical genres, isn't entirely suited for absolute novices. He might have done better, he felt, with something a bit more basic, such as *Baa Baa Black Sheep*. That might have had them standing in the aisles. As it is, they threw rocks.

Having resurfaced ten yards further out, Blondel decided to try a little lateral thinking. On the one hand, there were rather a lot more of them now, and some of them seemed to have grasped the principle of the sling-shot. If one chose to look on the bright side, though, one couldn't help noticing that they weren't terribly good marksmen. It might be worth giving it another ten minutes to see if there was any chance of them wiping themselves out with stray missiles.

A feeling of acute numbness in his toes argued against that, and Blondel came to the conclusion that getting cramp and drowning wasn't exactly the most positive step he could think of at this juncture; so he chose the least inhabited part of the beach and started to swim towards it. He was just about to come within easy boulder range and was wondering if this was the best he could do when an idea struck him, with a number of small, fast-moving stones.

It might justifiably be said that leaving it until now to reveal that Blondel had had a small, high-volume, waterproof personal stereo in his jacket pocket from the outset smacks of rather meretricious storytelling; however, since Blondel had only just remembered it himself, the omission is probably justifiable. He hadn't given the thing a second thought since he'd acquired it, as his introductory free gift on taking out a Galeazzo Brothers With Profits Ten Year Endowment Policy, just before the concert. Now he realised that even the things you get given for free can sometimes come in very handy. He trod water, fished the thing out, removed the headphones, turned the volume to maximum and switched it on.

It was an added bonus that the machine contained a tape of the massed bands of the Royal Marines playing *The Ride of the Valkyries*, although since all tapes for which one does not have to pay money have exactly the same thing on them, it probably was only to be expected. At any rate, it worked. The cavemen dropped their improvised weapons and fled. All except one, who reacted rather like a rabbit caught in the headlights of a fleet of oncoming lorries. The noise seemed to paralyse him, his knees gave way and he sat down heavily on a short, thick log. Perhaps, Blondel said to himself, the poor chap isn't a music lover. Or perhaps, rather more likely, he *is* a music lover.

He clambered out of the water, shook himself and started to squelch up the beach, trying not to startle the dazed caveman, who was sitting with his head between his knees, whimpering. Unfortunately the band chose that moment to launch into the Soldier's Chorus from *Faust*, and that seemed to do it for the caveman. He lurched violently and disturbed the log, which started to roll slowly towards the water.

Feeling slightly ashamed of himself, Blondel switched the music off and helped the caveman to his feet. He tried to apologise in sign language, but he didn't seem to be getting through, somehow.

'Come on, old chap,' he said. 'You run along and we'll say no more about it ...'

The log rolled to the edge of the water and fell in. Blondel realised that the caveman, far from being

251

paralysed with fear, was concentrating single-mindedly on the log and what it was doing.

'We'll,' the caveman repeated. '*We'll!*'

He scampered to the water, fished the log out, lugged it back up the beach and set it rolling again. 'We'll!' he yelled.

'Oh *bother!*' said Blondel to himself, 'I've done it again.' Then he trudged off to find the tunnel.

Back in the tunnel, Blondel felt simultaneously relieved, dry and very, very lost. The last feeling was the worst, and it wasn't helped by the discovery that the water in the cave pool had turned his map to sticky and illegible porridge. It would have to be intuition again. He turned left and ran down the tunnel.

Fifty yards or so further on, he discovered the flaw in his basic strategy. A squad of heavily armed men were coming down the tunnel towards him. They seemed pleased to see him, a feeling he found it hard to reciprocate. He skidded to a halt, turned athletically, and ran back the way he'd come. Mistake number two.

If he hadn't been so preoccupied he'd have seen himself coming; as it was, he collided with such tremendous terminal velocity that both of him were thrown backwards. For a moment, he was both stunned.

'You clumsy idiot!' he panted, simultaneously.

'Look who's talking.'

'Why don't you look where you're going?'

'I like that, coming from you.'

'Look,' said his later self, 'I'm being chased by a platoon of Time and Motion, I haven't got time ...'

'So am I,' replied his earlier self.

'But they're not behind you,' replied the later self, 'they're behind me. You're heading straight for them.'

'I am?'

'Yes.'

The earlier Blondel gave his later self a funny look. 'How do you know?' he said.

'Because I nearly ran straight into them, idiot,' replied the later Blondel, 'that's how. Now, if you don't mind ...'

'Before or after you ran into me?'

'Before. No, after. Look, does it matter?'

'But that's crazy,' replied Mark I. 'It's impossible.'

'Is it?'

'Must be,' said Mark I, backing away slightly. 'Because I – we – can't be just about to run into them, because you've just warned me they're coming.'

Mark II tried, very briefly, to think about this, and then came to the conclusion that now wasn't the time. So to speak.

'Look,' he said, 'will you just ...?'

Mark I shook his head. 'Oh no you don't,' he said. 'If one of us is going to turn round and carry on running in the safe direction it might as well be me.'

Mark II stared. 'How do you make that out?' he said.

'Well,' Mark I replied, 'I'm not the one who went blundering into them in the first place letting them know where I was, am I? No, I reckon the best thing would be for them to catch you, so's I can get away.'

'Look ...' Mark II said angrily, and then tailed off. 'Why don't we both ...'

Mark I gave him a look. 'Don't be silly,' he said.

Down the tunnel came the sound of heavy boots

running. 'But if they catch you,' said Mark II frantically, 'they'll catch me too.'

'And vice versa.'

'Toss you for it?'

'Do I look like I was born yesterday?'

'Right now,' Mark II replied, 'I wouldn't like to bet on it. For all I know you probably were. And tomorrow. Now can we adjourn this and do some running away, because —'

'If we toss for it,' Mark I went on, ignoring him(self), 'you'll know which side the coin came down, because you're later than me and . . .'

This is crazy, said Mark II to himself; a third self, presumably. Perhaps that's what's meant by a multifaceted personality. Or terminal schizophrenia. 'All right,' he said, 'you can call.'

'Ah yes,' Mark I replied smugly, 'it's all right for you to say that, because you know I called wrong and so . . .'

Blondel took a deep breath, shouted 'Behind you!' and, while his head was turned, kicked himself in the reproductive organs. Then, while he was lying on the ground groaning weakly, he jumped over himself and ran.

Straight into an oncoming TAM patrol.

He turned and fled. It wasn't exactly easy running, not with this awful pain in his lower abdomen, but somehow he managed. Fear probably had something to do with it. Also a very great desire to find himself again and kick his head in.

About fifty yards down the tunnel, he collided again.

'Right, you,' he chorused, and let fly a powerful right hook. His two right hands landed in his two left eyes at exactly the same moment. He fell over and went to sleep.

'Straw.'

'No.'

'Shadows.'

'No.'

'Spiders' webs.'

'That's two words.'

Guy snarled quietly. 'Very true,' he said, 'but are they the right two words?'

'No.'

'That sounds like a very interesting game,' said the voice pleasantly, from his corner of the cell. 'Would you mind explaining the rules to me?'

Guy turned his head. He prided himself on his adaptability, but the prospect of this state of affairs continuing much longer wasn't exactly cheering him up. 'It's a very boring game, actually,' he said. 'Sand,' he added.

'There isn't any sand,' Isoud replied.

'How do you know?'

'She's right, actually,' the voice broke in diffidently. 'Or at least I haven't come across any. Not yet, that is. I may be wrong, of course.'

'What we do,' Isoud said to the voice, 'is I think of a word and then I say I Spy With My Little Eye Something Beginning With S. That's a clue.'

'Oh yes?' said the voice.

'That lets you know the word begins with S.'

'Excuse me if I'm being a bit slow,' said the voice, 'but what if the word begins with something else? G, for example, or T. Or can you only choose a word beginning with S?'

'No,' said Isoud, 'if the word began with G, I would

say I Spy With My Little Eye Something Beginning With G.'

'Oh I *see*,' said the voice. 'Can I have a go?'

'I haven't finished yet,' Guy said irritably. 'Stones,' he suggested.

'No.'

'It must be stones,' he protested. 'There isn't anything else beginning with S.' He looked around sadly. 'There's not a hell of a lot beginning with anything, really.'

'Well that's where you're wrong, Mr Clever,' Isoud replied smugly. 'There's sandstone, frinstance.'

'Is it sandstone?'

'No.'

Sotto voce, Guy asked God to give him strength. 'All right,' he said, 'I give in, now tell me what it is before I go completely round the bend.'

'Shank,' said Isoud proudly.

'*Shank*?'

'The shank,' Isoud explained, 'of the lock. I told you it was a clever one.'

'Very clever indeed,' said the voice, 'if I may make so bold.'

'*Shank*?'

'There is such a word,' Isoud said defensively.

'Yes,' Guy replied, 'but you can't see it.'

'Yes I can.'

'Then you must have bloody good eyesight,' Guy snapped, 'because the shank is part of the works, ergo it's inside the lock, ergo you couldn't see it from here even if it wasn't as dark as a bag in here, which it is. I win.'

'Be like that, then.'

'Actually ...' said the voice, and then became aware, no doubt by some form of low-level telepathy, that he was being glowered at by both parties. 'Sorry,' he said, and went back to plaiting spiders' webs.

'My go,' said Guy firmly.

'It's not,' Isoud said, 'you cheated.'

'I did not cheat,' Guy said. 'A shank is part of the works of a lock, ask anybody. If you like, I'll call the warder. He should know about locks if anybody does.'

'I'm not playing with you any more.'

'Good.'

A rat nuzzled affectionately up to Guy's hand and was both shocked and profoundly disillusioned when the hand tried to swat him. He retreated into a distant part of the cell and, since rodents can't cry, started to gnaw at a splinter of wood.

'Of course,' Guy said suddenly, 'it could be that we've been missing something important here.'

'Oh yes?' said the voice eagerly. 'Do tell.'

Guy reached inside his jacket and felt for something. To his great relief it was still there. 'All we have to do in order to get out of here,' he said, 'is to open the door, right?'

'That would help, certainly,' the voice agreed. 'But, and far be it from me to play devil's advocate or anything, isn't that going to be —'

'Not,' Guy said, 'if I shoot the lock off.'

'Gosh!' The voice sounded impressed. 'Can you do that?' it asked.

Guy drew his revolver and screwed up his eyes. There was just enough light to see that it was loaded. 'Don't see why not,' he said. 'Stay well back, everyone.'

He advanced to the door, felt for the lock, placed the

muzzle next to it, and fired. The noise, which was ear-splitting in the confines of the cell, slowly died away. From the other side of the door came the sound of someone saying, 'Look, do you mind?' in a querulous tone. Guy tried the door. It was solid. There was a bullet-hole clean through the wood about an inch above the lockplate.

The peephole in the door slid back, filling the cell (or so it seemed) with a beam of blinding light.

'See that?' said the warder.

'Pardon?'

'That's a brand new hat, that is,' the warder went on. 'And now look at it.'

Guy blushed. 'Sorry,' he said.

'Bloke can't pull up a chair and take forty winks in this place without getting holes in his hat,' the warder grumbled. 'What's the world coming to, that's what I want to know.'

'It was an accident,' Guy said. 'Honest.'

'Oh yes?' The warder didn't sound impressed.

'It was,' Guy insisted. 'I was trying to, er, shoot off the lock, and I must have ...' He closed his eyes and tried to swallow the shame. 'Missed.'

There was a long silence.

'Missed.'

'Must have.'

'I see.'

'Good.'

'I was,' the warder went on, 'going to come in there and take that thing off you as an offensive weapon. Still, seeing as how you can't even hit a lock, I don't think I'll bother.' The peephole cover slid back, flooding the cell with darkness, and Guy put his revolver back in its holster. More than anything else in the world, he realised, he hated hats.

Blondel opened his eyes and looked round. To his relief, he found that he wasn't there any more.

Lying next to him, however, were a large number of recumbent bodies; about thirty of them. They looked as if they'd been in a fight.

One of them groaned and lifted its head slightly. The effort proved too great, however, and it sagged back.

'Hello,' Blondel said, 'what happened to you?'

The soldier looked up and instinctively reached for something at his side. Blondel put his foot on it and smiled.

'Not now,' he said. 'What happened?'

'It was those other blokes,' the soldier said.

'What other blokes?'

'The ones who came down the corridor a few minutes after we got here,' the soldier replied. 'We were just about to take you into custody when they got here and started arguing the toss. Said it was their collar and why didn't we back off. Well, we weren't standing for that. There's a reward.'

'Oh yes?'

'Too right.' The soldier grinned. 'We showed them all right,' he said, and fainted.

Blondel sighed. It was at times like this that he wondered why he bothered. He had this strong suspicion that all he really had to do was wait quietly and everybody would beat the springs out of everybody else without him having to lift a finger.

He stood up and counted the bodies. It came to an odd number. Not so good.

In the distance, he could hear the sound of running feet.

'Listen,' he said out loud, and pointed towards the direction the sound was coming from. 'You go that way, right?' Then he picked up his feet and ran the other way.

He hadn't gone far when he stopped. Not voluntarily; there was this door in the way.

Blondel picked himself up off the ground, rubbed his nose and looked at the door warily. Something told him that whatever there was on the other side wasn't going to be friendly. It had that sort of look about it.

Behind him he could hear footsteps, getting closer. They sounded like the footsteps of heavily armed men who have just had a fight with themselves and are dying to vent their embarrassment on an unarmed and vulnerable third party.

On the other hand, it was perhaps the least prepossessing door he'd ever seen, in quite possibly a uniquely wide experience of the subject. Not only did it have the words *No Entry* written on it, but also the word *Honestly*.

Behind him, Blondel could hear voices. They seemed to be discussing, in a breathless but enthusiastic way, who was going to have the privilege of mutilating which part of him.

When is a door not a door?

When it's a jar.

Obviously.

'... Which, together with a balanced portfolio of Beaumont Street Gilt and Fixed Income Trust units and a modest cash balance in, say, the Beaumont

Equitable Building Society, provides for maximum income potential without undue prejudice to long-term capital growth. What do you say?'

'No.'

Giovanni sighed. It was cold down here in the cellars and he was getting cramp. On the other hand, he enjoyed a challenge. 'Fair enough,' he said. 'How about putting the bulk of the capital sum into Carribeanis $9\frac{1}{2}\%$ Convertible Treasury Stock, and investing the balance in something like, oh, I don't know, Second Crusade $3\frac{1}{2}\%$ Loan Stock 1192? Now you can't say fairer than that. Safe as the Bank of England, that is.' He remembered the investment package he'd worked out for the Chancellor of the Exchequer back in 2343. 'Safer,' he added firmly.

'No.'

'It so happens,' he said, 'I know of this horse running in the 2.15 at Doncaster. When I say running, what I really mean is ran, of course . . .'

'No.'

There are times when even the most persistent financial adviser has to call it a day. 'Ah well,' he said, 'it's entirely up to you, naturally. If you don't want to provide for your old age . . .'

'Talk sense,' the Antichrist replied.

It was raining. It was coming down in bucketfuls and nobody had invented the umbrella yet. Mountjoy, who generally insisted on dressing in period ('When in the Renaissance, do as the Renaissancers do') looked out from under the soggy top edge of his cowl and blew a raindrop off the end of his nose.

'He's late,' he said,

'With respect, sir.'

Slowly, the Anti-Chaplain turned his head and scowled at his chief henchman. Acting Chief Henchman; he'd asked for White Herald, but apparently Maintenance were all out of 63B knee joints.

'You said something?'

'Yes, sir,' Clarenceaux replied. 'With respect, sir, given that we are presently in a temporal anomaly, with respect, um, how *can* he be late, sir? I mean ...'

Mountjoy let him tail off without interrupting. He felt it would be more humiliating. 'Have you quite finished?'

'Sir.'

'Then shut up.'

Clarenceaux mouthed the word *Sir* and continued to stand to attention. After all, he said to himself, I may be the lowest form of life and completely unintelligent and little better than a robot, but at least I've got the sense to wear oilskins.

Mountjoy was just beginning to suspect that this was some sort of practical joke when a small figure appeared on the opposite side of the bridge. He was carrying an umbrella. Typical.

'Sorry to have kept you,' Blondel sang out as he approached, splashing through the puddles in his green wellington boots. 'I got held up on the way here.' He turned his head and nodded to the castle on the other side of the river. 'Not there, of course, but the castellan turned out to be a fan and they insisted I stay for a glass of mead. One does like to be polite, you know.'

Mountjoy glowed peevishly, evaporating a pint or so of rain out of his cowl. 'It doesn't matter,' he replied, 'you're here now.'

'So I am, yes,' Blondel said. 'Look, do you think we could just step in out of the wet somewhere? This is my sister's umbrella, and it's a bit small for me.'

They found a degree of shelter under a small tree, and Blondel put the umbrella down. It was a sort of beige-fawn colour with rather restrained black patterns, Mountjoy noticed. So that was what women went in for. One of these days, it might be quite intriguing to meet one. Or maybe not. He flickered in the cold, and cleared his throat.

'Right,' he said, 'let's get down to business, shall we?'

'With pleasure,' Blondel opened the flap of the small leather satchel he was carrying round his neck and produced a tape recorder. 'You don't mind if I take notes, do you?' he said. 'I find my memory isn't what it was these days.'

'Please yourself,' Mountjoy replied frostily. 'I had assumed that we could trust one another, but —'

'I know,' Blondel replied. 'Wretched, isn't it? Actually, it wasn't my idea, it was my agent's. There's a born negotiator for you. Spent the last few days trying to sell your boss life insurance.'

Mountjoy looked down his nose. 'Unsuccessfully, I assume.'

Blondel grinned. 'Not entirely,' he replied. 'Didn't manage to kid him into taking out any life cover, but he did manage to interest him in an accident policy. He's now fully covered in the event of loss of limb.'

That, Mountjoy decided, was enough small talk. It was time to show his hand.

'It might interest you to know,' he said, wiping rain out of his eyes with the heel of his hand, 'that we have some guests staying at the Chastel at the moment.'

'Oh yes.'

'Friends of yours,' Mountjoy said. 'Or rather, one friend and one relative.' He smiled stroboscopically (a neat trick, if you manage it. Being two-faced, like Mountjoy, does of course help).

If Blondel was disconcerted for a moment, he recovered quickly. Someone who can teach themselves tightrope walking at the first attempt shouldn't have any problem with mere mental agility.

'Oh,' he said, 'you mean that Goodlet chap and my sister Isoud. Perhaps I ought to warn you that unless Isoud has a cup of tea first thing after waking up she's about as sociable as a puma. Or have you found that out already?'

'La Beale Isoud,' Mountjoy replied, 'has the sense to realise that she has more pressing things to worry about than where her next cup of tea is coming from.'

'Are you sure we're talking about the same person?' Blondel said. 'About this height, sort of mousy blond, keen on carbohydrate-rich foodstuffs?'

Mountjoy ignored him. 'I am told,' he went on, 'that they have already made one fumbling attempt at escape, which naturally ended in failure. You may be sure that they won't be in a hurry to try again.'

A gentleman, Blondel's mother had always insisted, is unfailingly polite at all times, even when being lowered into a pit full of scorpions by black-hearted and incorrectly dressed Infidels. He shrugged slightly.

'Clever old you, then,' he said. 'I take it you're going to suggest an exchange of hostages.'

'That was my idea, yes.'

'Fair enough,' Blondel replied. 'Swap me King Richard for the Antichrist, and I'll let you have the two Julians for Guy and Isoud.'

'Certainly not,' Mountjoy replied with an unpleasant little snicker. 'That would be grossly unfair to us, given that the Pope and the Anti-Pope are one and the same person.'

'But wearing different hats,' Blondel replied quickly. 'Hats make an awful lot of difference. You ask my friend Guy about hats.'

'Nevertheless,' Mountjoy replied, 'the terms are unacceptable.'

'How about if I get my agent to throw in a free radio alarm clock?'

Mountjoy scowled, making the world momentarily dark. 'If I were you,' he said, 'I would advise your

265

friend Galeazzo to stay off the topic of free radio alarm clocks, particularly when he's in the presence of My Lord.'

A terrible thought struck Blondel, and he struggled with his muscle control in a desperate attempt not to giggle.

'You don't mean ...' he said.

'Shortly before the date scheduled for the Day of Judgement,' Mountjoy intoned, 'My Lord, on the advice of his legal advisers, took out a public liability policy. Part of the package offered by the insurance broker, it appears, was a free radio alarm clock, which subsequently failed to go off on a rather important occasion. As soon as My Lord has finished with you, Master de Nesle, I rather fancy he means to take the matter up with the broker in question.'

Blondel, who had closed his eyes in the interests of mirth suppression, opened them again and nodded. 'Fair enough,' he said, 'we'll scrub round the alarm clock. But don't you think a deal whereby you give me two relatively unimportant civilians in return for two high-ranking clerics and the Antichrist is a bit, well, one-sided. If you'll forgive the pun,' he added.

'It depends,' Mountjoy replied luminously. 'Unimportant to us. Unimportant, indeed, to history. But unimportant to you ...'

Blondel frowned, and noticed something out of the corner of his eye. 'Hello,' he said, 'is that my old friend Clarenceaux under all that oilcloth? How's things, Clarenceaux?'

Clarenceaux, who had set in a position that was half standing to attention and half frozen rigid by the cold, stared straight in front and replied, 'Sir.'

266

'Bad as that, are they?'

'Sir.'

'Oh well,' said Blondel sympathetically. 'Stiff upper lip and all that.'

'Sir. Ran out of my size again, sir,' Clarenceaux explained. 'Quartermaster said it'd soon bed down, sir.'

'I see.' Blondel shrugged and turned back to Mountjoy. 'Tell you what I'll do,' he said, 'and I'm cutting my own throat, I really am. I'll let you have the two Popes and the Antichrist, you give me the King and Guy, and you can keep La Beale Isoud. Now I can't say fairer than that, can I?'

Mountjoy, for all his phosphorescent detachment, was shocked. 'You'd sacrifice your own sister?' he said.

Blondel tried to look innocent. 'Absolutely,' he said. 'A man's first duty is to his king, and next to that, to his fellow knights. Sisters just do the washing.'

Mountjoy's brain turned like the dials of a fruit machine. He remembered what the warder had told him the woman had said when he brought her her rations. They had enough trouble filling the existing staff vacancies without looking for another warder. 'I wouldn't dream of it,' he said.

'Pity.' Blondel sighed. 'Right, then, this is my very last offer, take it or leave it. You release Richard, Guy and Isoud, and you can have your lot back plus me.'

'You?'

'Certainly. You can ship me off to the Archive of your choice, and I promise you faithfully that you won't know I'm there.'

Mountjoy shook his head, diffusing second-hand rain. 'That would be, Messire, because you weren't there. You've been in one Archive already and escaped.

We wouldn't be able to sleep at night. No, our terms are quite straightforward. Goodlet and La Beale Isoud in return for My Lord and Their Excellencies. Otherwise ...'

'Otherwise what?' Blondel asked innocently.

'Otherwise,' Mountjoy replied, 'your sister and your friend won't even be fond and fragrant memories. They will never have existed. Do I make myself plain?'

'Absolutely, my dear fellow,' Blondel replied. 'After all,' he added, 'it'll just mean we're back to where we started.'

'Not quite,' Mountjoy said. 'If we were back where we started, none of this would be necessary.'

'Sorry?'

'I said,' Mountjoy repeated, 'if we were back where we started, none of this —'

'No,' Blondel interrupted, 'you're wrong there. If *you* were back where *you* started, then I wouldn't be here. We'd all be in the future, surely.'

'That's not the point,' Mountjoy retorted. 'If *we* were back where *we* started, then *you* wouldn't be here, but *we* would.'

Blondel shook his head. 'But surely in that case we wouldn't be we, we'd just be you.'

'That's what I said.'

'No, what you said was —'

'Hold on,' Clarenceaux interrupted. 'I think I see what's gone wrong. Mountjoy is taking a view of events as they would have occurred in Basic Time, while Blondel is looking at it all from an Overtime-based perspective which would naturally lead him to inter-pret ...'

He stopped. He had this feeling that everybody in the world was looking at him.

'Sorry,' he said, and died of embarrassment.

'Anyway,' Blondel said, 'I suppose it's a deal, then. Shake on it?'

'No thank you.'

'Suit yourself.' He stepped out from under the tree and opened his umbrella. 'I'll meet you back here, same time, same place, this week. All right?'

'Agreed.'

'Ciao, then,' Blondel said, and walked away over the bridge.

Half an hour later, a battered red pick-up came and collected Clarenceaux and took him back to the depot. Because of an acute shortage of embarrassment neurons at Central Dispatching they had to close off the circuits and double-bank the guilt centres to make up; with the result that, in the six weeks until he next died and they had a chance to take him to bits and do the job properly, he had a distressing tendency to burp in mixed company and then feel awful about it for days afterwards.

Blondel was driving the cart. It was difficult, because the cart was about seven inches wider than the tunnel, and it was only because of strange distortions caused by anomalies in the temporal field that he was able to get the blasted thing through at all. The key thing was, at all costs, not to meet himself coming the other way.

'Hold tight, everybody,' he said, 'this is our turning.'

Giovanni looked up to see a low, narrow doorway the size of a coal chute, with a picture of a cart in a red circle with a diagonal line through it stencilled on its central panel. Although he was used to this sort of thing, he closed his eyes and ducked.

It was already dark when they reached the bridge. It was also raining. Of course.

Under a tree by the side of the road at the other end, Blondel could see Mountjoy, Clarenceaux and, of course, himself, working out the terms of the exchange. At least there would be reliable witnesses in the event of any dispute about the terms. He made a chuck-chuck noise to the horse, pulled his hood down over his face and asked Marco if the lanterns were ready.

Two carts waiting at opposite ends of the bridge, in the pouring rain. For a while they just sat there. Then, on one cart, a lantern flashes three times. Then a lantern flashes three times on the other cart. The first cart flashes back four times. The signal is reciprocated.

There is no known reason for this performance, which is believed to be compulsory on these sorts of occasions. Presumably it's just tradition.

He had kept calm up till now; but the other cart hadn't moved, and Blondel began to worry. In keeping with the rest of his character, on the rare occasions when Blondel went to pieces, he went to very small, very numerous, very fast-moving pieces. In fact, you could use him to shoot clay pigeons with.

'For God's sake,' he muttered, 'what do they think they're playing at? Marco, you stupid idiot, don't just sit there, flash 'em some more. Come *on*, for God's sake.'

The other cart remained still. It flashed back; five flashes and then one more for luck. Blondel demanded angrily of the world in general what the hell that was supposed to mean.

Marco coughed politely. 'Maybe they're trying to remind you it's a one-way street, boss,' he said.

Blondel looked down at him. 'What do you mean, one-way street?'

'Well,' Marco said, marshalling his thoughts and hoping he was remembering this right, 'it means that if it's a north-south-only street, you can go from north to south but not south to north. If it's a south-north-only street, it means you can go from south to north but not north to south. If it's ...'

Marco suddenly found that his cap had somehow left his head and got wedged in his mouth. He took it out again.

'*Is* it a one-way street, Marco?' Blondel asked.

'Yes,' Marco replied, 'didn't you see the signs? It's a west-east-only street, that means you can go —'

'Yes, thank you,' Blondel replied, 'eat your nice hat now, there's a good lad. Silly of me not to have noticed, wasn't it?'

It made sense, after all. There was a serious risk that going through a No Entry sign in this particular context might result in something rather worse than a fine and two penalty points. He pulled himself together, chirruped softly to the horse, and moved the cart forwards.

'You're late again,' said Mountjoy. 'What kept you?'

'Got held up in traffic,' Blondel improvised. 'Anyway, I'm here now.'

Mountjoy flickered like a portable television in a thunderstorm. He hated getting wet; the last thing he needed to do at his time of life was to fuse. 'Can we get on with it, then?'

'You've come alone, then, like we agreed?'

'Of course I have,' Mountjoy replied wearily. 'For a start, nobody else'd be crazy enough to come out in this weather. Are they in the back?'

Blondel nodded. 'Want to check the merchandise?' he asked. This too was traditional.

'I trust you,' Mountjoy replied. 'I mean,' he added, 'if you can't trust slippery, devious little bastards, who can you trust?'

'Very true,' Blondel replied. 'But, since you're none of those things, I'd be grateful if you'd just lift that tarpaulin there.'

Muttering, Mountjoy did so. There was a loud protest in a distinctive female voice as rain came into the back of Mountjoy's cart. They were there all right.

'Any problems getting here?' Blondel asked.

'No,' Mountjoy replied suspiciously. 'Why?'

'Because every time I drive her anywhere,' Blondel replied, 'it's *Shouldn't you be in third gear?* and *I'm sure that was the turning back there on the left* all the bloody way. You must tell me how you managed it some time. Ready?'

'Ready.'

Mountjoy waved his hand. Pursuivant and Mordaunt jumped down and pulled two anthropomorphic bundles out of the cart. There was a bump as they hit the ground.

'That's fine,' Blondel said quietly. 'Giovanni, Marco, Iachimo, give me a hand, will you?'

The Galeazzos unloaded their cargo, plus a free simulated calf attaché case and solar calculator each, and laid them on the damp roadway. The two carts moved forward a few paces and took on their new respective cargoes.

'Right,' Blondel said. 'That's that, then. Pleasure doing business with —'

'*Seize them!*'

Blondel gave Mountjoy a very brief look of utter contempt, and then cracked the reins sharply. A moment later, his cart was surrounded by dark shapes; looming, ominous shapes, all the more disturbing because their visors were down over their ...

'Look, Guy!' Blondel shouted. 'Hats! Iron hats! Lots and lots of them!'

There was a loud crack, and the sound of a bullet ricocheting off the crest of a helmet. A dark shape swore loudly and ran for its life. Or at least its five-hundred-year parts and labour warranty. The cart lurched forward and trundled off.

'After them!' Mountjoy yelled. The dark shapes stayed exactly where they were, all apart from one, who was wandering around bumping into things. Later they explained that you can't hear a damn thing inside those bleeding steel helmets.

From the back of Mountjoy's cart came a loud and authoritative protest. You'd have had no problem hearing it through six inches of plate steel.

'Good,' it added. 'Now don't just stand there, get after them.'

'Do you know,' Blondel said, as the cart thundered down the road, 'I'm getting just the teeniest bit sick and tired of all this running about and being chased by people, aren't you?'

Guy nodded. He was more than the teeniest bit sick at the way the cart was lurching about, too, but it seemed so long since he'd eaten anything that that was probably academic. He found what seemed to be a handrail and clung on to it fiercely.

'Ouch,' said Marco.

'Sorry,' Guy said, letting go of his ear. 'What are you doing down there?'

'I'm looking for my cap,' Marco replied. 'It fell off when we —'

'Forget it.'

'But it's nearly new,' Marco said. 'It's got a feather on it and —'

'I said,' Guy repeated, 'forget it.'

The cart went over a pothole rather too fast, sending everyone up in the air about six inches. There was a cracking sound and a great deal of turbulence. Then the cart stopped.

'The axle's snapped,' Giovanni said. 'Now I bet you're glad you decided to have the Fully Comprehensive.'

'Shut up, Giovanni,' Blondel said, 'and you, Isoud.'

'I didn't say a —'

'Then don't.' Blondel jumped down from the box. The lanterns of Mountjoy's cart weren't far behind. 'Come on,' he shouted, 'this way.'

'Why this way?' Isoud said.

'Look —'

'I think we should turn right.'

'*Look* —'

'It says on the map —'

'*This way!*'

They set off at a run, and made the cover of a small thicket just as Mountjoy's cart, heavily laden with dark shapes, failed to notice the obstruction in the road in time to stop. There was a pleasant crunching noise.

'I think,' Blondel observed, 'something just ran over Someone's foot.'

Dark shapes spilled out of the cart. Lanterns were

waved about, Mordaunt slipped in the mud, fell, impaled himself on a broken spear, died, and was accused by Mountjoy of skiving. Then the lanterns began to head towards the thicket.

'Oh bother,' Blondel said. 'Come on, everyone, all except you, of course, Isoud. I expect you want to go that way. The rest of you follow me.'

'Where the hell are we going?' Guy demanded.

'Back to the road, of course,' Blondel replied. 'Use your head.'

'But —'

'And when we get there,' Blondel continued, 'we're going to go up it. That's east-west to you, Marco. It's a one-way street, remember?'

'When are we?' Guy asked.

'At least it isn't raining,' Blondel replied. 'Come on, you two, I'll buy you each an ice cream.'

They walked towards the source of the noise and then, subconsciously adjusting their pace to the context, strolled. It is impossible to do anything other than stroll at a church fête, especially if it isn't raining.

'What happened?' Guy said. 'I mean, one minute we were running directly at those ... And then, bang! Or rather,' he added, puzzled again, 'not bang.'

'Oh look,' Blondel said, 'they've got a band. Salvation Army, probably. I like silver bands, don't you?'

'I suppose,' Guy continued, 'it was because it was a one-way street, and therefore, by implication, there was a no entry sign, and that meant it was somehow linked into the time tunnel network. Does that always happen when you go the wrong way up a —'

'Probably,' Blondel replied. 'Personally, I've never tried it before. Have you?'

'Well, no,' Guy admitted. 'When do you think this is?'

Blondel looked round with the eye of experience. 'Twentieth century,' he said, 'second half, definitely. Of course, the twentieth is a right little tinker to get your bearings in, because you can't go by the clothes. They were always having nostalgia. You could be strolling along looking at the hemlines and the shoulder-pads and thinking, Yes, I know when this is, perhaps there's a new Elvis Presley picture on at the cinema, and the next thing you know you're nearly knocked down by a Datsun. Cars, though, are a dead giveaway. You can date things by cars to within six months, usually.' He stopped, looked round and nodded. '1986,' he said. 'Funny sort of place to end up, 1986.'

'Is it?'

Blondel nodded. 'Nothing happened,' he explained. 'You may not have noticed, but there's a strong tendency when you leave the time tunnels at random to come out at a turning point of history.'

'You mean like Caesar crossing the —'

'Yes,' Blondel replied sternly, 'and keep your voice down. I don't want anybody finding out that was us. I don't know why it is,' he went on, 'this forever popping up at crucial moments. Maybe they've just got a stronger temporal field than your average wet Thursday in Dusseldorf. Anyway, as far as I can see, nothing of any significance whatsoever is happening here.'

'Good,' said Guy, and added, 'you mentioned something about an ice cream ...'

Blondel nodded, borrowed five pounds from Giovanni – or rather, borrowed the use of his Beaumont Express Card – and wandered off in search of the refreshments tent. The Galeazzo brothers found a hoopla stall, which they proceeded to strip bare. Guy and Isoud sat down under a chestnut tree.

'Well,' Guy said awkwardly, 'here we are.'

'Yes,' Isoud replied.

'Um,' Guy continued, feeling it would probably be easier as well as nicer to try wading through waist-high custard, 'about this future of ours. The getting married and everything.'

'Yes,' Isoud said. Expressing oneself in unhelpful monosyllables in the course of extremely embarrassing conversations is a woman's prerogative, Guy remembered, and the thought struck him that his father had probably had a conversation like this, or else he wouldn't be here. And his father, and his father before him, right back to the period of human history when it was socially acceptable to crack girls over the head with clubs and drag them off by their hair. It was a wonder the world was populated at all.

'Don't get me wrong,' Guy went on, 'but, well, in a sense ...'

He realised that he hadn't the faintest idea what he was going to say next, and was just about to change the subject and point out a perfectly ordinary tree on the other side of the green when Isoud turned to him and said 'Oh, Guy!'

There you go, monosyllables again. I think all the bride's lines in the wedding service are made up of monosyllables. Follows.

277

'Yes, well,' he said, 'like I was saying, we really ought to consider —'

'Kiss me, Guy.'

'Sorry?'

'I said,' said Isoud, with just a touch of residual personality showing through, 'kiss me.'

Guy wanted to say, Hold on a minute there, I think you've got hold of the wrong end of the stick, because what I was going to say was that now that we've found out how flexible and adjustable time is, perhaps we won't have to get married after all, and since neither of us is desperately keen on the idea ... But since he'd been taught not to speak with his mouth full, he didn't.

'Hello, you two,' Blondel said, grinning at them over a mobile barricade of white froth. 'Thought so.'

Isoud detached herself, leaving Guy realising what a rock must feel like when there are limpets about. She blushed prettily, said something about having a look at the white elephant stall, and skipped away, for all the world, Guy reckoned, like a radiantly happy electromagnet.

'Have an ice cream,' Blondel was saying. 'So Isoud showed you the family photograph album, did she?'

'Gug,' Guy replied.

Blondel shrugged his shoulders. 'Took me a long time to find you,' he went on. 'Well, to be honest, I wasn't looking all that hard, what with searching for the King and everything. Still, better late than never, I suppose.'

'Hold on a minute,' Guy said. There was ice cream all over his nose, but he didn't care. 'You mean you ... you *chose* me specially? I thought it was just a coincidence or something.'

'Hardly,' Blondel replied. 'I don't want to sound rude, but if I'd had a free and unrestricted choice of assistants, I think I'd probably have chosen someone who's a rather better shot. Not that you've done badly,' he added. 'Just the reverse. But you see what I mean.'

'Yes, I see,' Guy lied. 'You mean, Isoud and me, it's been sort of, fated ...'

'If you like,' Blondel replied. 'That is, we knew the ending, all we had to do was reconstruct the plot a bit. Your ice cream's melting all down your sleeve, by the way.'

'How long has it been –' Guy winced; the word was so bloody *fey*, '– fated, then?'

'Ever since we got the photographs back from the developer,' Blondel replied. 'That's one of the weird things about living in a timewarp. You get the photos back centuries before they're taken and sent off, rather than the other way round, which I believe is the usual way. So we knew it was going to be you Isoud would fall for, it was just a case of finding you. And while you were handy, of course, you might as well make yourself useful in the quest.'

'I see.'

'Honestly,' Blondel continued, chuckling quietly, 'you should have seen Isoud's face when she first saw the picture. Talk about horrified disbelief! Still, I think she's just about come round to the idea.'

'Thank you very much.'

'Don't mention it.'

'Yes,' Guy said, 'that's all very well, but it still doesn't explain why you dragged me out of my century —'

'You were just about to be killed,' Blondel interrupted. 'Remember?'

'Was I?'

'Didn't I mention it? Oh yes, you wouldn't have stood a chance if I hadn't ... well, there we are. Couldn't have you getting killed before the wedding, it would have messed things up terribly. Not,' he added, 'that anyone wants you to get killed after the wedding, needless to say.'

Guy frowned. 'Not even Isoud?' he said. 'I still don't think she's likely to have changed her mind that much. She doesn't have a terribly high opinion of me, I reckon.'

'And that,' Blondel replied, 'is a prerequisite of a successful marriage, as far as I can tell.'

Guy thought about it for a moment, considering all the examples in his experience of happily married couples. Yes, he definitely had something there.

'Even so,' he persisted, 'if it was fated, why did you have to go to all the trouble finding me? Wouldn't I have just turned up anyway?'

'Probably,' Blondel replied, 'but it might have taken ages, and I've always been particularly keen to get the wedding over and done with. Partly,' he said, grinning, 'because I have this rooted aversion to mashed potato, but mostly because, in the wedding photograph you haven't seen, the man giving the bride away at the wedding is Richard Coeur de Lion.'

Guy choked on his ice cream. Blondel patted him on the back.

'So you see,' he went on, 'I've been quite shamelessly fiddling about with your destiny for my own purposes, just like you were going to say yourself. Hope you don't mind. Anyway, you'll understand what I'm getting at when I say that I'm not a believer in long engagements. Ah, here she is.'

Isoud was walking back, holding a lampshade, a sink tidy and a colander. It's started already, Guy said to himself. A door marked *No Entry* would go down very well at this juncture.

'Come on,' Blondel said, 'let's go and have a look round the sideshows. I think we can all afford an afternoon off, in the circumstances. No, Guy, I'd stay clear of the rifle range if I were you, there's a man in a cap just over there and I don't think he'd be too ...'

'Blondel? What's the matter?'

Blondel was staring, so hard that his eyes were almost circular. His mouth had fallen open and his face was wet with sweat.

'What is it?' Guy said.

'Look,' Blondel croaked, and pointed.

Guy followed the line of his finger, and saw one of those rubber inflatable castles designed for children to bounce up and down on. It was doing good business, as far as Guy could tell, and the proprietor was throwing two little cherubs off it for trying to puncture the inflatable bit with a penknife. 'So?' he said.

'Look,' Blondel repeated. 'Are you blind or something?'

Guy looked; and noticed that there was a pattern of little teardrops painted all down the side. And he began to wonder.

Blondel had broken into a run. The proprietor, seeing him coming, let go of the two little cherubs and stared at him. A policeman on duty in the beer tent came out, wiping his mouth. Guy looked across at Isoud, and ran after him.

'Here,' said the proprietor, 'you can't go on it, it's just for the kids. Here ...'

Blondel was standing in front of the moulded rubber gate. The musical attachment stopped in the middle of the tune it had been playing and then started to play something else. Guy recognised the tune at once. He'd heard it a lot lately.

Blondel waited for a moment, counting the bars for the start of the vocals. Then he sang:

'L'amours dont sui epris
Me semont de chanter;
Si fais con hons sopris
Qui ne puet endurer ...'

The policeman stopped dead in his tracks and let his hands fall to his sides. Everything was quiet, except for Blondel's voice, soaring away into the clouds and ranging outwards in every direction, until it seemed to fill the entire world.

'A li sont mi penser
Et seront a touz dis;
Ja nes en quier oster ...'

Guy felt like a diver who has miscalculated and can no longer hold his breath and is still a long way from the surface. The air seemed to tighten unbearably round him, crushing him until he could feel his ribs and the sides of his skull being driven inwards. And then, from somewhere a long way down inside the inflatable rubber castle, a voice sang:

'Remembrance dou vis
Qu'il a vermoil et clair
A mon cuer a ce mis
Que ne l'en puis oster ...'

The voice sounded like an air-raid siren with bronchial trouble. It was the most beautiful sound that Blondel, or Guy, or Isoud, or even the Galeazzo brothers (who had been on the point of interesting the vicar in their exclusive range of tax-free clerical pension schemes when the music started) had ever heard in their entire lives.

The voice fell silent, and Blondel sang again. He sang like the first green shoot of spring, the first snowdrop, the first drop of rain in a dry season. He sang:

'*Plus bele ne vit nuls*
Ne cors ne de vis;
Nature ne mist plus
De beaute en nul pris
Por li maintaindrai l'us
D'Eneas et Paris,
Tristan et Pyramus
Qui ameraient jadis,'

and it seemed like the whole world, the entire human race, eight centuries of it suddenly realising their mistake and being glad that things were right now, joined in and sang:

'*Or serai ses amis*
Or pri Deu de la sus.
Qu'a lor fin soie pris.'

Giovanni blinked and reached for his handkerchief. He was crying for pure joy. He was thinking of the royalties.

Talking of royalties; the castle suddenly deflated and fell to the ground, and out of nowhere stepped a man. A tall man, dazzled by light he hadn't seen for eight hundred years, a man stooping and stiff, nursing his pet rat. A man who had been wronged, and who was going to set things right.

'Blondel, my dear chap,' he said, 'this really is most awfully decent of you, you really shouldn't have

283

bothered, you know, I was getting on splendidly, digging tunnels and so forth. But . . .' He stopped, and breathed in the pure, wild air, and soaked up the light until he seemed to glow with it. 'Thank you, my dear fellow,' he said.

'Your Majesty,' Blondel replied. He was kneeling. There were tears streaming down his face, just like the teardrops painted on the side of the rubber castle. 'Your Majesty,' he repeated. 'It was nothing.'

The King reached out a stiff hand and raised him up. The light didn't seem to be troubling him now; indeed, he looked like a man who would never be troubled by anything ever again.

'Right,' he said. 'Now, then.'

Timestorms are, of course, much rarer these days than they used to be in five hundred years' time, thanks to the tireless efforts of the Time Wardens, and as the threat they will pose receded, humanity will forget the almost indescribable chaos they will cause and will have neglected to be about to take even the most elementary precautions, such as having their names and dates of birth tattooed indelibly on their foreheads.

In a timestorm, events which in the usual course of things will have happened or will happen consecutively suddenly happen concurrently. In other words, people are born, live long and purposeful lives, select a pension scheme which will grow with them, marry, spend small fortunes on carpets, have children, age gracefully and die all at the same time. Trees are simultaneously acorns, oaks and HB pencils. All the days of the week take place at once. Endowment policies mature on payment of the first premium, and vintage wines suddenly fall drastically in price. Such concepts as relativity, the laws of thermodynamics and early closing cease to have any meaning. Giving up smoking becomes easy but pointless.

One kind of timestorm has effects that are so devastating as to be almost without exception terminal; and it was with some relief that the Caernarvon Commission was able to report that none of the reported instances of such a catastrophe having taken place could be factually substantiated.

Once someone has become caught up in one, he can never get out again; and nobody undergoes the phenomenon without incurring material ruin, irreversible psychological damage and a free digital stereo alarm clock radio.

'Where are we?' Guy shouted.

He didn't want to, but it seemed that his role in life, over the last however-long-it-was-now, was to ask that sort of question; as if some sort of unseen Narrator needed him to establish the mise en scène.

'I don't know,' Giovanni yelled back. 'Do you honestly think it matters?'

Well, no, Guy conceded, probably not. Not particularly likely that anything matters, or will ever do so again. I mean, this is it, isn't it?

A tiny voice in the back of his mind agreed that yes, it probably was.

Time and space are, of course, connected at a fundamental level. To give a basic example: because of tectonic shift, the various land masses are no longer where they used to be, and the people who invested in valuable building plots on the strip of land joining England and France have long since given up trying to get hold of the representatives of Beaumont Street

Realty who sold them to them, and died.

In other words, where you are depends to a great extent on when you are. However, when you are in the middle of a timestorm so massive in scale that eight centuries of history are being rolled back like the duvet on the bed of Causality, the whole thing becomes academic, and the only really important question to consider is whether or not it's ever going to stop.

'What was that?' Guy screamed dutifully.

'1789,' Giovanni replied, emerging from under a log. 'Didn't you see its markings?'

The huge shadow that had momentarily blotted out the sun receded into the distance, became a small, vividly bright spot on the sun's disc, and exploded like a firework. About fifteen seconds later there was a soft, distant plop.

'Pity,' Giovanni said. 'We did good business in 1789. The French Revolution, you know.'

'Ah,' Guy replied. He listened, and noticed the absence of a sound. It had been going on for some time, getting louder and louder and worrying him very much. If it was worth trying to find something inside his own experience which came within long rifle shot of resembling it, he would suggest that it sounded like enormous reels of film ticking through the gate of a projector backwards.

He lifted his head and looked around. Something very strange had happened to the surface of the earth.

It had happened quite quickly. One moment, there had been King Richard and Blondel and, in the background, the sagging rubber castle and a crowd of bemused villagers. The next moment; well, moments had been pretty plentiful after that. The trick had been

287

not to be hit by them as they ricocheted off each other and sang screaming through the air. As for the landscape, it had sort of faded away. It was as if (and the librarian of Guy's meagre archive of imagery started to giggle hysterically when the request came through for this one) the world was a huge watercolour painting which had just been put under the cold tap. First it had run, and then it had been washed away.

'Giovanni,' Guy asked quietly, 'are you still there?'

'Depends,' Giovanni replied. 'It's all down to criteria really, isn't it?'

'You what?'

By way of illustration, Giovanni stuck his fingers into Guy's eyes.

'Look,' Guy said, 'just stop clowning about and answer me. Are you there or ...?'

'You didn't feel that, then?'

'What?'

'Or this?'

'*What*?'

'Or,' Giovanni said, grunting with the effort, 'this?'

'Look,' Guy said, 'will you stop it and ...?'

Giovanni put the knife down. 'Part of me's here,' he said. 'Part of you, too. The rest ...'

They both ducked. There were three large bangs as the main factors leading to the Industrial Revolution were torn up by the roots and flung into the air, or at least flung. Snippets of speech floated down and settled round them, still gibbering faintly. Fortunately for Guy's sanity, they weren't in languages he knew.

'Stuff it,' he said, 'would it make it any easier if I didn't want to know what was happening?'

Giovanni shrugged. 'No,' he said. 'What's happening

is that the historical part of you, and me, has been vaporised. All that's left is what …' Giovanni considered for a moment, during which time a splinter of the American War of Independence floated down like a sycamore seed and lodged in his hair. 'What you're really made up of, I suppose,' he concluded lamely. 'In your case, inquisitiveness, fear and a certain amount of angry disbelief. In my case a strong will to self-preservation coloured by a strong dash of financial acumen. Have you any idea,' he added, 'what this lot's doing to the exchange rate?'

'But …'

'Exactly,' Giovanni replied smugly. 'The first time I met you, I put you down as a but-and-three-dots sort of person. Me, I'm more of a therefore.'

But Guy wasn't listening. He was looking up at what he stubbornly persisted in thinking of as the sky. The greatest motion picture of all time was about to start.

It started far off in the future, and it employed a range of split-screen techniques beyond the wildest dreams of any mortal director. There were billions of them, tiny little images, each showing a tiny segment of an overall image which, taken together, Guy supposed was The World. And each individual film crew was using that rather arty style whereby the camera is supposed to be looking through the hero's eyes. To make it that bit more baffling (although Guy knew several people, most of whom wore scruffy old tweed jackets and smoked pipes, who'd undoubtedly have approved) the whole thing was being shown *backwards*.

He looked round for Giovanni, but he'd gone. In the darkness, Guy could make out a tiny figure walking across the blurred and naked foreground, not looking at the sky. He had a torch in one hand and a tray round his neck. He was, Guy realised with grudging admiration, selling popcorn.

The film show moved with considerable pace; and although the voices were all so faint that he couldn't hear any of them, he found that he was able to follow what was going on. This was the Sixth World War; then the foundation of the United States of Oceania and the Eurasian People's Republic; the 2120 World Cup; the Macclesfield Missiles Crisis; the restoration of the Jacobites; the Fifth, Fourth and Third World Wars; the Berlin wall; the Second World War ...

'Hey,' Guy shouted, 'that's me ...' Then the screen he'd been looking at suddenly went blank, and he suddenly didn't want to watch any more.

The film show went on, however, gaining momentum as one spool grew bigger than the other, so that the discovery of America and the reconquest of Spain seemed to merge into one another, and the Apaches merged seemlessly with the Moors. The Moors became Turks under the walls of Constantinople, then Mongols streaming across the steppes of Russia, and then Saracens laying siege to Antioch ...

Then the film stuck, as if a huge hair had got itself jammed in the gate of Time; and, as always seems to happen, the film seems to crackle, and little wisps of smoke ...

'Satisfied?'

'All right,' said a muffled voice from inside the rubber castle, 'there's no need to make a bloody great performance about it.'

'Come out, then.'

The rubber castle stirred uneasily. One of the small children who had been bouncing about on it a few minutes before dropped its ice cream and started to yell.

'Can't we talk about this like sensible adults?'

'No.'

'How about arbitration?'

'No.'

'Toss you for it?'

'No.'

The castle writhed a little, like a dyspeptic python. 'Best of three?' it said hopefully. 'Use your own coin?'

'No.'

'Look, there really isn't anything personal, it's just ...'

King Richard raised his sword again and pointed at the ground in front of him. He was smiling, but his smile had about as much to do with joviality and bonhommie as a cap pistol with a Howitzer.

'You wouldn't,' said the castle, shaking like a crenellated jelly.

'Watch.'

'But opening the Archives ... You haven't got the faintest idea ... Thousands of years ... They just won't *fit* ...'

King Richard raised the sword in both hands, whirled it round his head, and brought it down in a flashing circle of light that seemed to cut a section out of the sky. A fraction of a second before it hit the ground, he checked the stroke and wobbled furiously. The castle unhuddled itself.

'Very funny,' it said, and its voice was on the thin edge of hysteria. 'Knew you wouldn't have the ... No!'

The sword rose.

'*All right*!'

And where the rubber castle had been, there stood a gateway, and behind it, mile upon mile of winding battlements and cloud-topped watchtowers and sun-spearing keeps and mottes and baileys and . . .

And the gate was open.

Something fell from nowhere and landed at Richard's feet. It was a small, brass Yale key, attached to a scruffy rectangle of cardboard by a broken rubber band. On the cardboard someone had written, Chastel des Larmes Chaudes. If nobody in, leave with Number 47.

Guy stood up and looked around.

About forty yards behind him lay the burnt-out wreckage of his plane. Somehow, he realised, he had got out of that thing before it blew up. Pretty impressive; shame he hadn't the faintest idea how he'd done it.

Nor, he realised, had he very much idea where he was. France, presumably; which meant his troubles weren't over yet. It would probably be a good idea to run somewhere.

'M'sieur!'

He looked round, feeling more foolish than anything else. 'Hello?' he said.

'M'sieur!' the voice hissed again. 'Allez! Allez vite!'

Ah yes, you (plural) go fast. Just what I was thinking, miss. Where, though?

The owner of the voice appeared out of the darkness, and Guy allowed himself to relax slightly. Not likely that the Germans were recruiting seventeen-year-old

French girls into the SS. More likely, this was a friendly native.

'Hello?' he said. 'I think ... I think I've banged my head.'

The girl scuttled forward, grabbed him by the arm and dragged him behind a bush. Ambiguous, Guy said to himself; but she's probably hiding me from a German patrol. Ah yes, there they go. Let's not say anything for a minute or so, until they go away.

When they had gone, the girl hauled him to his feet again – just when he was getting comfortable, but that's women for you – and bundled him off into a sort of small wood. He followed her, trying to trip over as little as possible, until they came to a little cottage. There was a light in the window. The girl stooped down, picked up a small stone, and threw it against the pane.

'Here,' Guy said, 'don't do that, you could break something —'

'Tais-toi, idiot,' the girl hissed (a high-class hisser, this one; of course, French is a much more sibillant language than ...). The light went out, and the door opened. Probably the householder, come to give us a piece of his mind.

'Isoud,' came a low voice from the darkness, 'c'est toi?'

'Si. On arrive.'

Guy felt himself being dragged towards the cottage. A young man appeared and grabbed his other arm. Tall chap, light blond hair, moustache.

The young man closed the cottage door and the girl pulled down the blinds. 'Etes-vous blessé, m'sieur?' the young man said – are you (plural) wounded, sir? Oh I *see*, am I all right?

'I'm fine,' Guy replied. 'I think I may have banged my head ...' Then he fell asleep.

When he woke up, he discovered that the girl's name was Isoud and her brother was Jean, and they were with the Resistance. Nice girl, too. Reminded him of someone, too, but for the life of him he couldn't remember ...

Out of the gate had ridden an army.

There were knights, and squires, and men at arms, landschnechts, halberdiers, bombardiers, longbowmen, crossbowmen, arquebusiers and, somewhere near the back, Pursuivant, Clarenceaux, Mordaunt and White Herald, with their eyes tightly shut. In any military force, there are always a select of body of men whose job it is in the event of an ambush to clutch their sides, scream convincingly and fall off their horses. It's a lousy job, but somebody's got to do it. Poor bloody henchmen.

At the head of the army rode a figure in half a suit of shining, night-black armour. The way in which he stayed on the horse is best left to the imagination.

The procession halted, and two trumpeters cantered ahead to blow the parley. A rather bemused sun glinted off ten thousand jet-black spearpoints. Behind the Antichrist's shoulder, two identical figures sat impassively in their saddles and looked down. By this stage, the only way they could stay materialised simultaneously was to sit absolutely still and breathe once every ten minutes.

'Well now,' said the Antichrist, 'here we all are, then.'

Richard (who had acquired some pretty impressive

armour of his own from somewhere; probably a while-you-wait armourer caught up in the gales of time) lifted his visor and smiled.

'Yes indeed,' the Antichrist went on, 'you with your victorious hordes.' He counted on his fingers; he had enough. 'Me with my ten thousand defeated but still quite highly motivated spectral warriors. Bit of a turn-up, don't you think?'

Richard continued smiling and saying nothing.

'Nice firework display,' the Antichrist continued. 'Looks like you rolled back – what – eight, nine hundred years there. Neat trick. And now you've won.'

Richard nodded. 'Apparently,' he said.

'So?'

'So what?'

The Antichrist leaned forward in his saddle. Cautiously.

There was a long, significant silence. Nature waited. Time listened.

'Um,' said Richard.

The Antichrist leaned forward in his saddle. Cautiously.

'Sorry,' he said, 'didn't quite catch that. Bit deaf on this side, to tell you the truth. What was it again?'

King Richard suddenly found the toe of his chain-mail socks very interesting. The Antichrist raised an eyebrow.

'I mean,' he went on, 'you must have had a bloody good reason, mustn't you? Winding back eight hundred years, threatening to open up the Archives, bringing the Chastel des Larmes Chaudes to its knees. Or rather knee. So, just give us the word and we'll get on with it.' He paused. 'Whatever it is.'

Something complicated seemed to be going on in the King's mind.

'If you'll bear with me a tick,' he said, apparently to his sock, 'I just want to, um, talk things through with my advisers. Get things straight in my own mind, you know.'

'That's fine,' the Antichrist replied. 'All the time in the world.'

Richard took two steps back and pulled Blondel and Guy into a huddle. The Galeazzos drifted up, like iron filings to a magnet.

'Quick,' Richard hissed sideways under the nose-guard of his helmet. 'Think of something.'

'Sorry?'

'Something to ask for,' Richard whispered. 'Demands. That sort of thing. Quickly.'

There was a deathly hush.

'How about,' Guy started to say. 'No, that'd be ...'

Five anxious voices assured him that it was fine. They really wanted to hear from him. This administration accorded the very highest value to the voice of public opinion.

A moment later, Richard stepped forward.

'Ready?' said the Antichrist.

'Yes,' Richard said, looking round over his shoulder. 'In just a ... Yes. Ready.'

'Well?'

'We demand – and we won't take no for an answer.'

'Yes?'

'Sorry?'

'You were demanding something.'

'Oh yes, that's right. We insist that you, er ...'

'Yes?'

'Do something about the way it gets dark so early in December,' Richard said. His visor had fallen down over his nose, muffling his voice. He didn't see in a hurry to do anything about it.

The Antichrist blinked. 'Granted,' he said.

'I mean,' Richard mumbled, 'it's a disgrace.'

'Agreed,' the Antichrist said. 'So what shall we do?'

'Sorry?'

'About the long winter evenings,' the Antichrist said patiently, and with malice. 'I mean, do you want more sun in winter, which will bugger up the crop cycles but never mind, or less daylight in summer, which'll —'

'Surely that's your problem,' Richard muttered quickly. 'Just do something about it, all right?'

'Fine.'

'Right, then.'

The Antichrist leaned further forward still, until his ribs were almost on his horse's ears. 'That's it, then, is it?' he said. 'Shorter winter evenings. All this was about shorter winter evenings?'

Giovanni pushed his way forward. 'Go on,' he said, nudging Richard hard in the ribs, 'tell him. Tell him about the calendar reforms.'

'Ah yes,' Richard said, with a strange edge to his voice. 'I was, um, forgetting. You tell him,' he said desperately.

'We demand,' Giovanni said, doing his best to speak with a palate apparently composed of leather, 'that something is done about the calendar. I mean, it's a disgrace.'

'Absolutely,' Richard boomed through his visor. 'A scandal.'

'Infamous,' said Blondel.

'Outrageous.'

'And we won't stand for it.'

'You can say that again.'

'We won't —'

'Shut up.'

'Sorry.'

'Is it now?' the Antichrist said. 'Do tell me all about it.'

'I mean,' Giovanni went on, giving the impression that somebody had wound his tongue up with a large metal key, 'you've got some of your months thirty days long, some of them twenty-eight, some of them thirty-one. Just think of the havoc it plays with watches.'

'Watches?'

'You heard me,' Giovanni snapped. 'Calendar watches. How the hell is a poor dumb machine supposed to know which months have twenty-eight days and which ones have —'

'And there's leap years,' Blondel added loyally. 'Somebody's bright idea, I suppose.' He tried to find a bitter twang in his vocal repertoire, and failed.

'Right, then,' said the Antichrist. 'Winter evenings shorter, reform the calendar. No problem there, I mean, they might have a bit of trouble fiddling the moon's orbit, but let nobody say we're not ready to give it a go. Are you sure there wasn't something else? Something,' he hissed viciously, 'almost equally important?'

'Um,' Richard said.

'I mean,' the Antichrist rasped unpleasantly, 'otherwise I think that when you come to explain all this' – and he waved his hand at the horizon – 'to the Boss and say it was all to get the calendar sorted out and tack an extra hour on before lighting up time in December, He might get just a bit aereated, don't you?'

As if on cue, the sky darkened. Clouds knitted together like huge eyebrows. The Antichrist's grin widened, until it stretched from ear to ... to ...

'I mean,' he said, 'Somebody Up There might take a less than tolerant view. Words like irresponsible and troublemaker might be used, don't you —'

SHUT UP

'Who said that?' Guy asked. Nobody could accuse him, he felt, of taking his duties lightly.

I DID, YOU CLOWN.

'How did you all manage to say that without moving your —'

AND AS FOR YOU, YOU CAN TAKE THAT GRIN OFF YOUR FACE.

The Antichrist looked straight up at the sky and wilted. Then he slid down the side of his horse like an oily raindrop.

THROWING YOUR WEIGHT ABOUT LIKE THAT, YOU OUGHT TO BE ASHAMED OF YOUR-SELF. NOW, IF YOU'VE ALL QUITE FINISHED MUCKING ABOUT, LET'S GET THIS MESS CLEARED UP AND WE'LL SAY NO MORE ABOUT IT.

'But,' the Antichrist said, and then clung frantically to the patch of air his horse had occupied before the lightning hit it. That, it occurred to him, was a hint. Bloody good hint, too.

Guy leaned over and whispered in Giovanni's ear. 'Is this what they call a *deus ex machina*?' he said.

'I wouldn't,' Giovanni whispered back, 'not if I were you.'

299

'All right, don't tell me, then,' Guy said. 'And you can all work it out for yourselves for all I care.'

The clouds swirled. A patch of cumulonimbus raised itself.

'And that,' Guy shouted, 'goes for you too.'

Suddenly he was alone. It wasn't another temporal shift or anything like that; it was just that everybody had suddenly realised how sensible it would be to be somewhere else.

WHAT DID YOU SAY?

'I'm fed up,' Guy yelled, 'and I want to go home. Nobody ever tells me *anything*.'

There was a long silence. A small thorn bush a few yards to Guy's left started to smoulder quietly.

DON'T THEY?

'No,' Guy said, 'and I'm not standing for it any longer, understood?' He raised his fist in a gesture of defiance, realised how silly he looked, and lowered it. 'If you were wearing a hat ...' he wailed.

ALL RIGHT.

'Sorry?'

I SAID ALL RIGHT. YOU WANT TO KNOW WHAT'S GOING ON AND I'M GOING TO TELL YOU, READY?

'Well, yes,' Guy said. 'Um ...'

IN THE BEGINNING ...

'He's asleep,' said Blondel.

'Good,' Isoud replied, pounding the boiled potatoes with a wooden spoon and a great deal of force. 'Did you really have to hit him like that?'

'If he thinks he's got concussion —'

'He has got concussion.'

'Let me rephrase that,' Blondel poured himself a drink and held it up to the light. 'If he thinks he got concussion getting out of the plane, he won't be surprised at not being able to remember anything. Best way,' he added. 'Santé.'

Isoud added a drop of milk to the potatoes. 'You know,' she said, 'he seems much nicer than he did.'

'That's just because he's incoherent with concussion,' Blondel replied. 'I've noticed, you women tend to go for the concussed type. Brings out the nursing instincts, I suppose. Can I get you one, sir?' he said, turning to the man sitting in the shadows in the corner of the room.

'Thanks awfully,' said the man, 'but not for me. Well then, that just about wraps it up for now, then, don't you think?'

'More or less,' Blondel replied. 'Thanks ever so much for dropping us off here, by the way. It'll make things much easier for Isoud and Guy.'

'Don't mention it,' Richard replied. 'They've got their own lives to lead, after all.' Richard shrugged and grinned. 'Not like us.'

'Right,' said Guy. 'Thanks.'

YOU GET THE GENERAL IDEA, ANYWAY?

Guy rubbed his eyes. 'More or less,' he said. 'Only . . .'

MMM?

'That bit with the whale,' Guy said doubtfully. 'I mean, I've often wondered about that. You see, I always understood that whales couldn't swallow people, because of all this sort of mesh stuff they've got in their throats, so how come . . .?'

IT'S A ... THING.

'Thing?'

BEGINS WITH M. METRONOME, NO, META-PHOR. IT'S A METAPHOR.

'Oh,' Guy reflected for a moment. 'And that's allowed, is it?'

OH YES. PERFECTLY LEGITIMATE DEVICE, METAPHOR.

'Great,' Guy said. 'I didn't mean to imply ...'

WHICH WOULD YOU RATHER LISTEN TO, ANYWAY, A NICE STORY WITH A HAPPY ENDING AND A STRONG WILDLIFE ELEMENT, OR THREE HOURS OF TECHNICAL METAPHYSICAL JARGON FULL OF WORDS LIKE COUNTER-INTUITIVE AND NEO-TRANSUBSTANTIATION? SOME PEOPLE DON'T KNOW THEY'RE BORN.

'Thank you,' Guy said. If in doubt, his mother had told him, just say thank you. People will understand. 'Er ...'

NOW WHAT?

'Sorry,' Guy said, 'and really, I don't mean any disrespect or anything like that, it's just ...'

BEFORE YOU ASK, IT'S ANOTHER META-PHOR.

'What is?'

STANDS TO REASON, REALLY. EVEN IF YOU COULD HAVE A TOWER THAT HIGH, THEY MUST HAVE HAD SOME WAY OF TALKING TO EACH OTHER, OR ELSE HOW DID IT GET BUILT IN THE FIRST PLACE? JUST THINK ABOUT IT, WILL YOU? YOU'D HAVE HAD ONE LOT DIGGING OUT THE FOOTINGS ON ONE SIDE AND ANOTHER LOT —

'No,' said Guy, 'actually it wasn't that so much as ...'

OH. LOT'S WIFE, MAYBE?

'No,' said Guy, 'not Lot's wife.'

Silence. *SO YOU ACTUALLY BELIEVE ALL THAT STUFF ABOUT —*

'Yes. What I was going to ask was ... um ...' Guy nerved himself. It wasn't nearly as hard as he'd imagined. 'You're not Him, are you?'

There was a slight rustling sound as something shuffled about in the burning bush. 'How did you guess?' it said.

It turned out to be a little white gnome with no hair and singed eyebrows, which clambered out, dusted itself off and extended a sooty hand.

'Melroth the Pole-Star,' it said. 'Pleased to meet you. Now you know,' it added, 'why angels always wear white. Asbestos.' It coughed.

'I hope you aren't offended,' Guy said.

'Not a bit,' Melroth replied, 'only too glad to get out of that thing.' The thorn bush collapsed in a cloud of white ash. 'Now then, where were we?'

'Um,' said Guy, 'you do have ... I mean, I can take it you're fully authorised to ...'

Melroth stared at him for a moment and then winced slightly. 'Sorry,' he said, 'memory like a sieve. My identification.' He showed a small plastic square with a blurred photograph half obscured by a red inkstamp. That alone was enough to convince Guy that it was genuine.

'He couldn't come himself, you see,' Melroth was saying. 'I know He's supposed to, but it just doesn't work like that. I mean, He can't be everywhere, can

He? Well, He can, of course, but —'

'Thanks,' Guy said. 'Now, about this time thing.'

'Yes?'

'Don't you think we should —'

'Hold on a tick,' said Melroth. He looked at his watch and made a few notes on a clipboard. It was a clipboard of burning gold and it had appeared out of nowhere, but it was palpably a clipboard. Suddenly Guy found himself understanding something very fundamental about the nature of Time.

'Right,' Melroth said, 'fire away.'

'Time,' Guy said, and he took a deep breath. 'It's a bit of a mess, isn't it?'

'Well,' said Melroth indistinctly, 'yes, it is. A bit.'

'Wouldn't it be easier if there was just the one sort of time,' Guy went on, slowly so as to let Melroth take notes, 'the sort that people could understand? You know, hours and minutes and seconds, and things happening one after the other, and then not happening ever again. None of these Archives and editing and all that. No time travel. No timestorms. Just time.' He paused, and added, 'I'm sure it'd make things much easier for your lot, as well as us.'

A very long silence. Eventually, Melroth scratched his nose.

'Interesting idea,' he said. 'But no. Wouldn't work. Administrative inertia. Unions'd never stand for it. Manifesto commitments. Cost too much to implement. Limited budget resources for new capital projects. Um.'

'Are you sure?'

'No call for it. Weight of public opinion against it at this juncture. Tried in the past and found to be impractical. Careful studies carried out by highly qualified specialist research groups have shown. Constitutional reasons why not. Other unspecified reasons.'

'Sure?'

'Look.' Melroth diminished visibly, and the sleeves of his robe came down even further over his knuckles. 'It's not as if you're the first one to suggest it, right? It's just —'

'It's just,' Guy said, 'somebody made a cock-up a long time ago and nobody wants to admit it. Right?'

Melroth nodded.

'That's fine,' Guy said. 'Nobody minds. Nobody knows. Nobody need ever know. Just ... sort it out, and that'll be that. Do you see what I mean?'

Melroth looked at him. 'You reckon?' he said.

'Yes.'

'Um.'

Guy squeezed the last drop of determination out of the spongy mess he was keeping his brains in these days. 'You'll never get a better opportunity than this, you know,' he said. 'Think about it.'

'All right.'

'I know, that's easy to say, but ...' He stared. 'What did you say?'

'I said all right,' Melroth replied. 'Satisfied.'

'Yes,' said Guy, startled. 'That's fine, thank you.'

'I mean to say,' Melroth continued irritably, 'we do actually listen to what residents, I mean mere mortals, tell us, you know. It doesn't just all go in a great big shoe-box somewhere, or if it does we have to empty it out every month or so and things sometimes fall out and we pick them up and sometimes we read them and ... I mean, there is feedback. Definitely.'

'That's very reassuring,' Guy said. 'Really.'

'Good,' said Melroth. 'I think we understand each other.'

'Absolutely.'

'Well, then ...' Melroth hesitated. It's very rare these days for an angel to have to do something he's never done before, and he was nervous. He closed his eyes and took a deep breath. 'Thank you,' he said.

'Don't mention it,' Guy replied. 'Any time.'

Melroth turned and gave him a look. 'Any what?'

'Time.'

'Oh,' said Melroth slowly. 'That old thing.'

A wheelbarrow moving slowly across an infinite, blank landscape.

Behind it, doing the best he can with limited resources, a one-legged, one-armed, half-headed humanoid.

In the wheelbarrow, a large rubber sack with brightly coloured designs painted on it. Behind, a small knot of men carrying tea chests.

The servants of the Central Authority cannot, for fairly obvious reasons, be made redundant. But they can be redeployed, rationalised, reassigned and, in extreme cases, promoted sideways.

Of the Chastel des Larmes Chaudes staff, about ninety per cent had been seconded to the Parks and Amenities Department, where they were set to work whitewashing the stars and cleaning out black holes after interstellar conferences. They had been the lucky ones.

'Boss.'

The Antichrist looked round and noticed Pursuivant under three hundredweight of files and a typewriter.

'Well?' he said.

306

'What exactly are we going to do when we get there?'

'Shut up.'

'Yes, boss.'

Nobody spoke for the next ten minutes or so, during which time Mordaunt dropped the packing-case that contained the fax machine (probably on purpose) and Mountjoy tripped over the flex of the electric fan. Then they saw it, stretched out in front of them like a magnified sky.

'Oh *shit*,' said Pursuivant.

'All right,' snapped the Antichrist furiously, dropping the handles of the wheelbarrow and discovering that it was directly above his big toe, 'you can pack that in from the start. I mean,' he added hopelessly, 'it's not as bad as all that.'

'It isn't?'

'No.'

'Oh.'

Pope Julian, of course, had had it easy. Since he was by definition an incurable temporal paradox he had simply ceased to exist. Jammy little toad.

They had been standing there for a while when the caretaker came out. He was carrying three huge tins of blue paint, six moulting brushes, and he was grinning like a cracked wall.

'Here they are,' he said, 'the boys from the blue stuff.'

They ignored him. He chuckled unpleasantly, like a blocked drain.

'There you go,' he said, plonking the equipment down in front of them. 'And watch the bits round the edges. Gone a bit mouldy there, it has. You'll probably need to rub it right down and fill it before you can start.'

The Antichrist didn't answer. Somewhere on the other side of this lot the rest of his erstwhile subordinates were toddling about in a leisurely fashion, daubing a bit of glitter on a star here, polishing a red dwarf there. If ever he got his hand on that bloody de Nesle ... Well, there'd be trouble.

The caretaker handed over the keys to the tiny shed which was to be their home for the next ... for a very long time, and pottered away into the vast white distance, sniggering. The Chastel men stood for a while, staring; just as stout Cortez would have gazed on the Pacific if he'd just been told that he was going to have to walk home.

'Oh well,' the Antichrist said. He took a handkerchief from the top of the wheelbarrow and gripped it in his teeth while he tied knots in the corners of it with his hand. Then he put it on his head. 'The sooner we make a start ...' he said, and his voice seemed to drain away into the immensity in front of him. 'Anyway,' he said.

Then he and the others began to paint the sky.

The jury room of the United Global Criminal Court.

'Whose is the giblets?' called out the foreman of the jury. Eleven hundred and ninety-eight people shook their heads in turn; and then somebody nudged the eleven hundred and ninety-ninth juror, who had been staring out of the window, and who turned, shook himself, and said, 'Sorry, I was miles away.'

'Right,' said the foreman. 'Eat it while it's hot.'

The culture that had evolved in the jury room over the last eighty years was distinctive, to say the least. Only Mr Troon and Mrs Cartagena were left from the original panel; the rest were second, third or even fourth generation. When Mr Troon died – and he'd been in a coma for six weeks now, the poor old sod – nobody would be left who had heard the original evidence (Mrs Cartagena had, by her own admission, slept through the whole trial), but that was largely irrelevant. Opinion as to the guilt or innocence of the accused was now a matter of clan belief; and ever since the last outbreak of inter-tribal warfare, positions had become utterly entrenched. The politics of it all defied simple explanation; however, basically it came down to the fact that so long as the Macdonalds refused to give up their nine of the original twelve chairs and the Battistas clung on to their right to first choice of the bread rolls, further negotiation was a waste of everybody's time.

Stephen Ogilvy III (the foremanship had been hereditary in the Ogilvy family for as long as anyone could remember) banged on the table with the handle of his knife, and was rewarded with the usual silence.

'Right,' he said – as his father had said, and his father before him – 'have we reached a decision yet?'

Eleven hundred and ninety-nine voices answered him, and so it was time to start eating. At the far end of the table the Court Midwife announced that a new juror had just been enrolled.

Meanwhile, in their cell in the basement, the Galeazzo brothers lay motionless on their mattresses and reflected bitterly on the fact that, if they'd been found guilty in the first place and awarded the maximum sentence, they'd have done their time and been back on the street seventy-two years ago. But, as Someone had remarked at the outset, when the charge is one of mucking about with the very fabric of time itself, the interests of justice could only be served by ensuring that the lack of punishment really did fit the crime.

'Well,' said Blondel.

King Richard grinned at him and brushed confetti out of his hair. 'Got her off your hands at last, then,' he replied.

Blondel nodded. 'Took some doing,' he said. 'Have you decided yet?'

'Decided what?'

'What you're going to do,' Blondel said, looking away.

'I think so,' the King said. He sat down at one of the tables and watched as the wedding car bumped its way down the one cobbled street of the village. 'I saw an advertisement in the paper for a little pet shop in Poitiers, and I made enquiries. I reckon it's time to settle down and breed rats.' He leaned his head over his top pocket, made a cooing noise, and added, 'Isn't it, George?' A pair of small brown eyes gave him a look in return.

Blondel shrugged. 'Money in rats, is there?' he said.

'No,' Richard replied. 'But so what?'

'True. Anyway,' Blondel added, 'that's over at last. Now I can get out of this bloody collar.' He did so, and smiled.

'What about you?' asked the King, pouring the last of the champagne into a tumbler. 'Any plans?'

Blondel shook his head. 'The thing about life ...' he said.

'Yes?'

'Is,' Blondel went on after a moment, 'that there's

310

an awful lot of it, and the last thing I want to do is get involved. I mean, why break the habits of a lifetime?'

Richard sighed. 'I don't really think you can say you were never involved, Jack,' he said. 'You of all people.'

'Ah,' Blondel replied, 'but that's all over and done with, isn't it? I mean, all that history I mucked about with has been scrubbed. Clean slate. That means I'm a whatsisname, anathema. So long as I'm still around, can things really get back to how they should be? I'm not sure.'

'How come?' Richard said.

Under the canopy stretched across the village square, under the shade of the twisted old mulberry tree, a small, over-excited child was sick. 'Think about it,' Blondel said, lying back on the table and contemplating his fingernails. 'You were just the victim. I was the one who caused all the trouble. I was the one who went around singing *L'Amours Dont ... L'Amours ...* thingy all the time.'

'*L'Amours Dont Sui Epris,*' said Richard softly.

'That's the one,' Blondel said. 'Do you know, I've forgotten how it goes now. *L'Amours Dont ...* Ah well, never mind. I never liked it much anyway.'

'Didn't you?'

'No,' Blondel said, frowning. 'That bit in the third verse. Tum tum tumpty ... How *does* that bit go, can you remember?'

Richard shook his head. 'Sorry,' he said.

Blondel grinned. 'The hell with it,' he said, 'it's only a song, that's all. Some day somebody'll write another one, I expect. Anyway, I always reckoned it wasn't a patch on *Ma Joie Me ... Me ...* the other one.'

'Which one was that, Jack?'

'Can't remember.'

They sat quietly for a while, Richard remembering, Blondel just staring, while the last few friends and relations wandered away. A wedding guest hurried up, explained that some damn fool of an ecology canvasser had kept him talking for hours with some rigmarole about endangered seabirds, was told that he'd missed the ceremony and the reception, and clumped off in a huff. The sun went down.

'Anyway,' said Blondel.

'Anyway,' said Richard. 'Have you paused to consider that, if you put in a claim for overtime, you'd be the richest man in history?'

'No,' Blondel replied.

'Good,' Richard said, and fell asleep.

Blondel lay still for a few minutes more, gazing up at the battlements of the Chateau de Nesle in the far distance. Although he couldn't remember details, he had an idea he'd lived there once, a very long time ago. And, as the thought crossed his mind, he had the feeling he could hear somebody in one of the turrets singing a song which once he might have recognised.

'*L'amours dont sui epris,*' it sang,

'*Me semont de chanter;*
Si fais con hons sopris
Qui ne puet endurer.
Et s'ai je tant conquis . . .'

Blondel sighed, and grinned, and stood up. At the foot of the tower, a low door materialised and opened.

And Blondel strolled through it, hands in pockets, singing.

312

☐	Faust Among Equals	Tom Holt	£14.99
☐	Grailblazers	Tom Holt	£4.99
☐	Here Comes the Sun	Tom Holt	£4.99
☐	Ye Gods!	Tom Holt	£4.99
☐	Flying Dutch	Tom Holt	£4.99
☐	Expecting Someone Taller	Tom Holt	£4.99
☐	Who's Afraid of Beowulf	Tom Holt	£4.99

Orbit now offers an exciting range of quality titles by both established and new authors. All of the books in this series are available from:

Little, Brown and Company (UK) Limited,
P.O. Box 11,
Falmouth,
Cornwall TR10 9EN.

Alternatively you may fax your order to the above address. Fax No. 0326 376423.

Payments can be made as follows: cheque, postal order (payable to Little, Brown and Company) or by credit cards, Visa/Access. Do not send cash or currency. UK customers and B.F.P.O. please allow £1.00 for postage and packing for the first book, plus 50p for the second book, plus 30p for each additional book up to a maximum charge of £3.00 (7 books plus).

Overseas customers including Ireland, please allow £2.00 for the first book plus £1.00 for the second book, plus 50p for each additional book.

NAME (Block Letters) ....

....

ADDRESS ....

....

....

☐ I enclose my remittance for _____

☐ I wish to pay by Access/Visa Card

Number ⬚⬚⬚⬚⬚⬚⬚⬚⬚⬚⬚⬚⬚⬚⬚⬚

Card Expiry Date ⬚⬚⬚⬚